Hellhold
and Other Stories

by Sean Patrick Hazlett

Dedication

To my son Marius, for putting a smile on my face every day.

Table of Contents

Acknowledgements

I want to thank all the teachers and writers that helped me along the way, or, barring that, did not discourage me when they should have. My fifth grade teacher, Mrs. Umile, was instrumental in encouraging me to write my first fantasy stories. I want to thank internationally best-selling novelist David Vann for having patience with my early writing as a Stanford undergraduate. He never discouraged me and always provided productive critiques that helped me improve my work. The late Jeff Carlson inspired me to write fiction after sharing his wisdom and experience. He also graciously took the time to critique one of my first stories, pointing out all my rookie mistakes. I'm also thankful that *Writers of the Future* editor, David Wolverton, discovered and recognized my work. Mike Resnick has also been instrumental in supporting my early writing career by encouraging me and buying my stories. I also want to thank award-winning author and editor, Nick Mamatas, for his unvarnished and relentless critiques of my stories in one of his fiction writing classes. Most people hold back their criticism, but Nick never sugarcoated his feedback. Because of it, he made me a better writer. I doubt I will ever reach Nick's bar for excellence, but he definitely set a high standard. Lastly, I would like to thank my ever-patient wife, Claire, for sacrificing her weekends to edit my stories.

Introduction

This collection includes fifteen short stories I wrote from December of 2015 through October 2017. They have appeared in venues such as *Galaxy's Edge*, *Terraform*, *The Year's Best Military and Adventure SF*, *Year's Best Hardcore Horror*, *Abyss & Apex*, *Kasma SF*, *MYTHIC: A Quarterly Science Fiction & Fantasy Magazine*, and *Dark Moon Digest*, among others. The stories cover concepts as varied as demonic artifacts lurking in hidden dimensions, the lure of forbidden knowledge, the dark side of divinity, the wages of totalitarianism, robotic horrors, artificial intelligence gone terribly wrong, biological monstrosities, and the twisted end of innocence.

While I've been writing since I was ten years old, I only began a serious effort to publish my stories in the last few months of 2011. The one great thing about short stories is that they are tremendously useful for generating and validating ideas. They allow writers to test concepts relatively quickly without the time and commitment required to produce a novel. Moreover, they also provide writers with an opportunity to learn and experiment with their craft.

I've learned much over the last few years and have had a lot of fun bringing these new worlds to life. I plan on creating many more in the future. I hope you enjoy reading these tales as much as I've loved writing them.

Hellhold

"What say you, Henry Tuttle, are you guilty of witchcraft?" Jonathan Corwin asked, his stern voice resonating with the authority of a man who had already settled on the answer.

"Not guilty," I replied, knowing the futility of my answer.

"Tituba's prior testimony says otherwise, Mr. Tuttle. She claims that a tall man dressed in black came to her, Sarah Osborne, and Sarah Good in the night. This man forced them to sign their names in blood in a great book. Many in this town suspect you are that man. And Tituba claims that man was the Devil. What say you to these allegations, Mr. Tuttle?"

I wanted to scoff at Mr. Corwin's accusation, but the mood in the courtroom was tense and on the precipice of exploding into unrestrained lunacy. So I stifled the impulse. "I say before God, before whom I stand, that I know nothing of these charges."

"In what year where you born, Mr. Tuttle?" said the other magistrate, John Hawthorne.

The non sequitur was anything but. The magistrate clearly sought to entrap me. But as I had sworn an oath on the Holy Book, I was compelled to speak the truth. "I was born on January first, 1680 in the year of the Lord." Hawthorne smiled. "So that would make you, what, twelve winters old?"

And there it was. The not-so-subtle implication that I bore false witness. For I was a man full grown nearing slightly past the middle of my years. I lowered my head. "Aye."

Members of the jury guffawed as if Mr. Hawthorne had caught me in a lie. If only the truth of the matter were that simple. When I raised my head and observed the jurors' reactions, their cold, pale faces showed plainly a human menagerie of scorn, disbelief, and even bemusement.

Hawthorne raised an eyebrow. "So Mr. Tuttle, are we to believe that the middle-aged man who stands before us is really a twelve-year-old boy?"

I shook my head. "Of course not, sir. I swear before God and the Heavens above that I have a sound explanation behind this apparent discrepancy, an explanation that I will most happily lay bare before this court."

With the alacrity of a vulture that had sniffed a whiff of blood, Corwin swooped in. "Would that explanation have anything to do with your participation in acts of maleficium?"

Corwin had a point. Whichever way, they had me. I was either lying under oath or some devilry had been responsible for my unnatural aging. The truth of the matter was not so simple. Nor was there a delicate way to reveal my suspicion to these Puritans that something sinister had followed me home.

"The way I appear to you now is no mark of my participation in witchcraft. The letter I carry in my hand today and addressed to Cotton Mather should go a long way in explaining my plight. My testimony here will further illuminate how I have lived a lifetime while nary a decade has passed in our earthly realm."

"Then I would be most curious to hear your tale," said Corwin. And so I told them of my journey to that dark, desolate place.

❧

A dense fog rolled in just before twilight, obscuring Cape Cod's distinct fishhook. My father, Captain James Tuttle, raised his brass spyglass and cursed. At the time, I was but a young and ignorant cabin boy, watching my father struggle to see thirty feet beyond the ship's bow.

A ship emerged from the mist without warning like an apparition out of time. Startled, the crew scrambled to their stations. My father squinted through his spyglass. For a moment, he smiled. "We've nothing to fear. The vessel bears the Union flag."

An undulating sigh of relief surged over the crew. After a two-month voyage across the stormy Atlantic and this close to home, the crew lacked enthusiasm for anything more strenuous than sailing into port.

My father slowly raised his hand as he continued to observe the other ship through his spyglass. "No...wait," he said tentatively before shouting, "To your stations!"

Half the men hesitated as if their feet were mired in molasses. Others milled about in apparent confusion.

"Move!" Father bellowed, a trace of panic betraying his normally stentorian voice. "It's a bloody ruse! They're raising the skull and crossbones!"

The sailors of the *Harbinger* shambled to their stations like sleepwalkers. Weeks of passage through fierce gales had leached the fighting spirit from their bones.

But it was too late. I surmised the pirates must've stumbled onto the *Harbinger* through blind luck, having laid in wait near known shipping lanes. Regardless of how the raiders came upon our ship, they were too close to the *Harbinger* for it to escape.

Lights flashed and smoke billowed from the pirate vessel. A cannonball zipped across the *Harbinger*'s bow. Father hung his head low.

Clad in black, the elder and distinguished Lord Ellsworth Asquith of Herfordshire scrambled up to the deck, his eyes wide as doubloons. He faced Father. "We cannot allow them to board, James! I beseech you—resist!"

My father shook his head. "I'm sorry, but were I to fight, I'd condemn every man on this ship to certain death."

Asquith persisted. "If the pirates unleash what's in the hold, our crew's lives will be the least of our worries."

"Your concern is academic, but my dilemma is real. I am the captain of this vessel and I, and I alone, am entrusted with the burden of taking a decision."

Grasping my father's arm, Asquith redoubled his appeal. "Don't be stupid, my good sir!" The elder man glanced at me. "My God, Tuttle, your own flesh and blood is a boarder on this ship. Think not of yourself, but of his welfare. You are playing with forces greater than all of us."

With a shrug of resignation, Father gave the most humiliating order of his natural life: "Hoist the white flag."

∾

Hours later, the two captains had hammered out the terms of the *Harbinger*'s surrender. From decades of seamanship, my father trusted in the custom that pirates would not harm crews that surrendered their vessels without a fight. In exchange for the lives of Father and his crew and, ultimately, their freedom, Father would surrender the *Harbinger* and its cargo to Captain Howard and the men of the *Tempest*. In turn, the raiders would hold Father hostage in their ship's brig until reaching their port of call in Bermuda. For the nonce, the pirates would divide the crews amongst the two ships with the pirates assuming command of both.

Once Captain Howard's men consolidated their control of the *Harbinger*, they divvied up the spoils.

Events had happened so fast that I struggled to make sense of the sudden and irrevocable loss of Father's status. I was but twelve years old at the time. Frightened and alone, I clung to Lord Asquith for guidance and protection. Together, we made a mad dash toward the ship's hold.

"Stand by me, boy." Lord Asquith said, "It's vital this section of the hold remain undisturbed."

Three brigands pursued us into the musty dark, cornering us before the forbidden compartment. "Undo the locks," ordered their leader. "Captain Howard demands we inventory every item, especially if it isn't listed on the ship's manifest."

Asquith pushed me behind him, shielding me from the pirates with his frail form. "This is madness. The cargo is not listed on the manifest for good reason. Look at the wall, man!" Asquith pointed at hundreds of wards and sigils scrawled in chalk. "Break those at your peril, for the ancient seals beyond that wall are weakening. If you enter, you risk unleashing forces unto this earth that defy comprehension. Walk away, good sir. Walk away."

"Hogwash!" The lead pirate unsheathed his cutlass. "Step aside, old man."

Asquith held up his hands. "Don't be foolish."

In half a heartbeat, the plunderer gutted Asquith, shoved him aside, and entered the sealed chamber through a narrow door.

I rushed to Lord Asquith. With bloodied hands, he handed me a scroll with a wax seal. He told me, "When you return to the New World, deliver this letter to Cotton Mather in Boston, Massachusetts. And please, for the love of the Almighty, stay away from that infernal compartment lest you succumb to its accursed influence."

I shook with trepidation. What had these foolhardy marauders unleashed?

"Don't just stand there, boy!" Asquith yelled, coughing up blood. "Go! Get away from here!"

So I raced up to the deck, shivering in fear, leaving Lord Asquith in the hold to suffer a slow and most unsavory death.

A week later, weevils had decimated our grain stores. The crew dumped the infested grain and sequestered what was left in the hold.

Shortly thereafter, the ship's rat population exploded, finishing off what remained of the *Harbinger*'s already meager supplies.

The crew sparingly transferred biscuits from the *Tempest* until those provisions also became infested.

And so we ate the rats until the rats began to eat us.

I found helmsman Reynolds in his bunk, his face half-eaten and buzzing with flies. Maggots had burrowed into the abscesses of his bone and sinew. From then on, the crew began a concerted campaign to eradicate every rodent on the ship.

∞

Rigger's mate Jones was the first sailor to disappear. He was a pirate and by all accounts an impetuous one—after all, he'd cut down Lord Asquith without hesitation. Witnesses swore they last saw him entering the warded compartment of the hold. After an exhaustive search, the crew never found a trace of him.

Captain Howard suspected foul play from men he believed were loyal to Father. So to set an example, Howard forced carpenter's mate McReady, the last man to have seen Jones alive, to walk the plank.

∞

Within two weeks, amidst all the scurvy and starvation, the men who bunked closest to the tainted cargo began to fall ill. Not only were they drained physically, but they also teetered on the precipice of madness. It was as if over time, a miasma seeped from the artifact and spread like an affliction, a fell pox on man and beast alike. After three of them hanged themselves by their own entrails, Captain Howard sent four men loyal to my father—men he could afford to lose—to jettison the curst relic.

Those men never returned.

∞

Several nights later, I woke to pandemonium. Men milled about on the deck, their eyes cast toward the heavens. The night sky had changed. The constellations, topsy-turvy. Polaris no longer held sway in the northern sky, inexplicably erased from the cosmos. The *Tempest* had vanished in a dense fog. Our compass needles spun in all directions. Captain Howard himself conceded that the ship was woefully lost.

For three weeks, the *Harbinger* drifted aimlessly. For three weeks, the crew never saw the light of day; twilight alternated with darkness. For three weeks, we failed to spy land. All the while, our food stores dwindled and men grew desperate.

∞

They ate Mason first.

After they'd carved up his corpse, the man's disembodied head opened its eyes. Pure black orbs darted back and forth. Then it spoke: "It waits beyond the soul tides!"

The crew panicked. Men turned and fled, stampeding on the deck. Rigger Lawrence was trampled under a roiling wave of humanity.

"Hear me!" Mason's head rasped. "The only way to light is through darkness. The only way to pleasure is through pain. The only way to life is through death."

Captain Howard raised his hand, "Order!"

The commotion faded to a whimper. The sailors kept their distance, wide-eyed and shuddering.

"Retire to your bunks and rest easy," Howard ordered. "I'll see to this."

Howard held a private council with the unholy thing that had once been Mason. Afterward, with Mason's apparent consent, Howard fastened the man's head to the foremast. According to Howard's terse explanation, he'd done it to help the crew navigate through these otherworldly waters. From thenceforward, the crew treated all the newly fallen in this manner, the deceased's head staked to a mast. And as the crew's ranks dwindled, the ship became more alive, each head adding to its collective intelligence—more eyes to illuminate the primeval darkness.

ᘓ

The thing that had been Mason announced the sighting of a spit of land. The head's eerie singsong voice would have been mesmerizing had I not known its source. As the ship drew closer to its dark destination, I was struck by the utter oily blackness of the shore and rocks beyond. And sometimes the blackness slithered.

As the *Harbinger* drew closer still, towering monoliths covered the lonely landscape like rotten teeth guarding the portal to a festering pit. A sense of foreboding hung like a fetid fog over the starving and exhausted survivors. Yet we had no choice but to explore those wretched night lands, leaving behind a handful of men to tend to the ship.

For some indiscernible reason, Howard ordered the crew to unload the vile relic from the hold. It was a casket, nine feet long by five feet wide. It had faded esoteric symbols and wards chiseled throughout its surface. No man wanted to touch it, so Howard made my father's crew draw lots. In the end, Howard selected four unlucky men to convey the artifact to the dark continent.

ᘓ

Just hours after making landfall, we discovered we weren't alone. By lantern light, we found Boatswain White smothered by python-sized leech-things lurking in the shadows. Round mouths lined with needle-sharp black teeth had latched onto his body. By the time we'd hacked the creatures off, they'd sapped his lifeblood, leaving behind a desiccated husk.

As we ventured deeper into the interior, the leeches preyed on men who wandered a short distance from our column. After losing three more souls in this manner, Captain Howard ordered each man to coil rope around his waist and bind it to the next man to prevent them from drifting into the darkness.

Famished, we began to hunt and devour the leech-things. But their slimy, ichor-lathered flesh offered little sustenance. And some lamented that consuming it may have even been making us weaker.

We slept fitfully on that desolate land, measuring our days from twilight to twilight.

⅚

On the second day, I woke to the wails of yet more fallen comrades, their pale faces marred by bloated black tongues and bulging black eyes. As one, they spoke. "Offer the gift to those who slumber upon the obsidian peak."

None of us could fail to understand the message of the dead, for in the distance shined a red beacon upon a lonesome mountaintop.

Captain Howard and his loyalists conferenced with the dead. Through his profane intercession, Howard produced a map illuminated by the dismal stars of an alien sky.

⅚

And so we marched to that solitary peak through a ruin of monoliths and broken arches of some arcane civilization that had long since faded from this realm of eternal twilight. We waded through lichyards littered with the petrified bones of great leviathans that dwarfed Spanish galleons. And we fed on the filthy parasites that stalked us through that lonely land. But no matter how far we tread, the mountain was always out of reach.

We marched for days. Days became weeks and weeks became years. The vapors of that foul land slowly took their toll. Our elders grayed and shriveled before their time, many succumbing to unnatural deaths.

Yet strangely, none complained. Our fallen comrades had assured us if we delivered the artifact to its master—our souls would return to hallowed ground one way or another.

℘

By the time we reached the black citadel, I was a man, full grown. Many had perished along the way, succumbing to fever or old age. Now their heads adorned the casket to serve as our guides, for the dead can see what the living dare not face.

Perched atop its forlorn peak like a sore on a rotting corpse, the citadel dominated the black vale. Its sinuous spires curled toward infinity.

By the time we reached the summit, only four of us remained. We lumbered up stairs chiseled into the mountainside and followed them to a chasm surrounding the citadel.

When we set the artifact down on the chasm's edge, the citadel's drawbridge lowered until it was flush with the obsidian stairs. Across that narrow span, an iron portcullis rose, revealing a gaping maw of darkness.

I could sense a great deal of trepidation amongst the others. On the final leg of our journey, they all hesitated to step into that abyss.

A similar sense of fear and revulsion weighed heavily upon me. I wished to venture no further. The casket was heavy. Its timeworn wards and seals were fading into oblivion.

But some hidden force compelled us to press on, a phantom chain tugging at our souls. We crossed the drawbridge and into a cavernous throne room bored into the obsidian. An oozing black web hung from the arched ceiling. And in those corded threads, something stirred.

An oppressive presence invaded our collective consciousness, seeding our minds with thoughts both alien and infinite. It feasted on our memories and fears, consuming them with an insatiable hunger, sapping our will to live.

Once that dreadful entity had drained us dry, it revealed itself. Suspended from those oily fibers, four spindly and segmented arm-legs extended from a small spherical body connected to an oversized head shaped like an inverted pyramid. A single eye on one of the pyramid faces regarded us with a menacing intelligence.

All at once, the heads of our deceased comrades floated upward until the web had ensnared them in its black ichor. A voice inside my mind compelled us to carry the relic up the final steps to the throne at the room's center. We rested our burden upon the smooth obsidian floor, then collapsed.

∞

When I awoke, I found myself surrounded by Captain Howard's men from the *Tempest*. They told me a curious tale about how the *Harbinger* had vanished for an instant and then suddenly reappeared covered with screaming human heads. They'd found me, the sole survivor, in possession of a faded and sealed scroll addressed to one Cotton Mather. Once they'd evacuated me from the *Harbinger*, they'd torched the abomination.

If not for the words of my father, Captain Howard's men would have almost certainly executed me as a murderer and stowaway. For they recognized me not. After all, an instant earlier, I had been but a young boy. The crew had been on the verge of cutting me down until my father had interceded, asking me questions only his son could have answered.

And so now I stood before the august jury of Salem accused of witchcraft. It was a charge I readily accepted. For one cannot pass beyond the veil to other realms without bringing something back. But before they hanged me, I asked that they break the seal and read the letter aloud before passing it on to Cotton Mather. For it would lay certain matters to rest.

In his arrogance, Jonathan Corwin agreed to carry out my request as if he were performing an act of mercy.

If only he knew.

And so with the haughty arrogance of one of Salem's fathers, he opened the note and read it aloud:

Dear Cotton,

If this letter reaches your eyes, then I fear the worst has come to pass. The relic's seals have been decaying for centuries, and it is nary by the Grace of God I've kept the resurgent forces within it temporarily at bay. Should we fail to divine a more enduring remedy, the great transference shall damn us all. And this demonic artifact is the hook by which the Beast shall tether its essence to our realm.

I've consulted with every mystic and oracle of all the major religious traditions of the Old World, yet none has proffered a mechanism by which to entomb forever the fell powers within. But fear not, I've learned of a powerful conjuror called Hausis among the Colony of Virginia's Croatoan people. I humbly beseech you to seek her out before these unholy things are unleashed upon our earthly realm.

Your humblest servant,

Lord Ellsworth Asquith

When good Jonathan Corwin finished the letter, I smiled. The Tuttle boy's nagging suspicion that something had latched itself to his mortal coil was true. And now that I knew my adversary's true name, I cast aside Henry Tuttle's tortured soul and took possession of his body. For I am legion and from the husk of Henry Tuttle, I will extinguish the flame of the last being in this realm that could stop me. Then I shall spread my seed to the ends of the Earth.

END

Afterword

The inspiration from this story came from a 2016 story in *The Magazine of Fantasy and Science Fiction* by the late Gardner Dozois called "The Place of Bones." The story involved an interminable journey through a parallel dimension in the Alps to find the fabled Dragonlands. Dorzois's masterful storytelling and ability to propel a story through an endless sense of mystery greatly impressed me.

"Hellhold" is similarly about a journey through a blasted land in a disturbingly dark dimension. In this story, I used the Salem witch trials as a frame to set up the deeper enigma of Henry Tuttle's rapid aging. I wanted to engage the reader with an immediate mystery that would only be answered near the end of Tuttle's forlorn expedition through dismal lands.

I also explored the notion of the curse of ignorance and how it can wreak havoc when the ill-informed cross forbidden thresholds and stumble into horrors they could not scarcely have imagined.

This story first appeared in Galaxy's Edge in 2019 and was reprinted in *MYTHIC: A Quarterly Science Fiction & Fantasy Magazine*. Of all the stories in this collection, I think this one is the most psychologically disturbing. I hope you enjoyed it.

Evolution's Echo

"I feel like a fugitive from the law of averages."
– Bill Mauldin

One false step on the crags, and a man could plunge hundreds of feet into the Pacific's cold oblivion. But something worse lurked beyond the bluffs, lingering in the redwoods. And whatever it was, it'd drained these soldiers' brainpans dry, leaving their bloated bodies here to rot.

The sight of those dead-eyed soldiers and their hollowed-out skulls was too much to take; I puked inside my gas mask. But Sergeant Gonzalez didn't give a rat's ass about my feelings. He just chewed my ass for ruining my equipment.

Screw him.

I chucked that useless thing into the bushes first chance I got. To hell with bio-containment protocols.

From the bluffs, we passed through a redwood grove and then emerged into a clearing teeming with chest-high straw grass. For all its natural beauty, there was a sense of dread about this place, shrouded in a veil of mist. I could feel it in my gut. I could smell it in the fetid fog.

Then they came for us.

Waves of grass, like falling dominos, rippled toward our position. The grass swallowed Private Saunders, muffling his screams. Men shouted.

Disciplined three-round bursts devolved into a riot of automatic weapons fire. Errant rounds zipped past my head.

To my right, the grass stirred. I slewed my M4 rifle. A mass of spindly, segmented legs lunged forward. I fired three rounds.

"Cease fire!" Gonzalez hollered as he marched down my squad's column, waving his hand.

I lowered my weapon and checked my handiwork: the ruin of an eight-legged thing as big as a horseshoe crab. Fluorescent green fluid leaked from its shattered carcass. Its segmented legs extended from a mushroom-shaped central husk. Each leg terminated in a spiked hook. I kicked the thing, upending it. As if by instinct, it sprayed black dust at knee level. I stumbled back, relieved it'd missed my face.

The creature's underside had a round mouth lined with needle-sharp teeth. The longer I gazed at it, the angrier I got. The Army hadn't briefed us on any of this. The green machine'd just thrown us in MOPP suits and told us to recover bodies.

"Goddammit, Private Murphy! I'm talking to you!" Gonzalez bellowed, rousing me from my stupor.

"Ah, sorry, sergeant. What's up?"

"What's up? I need a SITREP. That creeper dust you?" Gonzalez said "creeper" with such authority I could've sworn he'd expected to find one here.

"Dust me?"

Gonzalez raised his voice. "You heard me, dammit!"

I tapped the dead creeper with my boot. "That one did, but I killed it."

"Any of it touch you?"

"No, why?"

He glared at me for a good thirty seconds as if his stern gaze would make me change my story. When I didn't bite, he said, "Good. Avoid that shit like it's dick cancer."

"Why?"

"That's classified. Grab your gear. We're moving out. We've got a mission to accomplish."

"What mission's that exactly?"

"That's need to know, private. And right now, you don't need to know."

I smiled, wondering what the hell had possessed me to forgo a world-class education at Columbia to enlist in the United States Army.

As we trudged deeper into the forest, I passed five body bags. Farther down the trail, ten wounded men slumped in a small clearing. A bloody "T" was smeared on Carson's pale forehead. Sergeant Belski, our platoon medic, lined a smooth stick along Carson's upper arm and wrapped a torn undershirt around both. The medic rotated the stick until the binding was tight, grabbed a machete, and lopped off Carson's forearm with about as much fuss as if he were mixing a smoothie.

Carson howled.

Several feet away, Private Lathrop coughed uncontrollably, his face blackened with dust. Others waited for Belksi to tend to more minor wounds.

‟

A month ago, Governor Brown had sent the California National Guard to Russian Gulch State Park to investigate cryptic reports of missing campers and park rangers in an ever-expanding string of disappearances.

By the time the 11th Armored Cavalry Regiment got involved, the National Guard had lost a battalion, and the President had declared martial law in the Fort Bragg-Caspar-Mendocino area.

Now, my unit was at the leading edge of our formation. The rest of my squadron was either behind us on the trail or securing the outlying bluffs we'd cleared earlier that day.

We descended further into a forest thick with fern and redwood. The silence of the woods unnerved me. No birds chirped in the gloom. No squirrels rustled through the trees. No buzzing mosquitos assaulted exposed skin.

A blight of black fungus marred the bark of the local redwoods. Thin hairs bristling from these malignant growths swayed as we passed. Wherever the fungus appeared, rot and decay spread. An oily mist coalesced around us like a swampy soup. It was as if some strange and alien ecology were coopting the natural order, subverting the ecosystem to its own malevolent ends.

When he was within spitting distance of a blighted redwood, Private Sanchez reached for one of the mushrooms.

"Stop!" I screamed.

The fungus dusted his face. He spun and fell. He slammed his Kevlar helmet against a rock. The Kevlar popped off his head like a cork and rolled down the hill into the swirling mist. His face was as black as charcoal. He hacked up bubbling phlegm as if gripped by an epileptic fit.
Belski raced toward him.

"Mask up!" I shouted.

In half a second, Belski was on his knees, pumping Sanchez's chest and administering mouth-to-mouth. The medic continued his effort until his labored breaths signaled exhaustion. Lowering his head, he pressed two fingers on Sanchez's carotid artery and counted silently. After several minutes, Belski shook his head, then shut Sanchez's eyes.

"What the hell happened?" Gonzalez said as he raced toward Sanchez's corpse. He glowered at Belski.

"Sanchez got dusted. I tried to save him, but he's gone now."

Gonzalez stared daggers at the medic. "What'd you do?"

Belski's clenched his jaw. He scowled at Gonzalez. "I gave him CPR. What the hell else would I do?"

"I see." Gonzalez's tone seemed to shift from anger to something like regret. "Belski, I want you on point."

"What the fuck?" The words left my mouth before I could shut it. "Sergeant Gonzalez, Sergeant Belski's a medic, not a rifleman. We need him in the rear with the gear, not on the front lines.

Gonzalez grabbed me by the throat. "Keep your thoughts to yourself, fucknut. We're all riflemen first."

I pushed Gonzalez away. "Fine, sergeant. How 'bout I take point instead?"

His face hardened into an unreadable granite mask. Then he whispered, "I appreciate your initiative, Murphy, but trust me on this one. I got my reasons."

Gonzalez turned toward Belski. "Grab your gear and head down the trail about five hundred meters. Tell Garvey he's relieved."
Belski shouldered his rucksack, grabbed his rifle, and said, "Fuck you, Gonzalez," before disappearing into the gray mist.

"What should we do with him?" I asked Gonzalez, jerking my thumb toward Sanchez's corpse.

"Leave him. Got no time to bury anybody. Let's get moving. I don't wanna be jerking off in this wilderness at night."

I couldn't have agreed with him more.

ಬಂ

Belski limped up the hill with two soldiers in tow. Both kept their distance from the medic. It was the first time I'd seen him since he'd taken point.

His neck had swollen. Dark growths blotted his exposed skin like a pimpled pestilence. He shivered like he was in the grip of an unrelenting fever. Vomiting in the decaying ferns, he left behind a steaming puddle of bile and blood.

As the medic passed, Gonzalez swung his arm over my shoulder and shook his head. "See. I told ya to stay away from those shrooms."

℣

They dive-bombed us like spinning buzz saws from the treetops. A round thing latched onto Specialist Longo's face, stifling his screams.

Men panicked, firing rounds indiscriminately. Hot lead whizzed past my head amid a riot of flying splinters and green goo. The carcass of an eight-legged scaly thing fell at my feet. Its legs stretched out from a central husk that was ninety-percent mouth and ten percent eyestalks. Fleshy, membranous webbing connected its spindly legs in perfect radial symmetry.

"You're welcome." Gonzalez lowered his rifle. "Get your dick out of your hand and take cover. Start taking these gliders out. I'm gonna get the rest of the boys organized before this shit-show turns into a proper cluster fuck."

Minutes later, the men were firing their weapons in deliberate three-round bursts and dropping gliders from the sky. Soon the attack ended, and we continued our slow, inexorable march toward God knows what.

℣

The redwoods were getting blacker and the mist, thicker, making it harder to breathe. The putrid miasma left a greasy residue on everything it touched. To protect myself from the corrosive fog, I tore an undershirt into strips and covered my nose and mouth. I put on my gloves to stop my hands from burning.

The infestation had taken a much firmer hold in these parts. Trees were pocked with fungus oozing a rank black fluid. Murky webs of a slick fibrous substance connected the fungi in a dense network of throbbing vines. The woods began to moan and growl at us in registers that could almost be mistaken for human voices.

Few of us had made it this far. Alpha Troop was at a quarter strength, yet squadron command still pushed us forward from a tactical operations center safety secured on the bluffs miles to our rear. We kept sending back torn and blackened bodies, but the brass clearly hadn't even begun to comprehend the horrors we were facing in this festering hellscape.

We were so deep in the bush now, and the fog was so dense it might as well have been night. It was relief to put on my night vision goggles. At least they'd protect my eyes from this caustic soup. And so we meandered through the blackness, viewing the world through artificial shades of green. Men shouted ahead. I checked my rifle, then stomped through a thicket of unmolested ferns. I emerged into a clearing. Bright stadium lights washed out my night vision goggles, forcing me to remove them.

Once my eyes adjusted to the light, I saw a chubby man wearing a gas mask and white clean suit. He monitored a tablet while sitting on a foldout chair in front of an olive drab canvas tent.

Captain Li, the squadron's intelligence officer, strolled up to the man and shook his hand.

I was incredulous. This was getting shadier by the minute. After everything I'd been through, after all the death and destruction, not a single officer had had the decency to tell us grunts what the hell was going on. So in the absence of orders, I acted and strode toward the tent.

"It's in the suitcase," Captain Li said.

"Good," said the fat man. "We need to get the ordnance as close to the hive's cerebral cluster as possible. No one knows how deep the organism has burrowed."

Captain Li noticed my presence. "Whoah! Who the fuck are you? You're not authorized to be here."

He could go fuck himself, because he hadn't given us jack shit for intel. I took a deep breath. It was the only thing I could do to stop myself from tuning the captain up. "Sir, no one's briefed me on what I can and cannot do. No one's told me why I'm here or what I'm facing. I've watched about three quarters of my platoon die or get maimed. So with all due respect, I've earned the right to go wherever the hell I want."

The captain's eyes narrowed on my collar rank and then on my nametag. "Well, Private Murphy, I'm giving you a direct order. Return to your squad and do your job."

"Do *my* job!" I yelled. "Over three-quarters of us are dead because you didn't do *yours*. 'Til I get some answers, I'm staying right here."

I could see from the glint in his eyes he wanted to forcibly remove me. I put my finger on my M4's trigger and dared him to do it.

"Private Murphy! What the hell you doing?" Gonzalez wedged himself between Li and me.

I pointed at the captain. "This is the dipshit who let us march here completely blind."

Gonzalez grabbed me by both collars. "Son, you need to calm down. It's been a rough day. But as crazy as shit seems, we're pretty damn close to accomplishing our mission."

"Which is?"

"We're to secure L-Z X-Ray just like Captain Martinez said in his operations order."

"Yeah, yeah. That's just a spot on a map. No one briefed us on why we needed to seize it. I'm still not sure what the hell we're fighting down here. This an alien invasion?"

Gonzalez laughed. "Nah. Nothing like that. But it's on a need-to-know basis."

"Right," I grumbled, "and I don't need to know."

"Look at the big brain on Murphy." Gonzalez grinned.

"Well, screw that." I sidestepped Gonzalez and stomped toward the pudgy man.

Surprisingly, Gonzalez didn't follow. Good noncommissioned officers were often that way. They'd enforce orders until the orders stopped making sense. And even then, they'd hold the line until their soldiers couldn't take it anymore. Then, when shit got really stupid, they'd relent.

When I reached the fat man, Li grabbed my shoulder and said, "I told you to leave."

I swung at the captain with every ounce of strength I had, dropping him like a deuce.

I turned toward his companion. "Sorry 'bout that. I just wanted to talk to someone who could give me some answers. You seem like someone who can."

The man glanced at Li, shrugged, and extended his hand. "Name's Doctor Eli Rosen. I'm working as a consultant on a classified joint NASA-DOD project."

"Let me guess. The project went tits up and now you're here to unfuck it?"

He chuckled. "Something like that."

"Why are we here?"

"Because we need to get a suitcase nuke as close to the source of the infestation as possible."

"Couldn't the Air Force have nuked this place from orbit?"

"Sure, but that wouldn't play well on CNN. Plus, the Air Force needs boots on the ground to ID targets."

"I see. Why all the secrecy?"

"Because for you, this is a one-way trip."

I shuddered. No wonder those fuckers said nothing. Made sense though. Telling soldiers they were on a suicide mission wasn't exactly the world's best motivational technique.

I motioned toward the surrounding forest. "What's all this?"

"This is Project Demeter, a top-secret program to bioengineer highly adaptable organisms to send into space and seed worlds for human colonization. Exogenesis in a box, if you will."

"So what happened?"

"Lack of oversight and hubris. The researchers here were experimenting with transgenic material, particularly with tardigrade genes. Tardigrades, or water bears, are the only known animal species able to survive the vacuum of space. The researchers spliced the DNA and RNA from animals, plants, bacteria, fungi, and viruses to design a hybrid species.

"Unbeknownst to the researchers, the organisms developed a hive intelligence, which we believe acquired the capacity to engage in directed evolution. By the time scientists figured it out, it was too late, and the hive had begun claiming large swaths of Russian Gulch State Park."

"Where's our target?"

Rosen pointed down the hill. "About five miles east. We're very close to the husk, but we'll need to be right on its doorstep to trigger the device."

"All right," I said. Then I asked the one question that had been gnawing on me since I'd met Rosen. "How'd ya survive this far? I mean, you're completely unscathed."

Rosen smiled. "That's classified at a level above Top Secret. Even if I told you, you wouldn't believe me. Suffice it to say, I can do things even the entity in the gulch fears. It's why the government calls me for all the weird stuff."

I felt a hand on my shoulder. "All right, Murphy," Gonzalez said, "Time to get moving. You find what you were looking for?"

I nodded.

"Good. Now keep your mouth shut. Not a word to the others."

Gonzalez was a cold-hearted bastard, but he was right.

We put our night vision goggles back on, then followed Rosen toward our final objective.

℘

"Murrrrphy," a voice whispered from the darkness. I didn't recognize the voice and wasn't even sure I'd actually heard it.

"Murrrrphy," the voice repeated.

"You hear that, sergeant?" I yelled over my shoulder.

"Hear what?"

"Never mind. It's probably nothing."

Intermittent gusts of wind punctured the silence.

"What the fuck you say, Murphy?" Gonzalez growled.

"I said 'never mind'."

Another gust blew past me and toward Gonzalez.

There was a crisp metallic click as Gonzalez charged his rifle. "If you wanna play this game, I'll be damn sure I shoot first."

I stopped in my tracks, lowered my rifle, and slowly turned toward Gonzalez.

"What's wrong?" I said.

The wind blew again.

Gonzalez fired a shot at me, the round clipping a branch above my head. I dropped to the ground and crawled behind a rock just off the trail.

"I won't miss next time, boy."

"What the hell's wrong with you, sergeant?"

Another draft wafted downwind, carrying my voice with it. Further down the trail and upwind, there was a hole in one of the redwoods. Inside, a fleshy disk spun like a pinwheel every time I spoke.

Another round ricocheted off the rock, churning up earth and dust.

I pulled out a notepad and scribbled a few words on a sheet. I tore it out and folded it into a paper airplane, then yelled, "Read this. If what you hear is different than what you read, something is warping my words."

The instant I spoke, the flesh wheel started spinning. Taking advantage of the wind, I threw the paper airplane toward Gonzalez.

He took another shot. I watched and waited.

Unfolding the sheet, he read its contents. "Shit. You better not be fucking with me, Murphy. Now listen very carefully. Sling your rifle and slowly walk toward me. Above all, keep your mouth shut."

I tentatively raised my hands in surrender, then ambled toward him.

He trained his rifle on me, his finger resting on the trigger.

When I reached him, he motioned for me to lay face down. He confiscated my rifle. "Why did you threaten to kill me?"

"I never did that. You just started shooting."

"You're lucky I didn't aim. I wanted to scare you. You were saying some really twisted shit."

"See that fleshy thing inside that redwood?" I pointed at the blighted tree.

He nodded.

"Each time I spoke, that thing spun, creating an air current. That must've been what distorted my words. What you heard wasn't what I'd said."

He shook his head. "Impossible. I heard you loud and clear. For that thing to twist your words it not only would need to speak English, but it would also have to account for an insane number of variables like wind speed, distance, and the volume of your voice. And then it would've had to alter the sound so the message I heard, while entirely different than what you projected, was still comprehensible."

"Remember what Doctor Rosen said about a hive intelligence? Maybe it's smart enough to figure it out."

Gonzalez shrugged and then spit. "I don't know, seems pretty unlikely."

The earth shook. A concussive blast knocked us backward. White-hot shrapnel ripped through the air. I dove for cover. My ears rang like a broken bell.

"The hell was that?" I said, unable to hear my own voice.

"Grenade," Gonzalez mouthed.

The hillside erupted with small arms fire.

Gonzalez leapt to his feet. "Let's go," he signaled.

I got as close to him as I could to prevent the hive from distorting my voice and yelled, "What if the hive intelligence is manipulating sound farther up the line?"

"Shit," he mimed.

"Assume it's hand signals from here on out unless guys are in handshake distance?"

Nodding, Gonzalez gestured, "Follow me."

By the time we arrived at the leading edge of the battlefield, five more men lay in bloody pools. All of them had gunshot wounds.

Only Rosen had survived.

He approached us silently, speaking only when he was within arm's length. "I tried to warn them about the mimics, but they wouldn't listen." He shrugged. "Let's go. We don't have much farther, maybe a mile or so. Captain Li is arming the suitcase bomb.

෪

It was against my every instinct. It rejected all my training. But to survive, we had to clump together and stay within arm's reach. As Alpha Troop's twenty remaining survivors, we protected our deadly cargo with our lives.

We radioed our progress every hour to squadron headquarters. Four more companies stretched from here all the way back to the bluffs. If we failed, squadron would send another company to take our place, then another, and then another until our resources were spent.

None but the highest-ranking officers knew the endgame. When we were five hundred meters from our objective, Colonel Nathan, our squadron commander, radioed us outside our normal hourly window. "Retreat. Retreat. Return to the bluffs."

I was speechless. The order made no sense. Odder still, the colonel wasn't following proper radio protocol.

Gonzalez radioed back. "Ironhorse Six, this is Alpha One Two, over."

"Retreat. Retreat. Retreat," Nathan replied.

Gonzalez looked at me and mouthed, "The fuck?"

I shook my head. "Something ain't right."

"Ironhorse Six, Alpha One Two. Specify which unit must comply with your last order, over."

"Retreat. Retreat. Retreat."

"This mission's compromised," I said. "We gotta get moving."

Gonzalez nodded.

Minutes later, we stumbled upon the husk in all its grotesque glory. Leathery vines whirled and whipped at soldiers pointing their rifles toward a vast and towering, eye-infested husk. Slithering vines enveloped soldiers and squeezed them to death.

Before we got organized, the swirling mass had dispatched half our force. Then our bullets kept the vines at bay. But it couldn't last. Our ammunition was running low. We were exhausted.

Gonzalez and I protected Rosen and Li while they configured the tactical nuke. The captain wasn't happy about the arrangement, but Gonzalez had smoothed things over.

"We can't hold 'em back for much longer," Gonzalez said.

Li shouted, "We just need three more minutes!"

Bullets streamed toward the writhing husk. The vines were now slinking forward, eating away at our shrinking perimeter.

"Faster!" I yelled.

"I'm going as fast as I can!" Li said.

We were gonna do it. We were really gonna nuke this thing.

Something rustled behind me. I turned and saw a soldier with a bloated and blackened face.

Belski.

Behind him hundreds of soldiers shambled out of the mist, infested with the same black spores. The vines continued their advance, forming the hammer. Our infested comrades, the anvil.

"Hurry up!" I shouted, emptying my last clip into the vines. But where one vine retreated, another advanced, ripping the suitcase from Li's grasp and sucking it into the whirling vortex.

Li's expression said everything.

I glanced at Gonzalez. "You thinking what I'm thinking?"

He nodded.

So we fixed bayonets and plunged into oblivion.

END

Afterword

"Evolution's Echo" explores the classic government folly of experimenting with dangerous technology that it arrogantly judges it can safely handle. Inevitably the technology develops to a point in which government scientists lose control of the experiment, and a crisis ensues. And it's always the least informed and most expendable people who are sent in to pay the price and clean up the mess.

This story is about those heroes.

"Evolution's Echo" takes place in Mendocino, California, an area of incredible beauty on the coast of Northern California. With towering cliffs overlooking the Pacific Ocean to massive redwood groves surrounded by ferns, the location is absolutely breathtaking. Obscure this beauty with a creeping fog and creatures intent on infecting the soldiers who trespass on a strange bioengineered organism's territory, and you have one hell of an unsettling tale.

In addition to be being a standalone thriller about an Army platoon that has to confront an unknown enemy in a classified military operation, "Evolution's Echo" also includes Dr. Eli Rosen, a recurring character in many of my stories. His uncanny ability to survive under impossible conditions is never explained in this tale, so you'll have to read some of my earlier Rosen stories to understand what makes this particular physicist stand out from the rest. But you will not be disappointed when you do.

This story appeared in *Dark Moon Digest* in 2017. I hope you found it riveting.

Roses in Winter

Rose made a hash of the rented one-room cabin, desperate to find her son asleep and hidden under a heap of toys and clothing. Shuddering, she tried to convince herself that her worst fears wouldn't be realized, but reason told her otherwise. Autistic children had a tendency to wander, and Kirby loved to explore.

Her heart beat with an accelerating crescendo as she imagined her helpless son freezing to death alone, buried amidst the silent snowdrifts of the high Sierras.

As she pulled her leggings over cheap white flannel undergarments, she glanced out a snow-fringed window. A pale yellow sliver of light slowly slipped beneath the horizon.

They had come here to get a break from the craziness and sorrow. Life as a single mother was hard, but raising an autistic child alone was harder still. Since oh-eight, Rose's world had gone topsy-turvy. Her husband's construction business had been riding high. Then the financial crisis hit, and they'd lost it all.

Rose burst out of the redwood cabin and into the misty twilight. She knew Kirby would've headed for the frozen lake. Since they'd checked into the cabin yesterday, the lake's diamond-like shimmer had enraptured the boy.

Trudging and stumbling through knee-deep snow, Rose raced past towering redwoods that bore silent witness to her terror. With her husband already dead, losing her son would destroy what was left of her sanity.

In debt, unemployed, and desperate for cash, Jed had done the unthinkable: he'd blown his brains out with his father's Smith and Wesson, leaving her and her infant son to make do in the middle of an economic apocalypse. Three years later, Kirby had been diagnosed with autism.

After cresting a small rise, Rose saw a solitary child leaning against a redwood sapling on the lake's shore.

Kirby!

He waved excitedly at something in the mist.

Rose sprinted toward her son. But before she could reach him, he bolted out onto the lake. Rose's heart sank. She ran faster, terrified her son might fall through the ice.

Upon reaching the shore, she spotted a group of urchins in the distance. Draped in rags, they swirled in a nearly perfect circle around a shadowy form. Faintly, Rose heard them singing a melody that seemed familiar but that she couldn't quite place.

The dance mesmerized Rose. She watched in awe as the children slowly and inexorably carved a ring in the ice with their steady, rhythmic footfalls.

The urchins swallowed Kirby into their orbit. In the center of the rotating ring, the dark silhouette embraced Kirby.

Enraptured by the strange, hypnotic dance, Rose forgot her fear. The urchins whirled and spun, repeating the song over and over again. The cold of the biting wind vanished from Rose's consciousness. The circle became everything.

The wind abruptly changed direction, swirling the mist in its wake. And in that brief moment, Rose caught a glimpse of Kirby's murky companion.

It was a crone.

The old woman wore a ragged dress ill-suited for the bitter cold. But somehow her attire seemed appropriate to Rose. And there was something familiar about the woman's eyes.

In the twilight, the mist hung in the air as if the lake were somehow stuck in time. A quieting stillness settled over Rose. Suddenly, her eyes caught a crack in the ice. Then another.

The dancing children had etched a circle into the frozen surface where water began to rise. As if choreographed, they raised their hands above their heads and then thrust them toward the surface. Then, in unison, they all dropped to their knees. A deafening boom resounded as a massive ringed fissure snaked its way through the ice, and the children fell into the lake's cold embrace. Rose gawked, enthralled by the spectacle. By the time she realized what had happened, her son was gone, and the crone and her ragged children had vanished into the lake.

Rose raced onto the ice, frantic with loss. She collapsed onto the surface and wept.

℘

Overwhelmed by her loss, Rose could barely articulate what had happened. When she tried to describe the mysterious crone and her urchins to the authorities, her words came out as an incomprehensible muddle. The police dismissed her story as the ravings of a distraught mother devastated by the loss of her only son.

The official report chalked the tragedy up to simple wandering. Nearly half of autistic children exhibit wandering behavior, so the story stuck, and the investigation was closed. But in the following years, the local police never found a body.

Each year to the day, Rose made a pilgrimage to the lake. And each year, she'd lay a scarlet rose on the snowy ice.

The memories of her son's ecstasy just before his death haunted her. She couldn't reconcile the cold-blooded brutality of it all. She could never come to terms with his loss. He was her everything, her reason for being. So she meandered through her melancholy life where she had neither hope nor solace.

⁖

For twenty-nine years, Rose repeated her grim winter ritual, marking the passage of the four seasons with a single blossom. She placed twenty-nine roses to mourn her loss; twenty-nine roses to bury the pain; twenty-nine roses to blunt time's erosion of spirit and memory. For nothing is more cursed than outliving one's only child.

On the thirtieth anniversary of Kirby's disappearance, Rose returned to the old cabin in the high Sierras to leave yet another flower on the ice.

As she slogged through the stubborn snow on the brink of twilight, her bones creaked with the weariness of age. She struggled up the modest slope and then carefully made her way toward the towering, gnarled redwood that had grown from a sapling thirty years prior.

She placed her hand on the tree's auburn bark as if she were greeting an old friend. The redwood had been one of the only other living things to bear witness to her annual pilgrimages since the beginning, and it would be here long after they ended.

She took a deep breath before reaching into her coat and pulling out the rose. Stepping onto the ice, she made her way to the spot where Kirby had vanished.

But today, she and the redwood weren't alone. Ahead, in the mist, she could hear the laughter of children. As she pressed forward, she saw ten shadows cavorting on the ice. Her heart fluttered. Could one of them be her Kirby? She quickly suppressed the thought given its absurdity. After all, if Kirby were still alive, he wouldn't be a child, but a man fully grown.

Her vision wasn't what it used to be. She squinted to get a better look, but even a young woman's eyes would have failed to penetrate the shrouding mist.

And yet, despite all logic, and full of hope, she called out, "Kirby! Is that you?"

Giggles met her query. So she pushed onward.

When she had nearly reached the children, she came to the realization that none of them were Kirby. How could they be? Kirby had long since disappeared into the lake. And now Rose feared this scene spelled the onset of dementia or some other cruel affliction of the mind.

Rose's sorrow must have been palpable, for one of the boys smiled, placed his hand in hers, and said, "My name's Bobby. What's yours?"

"Rose."

"You look sad. Stay with us a while. We promise we'll cheer you up."

Tears welled in Rose's careworn eyes, and a smile creased her lips. "Okay."

The children locked hands, formed a ring around Rose, and sang, "Ring Around Rosey."

Rose clapped and laughed as the pure joy of childhood innocence washed over her. Since before losing Kirby, she'd never felt this happy. She'd almost forgotten the feeling of bliss.

The children frolicked around her until declaring, "Ashes, ashes, we all fall down."

And fall they did, into a circle of shattered ice.

Rose struggled against the frigid water until it claimed her forever.

ജ

Rose emerged from the ice into a realm of eternal winter. Surrounded by her wayward children, she wandered the void in search of her little Kirby.

Forever young, the children amused themselves by dancing around their foster mother, singing "Ring Around Rosey."

In the endless winter through which Rose and her children roamed, she began to love them as if they were her own. Yet there was still a hole in her heart that longed to see her son once more.

On rare occasions, Rose and her adopted brood would pass into the mortal realm, always in the depth of winter and always on that lake of shattered hope. Her yearning for Kirby intensified to the point of desperation. But he never appeared.

No one ever did.

Through many winters, Rose and her children ambled along the frozen lake searching for Kirby. And each winter, the great redwood sentinel on the shore seemed to diminish in its majesty.

Just when Rose had all but yielded to despair's black abyss, she noticed a boy waiting at the lake's edge. She smiled, and her adopted children began to traipse around her. The lone child leaned against the adolescent redwood, waving and clapping at the display. Rose motioned for the distant boy to join in the revelry.

After some coaxing, the boy dashed onto the ice, and Rose's children quickly engulfed him into their fellowship. Blinded by hope, Rose laughed and danced with her brood until the boy collapsed from the cold.

It was only then Rose realized the child was not hers. Tonight some other mother would discover her son missing and suspect the worst. But now that the child had passed into Rose's care, she'd be his surrogate mother for all time.

&

When winter shadows rise over dark horizons and sunder the night sky, time's branches sometimes twist and fold, warping the veil between life and death in a temporal carousel, where endings are beginnings and beginnings are endings.

As Rose's children circled her in dance, she spotted another boy waving from the shore who reminded her of Kirby.

A small part of her resisted calling the boy out onto the lake, but another part – hardened and tempered by the ice – overwhelmed her with an insatiable need to pull the child into her eternal orbit.

Her immortal children spun and sang their eerie tune. The boy clapped and jumped to the spellbinding rhythm.

As the dance reached a fever pitch, the boy lunged out onto the ice and bolted toward the circle. Rose smiled in satisfaction.

In the distance, another figure darted toward the shore. As it came closer, Rose instinctively knew it was the boy's mother. But the dazzle of the dance was too much for the poor woman, who stood dumbfounded by the redwood sapling on the lake's edge.

The children's heels cut deeper into the ice, carving a ring that began to pool with water. The boy's dancing and clapping began to slow. He shivered. His lips were turning blue. As the death grip of hypothermia took hold of the boy, Rose looked back toward the young woman enthralled by the dance. Then, gazing into the eyes of the dying boy, Rose now knew beyond any doubt it was her Kirby.

With a start, she glanced back toward the shore and recognized her younger self. And in that instant, the ice broke, and she and her immortal children shifted back into the void between realms, that netherworld of dark dreams where the snowflakes of time and memory drift backward forever.

END

Afterword

I finished writing "Roses in Winter" in late May 2016. As I look back on this story over nine years later, I am astonished to find a story so rich in symbolism and meaning.

The process of creation is at once both deliberate and subconscious. Many of the things a writer places in a story are put there on purpose. However, in hindsight, many other story elements surprise even the author.

"Roses in Winter" is one such story.

In particular, the story is rife with circular imagery—the circle in the lake, the ring around Rose, and most especially the cycles of time. All three serve to cement the theme of temporal loops that connect the older Rose to her younger self in a cycle of profound and infinite sadness. I don't believe that I had deliberately placed this symbolism when I had originally written this story. Instead, it seemed to have been an emergent theme from my subconscious.

Another aspect of this story that is important to note is that like Rose, I have a developmentally disabled child. I have also struggled with the fears and frustrations of raising a child who doesn't respond in a typical way to normal stimuli and has difficulty communicating. Like Rose, I too lived through the volatility of the Financial Crisis and the destruction in its wake. Not surprisingly, many of these biographical markers made their way into this story.

"Roses in Winter" was ultimately published in *Kasma SF Magazine* in 2017. I hope you found the story engaging.

Serpent's Wall

Papa stormed into the cottage, tearing off his sheepskin *ushanka* in a huff. "The chickens are missing!"

Yulia's stomach groaned—an instinct she'd honed during the famine. "We'll find them. They can't have wandered far," she said, knowing full well Papa would've already considered that possibility.

He shook his head solemnly. "No. The coop was torn open and covered in blood. Wolves, I suspect, though I don't quite know what to make of the scorch marks."

"Scorch marks?" Some dim childhood memory reminded her that that detail was important. A warning from Mama when Yulia was small. Something about fires above, fires below, and fires within. Dismissing the recollection as a distraction, Yulia concerned herself with more practical matters like how she'd replace the *kolkhoz*'s missing livestock or how she'd explain their disappearance to the Bolsheviks. But before Yulia had a chance to formulate a plan, she heard a diesel engine rumbling outside. She shuddered. Ever since December 1943, when the Red Army had driven the Germans out of Denisi, the Bolsheviks regularly patrolled the area. To the West, the Red Army had pushed all the way to the outskirts of Berlin, where the Third Reich was desperately fighting for its survival. But the Nazis no longer concerned Yulia—the Bolsheviks did.

Papa nodded toward her cleavage. "Cover yourself."

Yulia blushed before donning a shawl. She'd been an awkward little girl during the German occupation. But now, at thirteen, Yulia was blossoming into a beautiful young woman at the most inopportune of times. She'd also begun to sense the unspoken whenever she was around others. Some villagers said Mama had been able to catch thoughts too, but Yulia'd never put much stock in those tales.

Papa opened the door to their state-owned cottage. Across a muddy field, a squat, slate-gray T-34 tank belched smoke like an old pipe. Three Bolshie soldiers climbed off a red star-stamped cupola and approached her and Papa.

Papa clutched her arm, trying to drag her back inside. She resisted. Like Mama had been, Yulia was fearless. The Bolsheviks, like the Germans before them, didn't scare her one bit.

Their leader was a bear of a man. Brandishing his rifle, he made it clear that Papa would be inviting him inside.

But Yulia could sense something else. She couldn't quite describe the feeling. It was as if she could smell his thoughts on the chill wind, thoughts that seemed eager for violence.

Papa and Yulia stepped aside to make way for the soldiers. As they crossed the threshold, the bear's lanky companions leered at Yulia.

Once inside, their leader said, "I'm Sergeant Gordunov and I'm searching for my comrade. His name's Anatoly." He held up a black and white photo of a boy with strong cheekbones and a wide smile.

Papa stared at the photo as if to make a point of taking the inquiry very seriously. He shook his head. "Can't say I've seen him. Perhaps he decided to take some leave?"

Gordunov scowled. "Anatoly's a loyal soldier. He's no deserter."

Papa held up his hands, palms facing outward. "I meant no disrespect. Just trying to be helpful."

"I bet the Nazis found you very helpful too," Gordunov said with venom. "You hear anything about his whereabouts, report it to me immediately." He pointed outside. "You can find me at our camp about a kilometer beyond that ridge." Gordunov turned toward Yulia and rubbed his belly. "I'm hungry. How 'bout a snack?" He grinned, revealing a mouth of missing and rotten teeth.

"Please," Papa pleaded, "the Germans cleaned us out. We've only just begun rebuilding the *kolkhoz*'s stores."

"See," Gordunov nudged his comrade, "these Ukrainians were very helpful to the Nazis." Then he gripped his rifle and glared at Papa. "I'm sure you'll be even happier to help us, no?" The towering Russian wound like a cobra poised to strike.

Papa lowered his head and meekly motioned toward the kitchen. The soldiers tramped through the cottage, leaving clumps of mud in their wake.

Yulia stewed as the men rummaged through what little food they'd been able to save after fulfilling their state-mandated quota. Pots and pans clanged, and cupboard doors slammed open and shut.

Ten minutes later, the soldiers returned, carrying the family's last two loaves of bread.

Papa placed his hand on Gordunov's arm. "Please," he whispered, "leave something for us. We'll starve."

Gordunov sneered. "Like the rest of the Motherland, you'll make do."

The men left with their loot, reclining on the back of their T-34 as it rumbled southwest toward the bank of the Dnieper.

જી

Yulia began tilling the field just before dawn. Her stomach grumbled. Later that night, her and Papa would dig up the bread they'd buried near the privy for emergencies like this.

With a drill plow harnessed to Olga, the *kolkhoz*'s last surviving horse, Yulia churned the loamy earth into narrow ribbons and sowed the grain that would sustain them through the next winter. It hadn't always been this hard. Papa had owned several of his own horses before the Bolsheviks had confiscated them when Yulia was a toddler, during Stalin's collectivization campaign.

When the red-orange sun crested the horizon, a winged shadow drifted from east to west across the field. Casting her eyes skyward, Yulia watched the pair of black wings glide lazily on a chill wind. She followed them to a lonely oak perched on a hill. There, a committee of vultures congregated.

Yulia pulled Olga's reins taut. The horse came to a stop. She dropped the reins, patted Olga on the nose, and then headed toward the tree.

At the hill's summit, she found the wake of vultures gorging on a corpse. The bald scavengers were so engrossed in their feeding, they ignored her approach. As she drew closer, she recognized the partially eaten face of the boy in the photo, Anatoly. His eyeless pits stared into the void.

Fearless, Yulia drew closer still. She gagged on the stench of decay, then held her breath. Upon more careful scrutiny, Anatoly's torso appeared to be charred and blackened, reminding Yulia of Mama's eerie warning all those years ago.

Gunshots!

Two vultures exploded in a hail of feathers. The others took to the air.

"You there!" a man shouted in Russian. "Don't move."

Yulia's heartbeat quickened. From the valley below, Gordunov and his two lackeys stomped toward her. The sergeant put his paw-like hand on her arm. "You and your papa will pay for this."

"Please!" she begged. "I had nothing to do with this. I just found the body."

"Shut up, you filthy little *suka*."

Gordunov's backhanded blow to her face nearly knocked her off her feet. She could taste the salty tang of her own blood.

She struggled to keep up with Gordunov's long strides as he dragged her back to the cottage. Her arm throbbed from his grip.

When she and the Russians were within a hundred meters of the cottage, she spotted Papa. He stood outside, transfixed by the spectacle unfolding before him. Gordunov hastened his pace, hauling Yulia through the muddy field.

The sergeant smirked when he saw Olga. Olga responded with a warning snort. Her ears went stiff and started twitching. Gordunov shoved Yulia into the mud. He unslung his rifle and shot the horse from his hip. Olga collapsed with an ear-splitting squeal.

Yulia scrambled to her knees and crawled through the muck toward her dying horse. Tears rolled down her muddy cheeks, obscuring her vision. She placed her hand on Olga's flank and sobbed.

"That's what you get, <u>suka</u>!" Gordunov roared.

Papa raced to Yulia. One of Gordunov's henchmen swept Papa's legs. Papa careened into the mud. When he tried to stand, Gordunov's henchmen battered him with their rifle butts.

Gordunov held up his hand. His cronies stopped pounding on Papa. "Who tortured and killed Anatoly?"

Papa's eyes widened. "I...I don't understand."

Gordunov kicked Papa in the face. A riot of teeth and blood sprayed from his mouth.

The two men resumed Papa's beating. Their anger now seemed completely unhinged. She could smell thoughts reveling in the bloodlust. And she knew for certain that if she didn't intervene, they'd kill Papa.

"Stop!" she yelled. The soldiers laughed while they pummeled her father.

She crawled back to Gordunov. The sergeant observed the savagery as if he were appreciating Russian folk dancing.

"Please," she pleaded. "Let my father go. If you kill him, you'll have to answer to your commander. And since the horse you shot was also state property, you might have to answer for that as well."

Gordunov's rotten grin evaporated. He looked down at Yulia with an expression of contempt. Folding his arms across his chest, he paused, then said, "Blokhin. Kablukov. Enough!"

The two men obeyed, backing away from Papa, who now lay quivering in a pool of blood.

Gordunov thrust his meaty index finger at Yulia. "You. You're too smart for your own good. If you don't supply names by tomorrow, we'll tell the Molokan your papa did it. Then we'll get a warrant to shoot him."

Yulia shivered. She'd only heard mention of the Molokan in hushed whispers among the villagers. It was widely rumored that he drank the milk of the soul. Yulia didn't put much faith in such stories, but she nodded with an enthusiasm that shamed her anyway. A bullet would kill Papa more surely than some superstition.

She clung to her broken father as the soldiers marched off.

&

Vivid images of smoldering fields and men engulfed in flames invaded Yulia's dreams. From the vantage point of some winged beast, she watched the world burn. The visions were so visceral, they roused her from her sleep. A sudden urgency burned inside her gut. She hastily got dressed and scrambled outside into the welcoming night.

Strangely, she felt drawn to Serpent's Wall, a series of ancient earthworks stretching across the Ukraine. A collection of oak, birch, walnut, and chestnut trees crowned the earthen mound, their leaves just beginning to sprout in the spring thaw. Built centuries ago by some long-forgotten people, the Wall exerted a magnetic pull on her.

As she trudged through the darkness like iron to a lodestone, something in the distance reflected the moon's silver light. As she walked further, she could make out an oval-shaped object nestled against the earthen mound. An egg as tall as she was rested against the wall.

She pressed her hand against the egg. It had the texture of a homemade clay pot, imperfections and all. The steady rhythm of a heart beat inside. Something deep within her mind's eye called out to her. Visions flooded her consciousness, overwhelming her senses. Images rife with scales, fire, and fangs buffeted her at such a furious pace she couldn't process them.

She yanked her hand from the egg. What did it all mean? What kind of creature could produce such a thing? Why was the being inside reaching out to her? While Yulia had more questions than answers, she knew deep within her bones that the egg was linked to Mama's secret: Mama's stubborn insistence that the family never stray far from Serpent's Wall, especially during the famine when leaving the farm could have saved Mama's life. No. Yulia had no doubt the egg was worth protecting. She just didn't know why. Unsure what to do, Yulia made her way back home, blundering south along the Wall.

"Who goes there?" a male voice said in Russian. A flashlight's bright rays washed out her night vision. The metallic click of a rifle echoed in the gloom.

"Yulia," she shouted, holding up her hands.

"Well, Yulia, a bit late to be wandering out in the dark, isn't it?"

She nodded.

Behind her, something rattled.

"What was that?" said the man. "Yuri, you and Dmitry go check it out."

"Yes, Lieutenant!" Yuri said. He and Dmitry bounded into the night.

Three other Bolshies stayed with the Lieutenant.

Yuri shrieked.

"Everyone, down!" the Lieutenant commanded.

He delivered the order with such authority that even Yulia dove into the dirt.

The flashlight's ray danced chaotically and then stabilized. A black, sinuous thing briefly darted into the light, then back into the blackness.

"The hell was that?" said the Lieutenant, his voice quavering.

Dmitry squealed.

The Russians unloaded their weapons. Yulia closed her eyes and curled into a ball, making her body as small as possible. Hot shell casings rained down all around her. The odor of gunpowder suffused the cold night air. Yulia covered her ears in a futile attempt to mute the deafening gunfire.

In minutes, the shooting stopped. Slowly, Yulia opened her eyes. Just meters away, something slinked in the dark, tearing into the Lieutenant's bloodied leg. Six glowing ruby-red eyes regarded her from a moon-cast shadow. Then, as quickly as it appeared, the thing slithered off into the night, leaving six dead Russians in its wake.

&

Yulia woke in her bed to the sound of splintering wood. After returning home, she'd decided to wait until morning to tell Papa what she'd witnessed. Now, she feared she might be too late.

A loud crash shook the cottage. Yulia leapt up in a panic. She dressed frantically.

Footsteps tramped through the cottage and then up the stairs toward Papa's bedroom.

"Get up!" Gordunov's distinctive voice growled through the wall.

Yulia bolted out of her room and slammed into Blokhin. She fell backwards. He caught her. He spun her so her back faced him. He pulled her toward him, then cupped her breast. She stomped on his boot, broke free, then slapped him. She rushed past the soldier and into Papa's room.

Gordunov had Papa by the scruff of the neck and was dragging him toward the door.

Papa shouted. "What's the meaning of this? I've done nothing!"

"Then why do our comrades keep turning up dead or missing near this farm? You lie! Who are you protecting, old man?" Gordunov backhanded Papa in the face, peppering the chalky wall with blood.

Papa regarded her with his rheumy eyes. "Run!"

Gordunov's lackeys made to grab her, but she bobbed and weaved until she passed through the shattered front door and into the furrowed field. A thick orange sliver pierced the eastern horizon.

A storm of anxiety raged within Yulia. She worried for Papa's safety. She imagined the worst when it came to his treatment at the hands of the Bolsheviks. She was troubled that they were also coming for her. And she fretted over the egg. What if the Bolshies had found it?

Yulia ran harder, terrified that if the Soviets had uncovered the bodies, they might also have discovered the egg. She feared she'd never see it again.

When she reached Serpent's Wall, the corpses were gone, but a blood trail led north. She shivered. If they'd come first, the Russians would've have taken the bodies <u>and</u> the egg. She had no desire to follow the trail, but she needed to know if the egg was safe. So she crept north along the Wall.

To her relief, the egg stood where she'd last seen it, untouched. She'd be damned if she let the Bolsheviks take it, so she gathered whatever sticks and twigs she could and covered the egg. Then she coated her scaffold with mud before she collapsed against Serpent's Wall and drifted to sleep.

ૐ

It was dark when Yulia woke. How she'd slept through an entire day was a mystery to her.

She sat up against the Wall. Six glowing eyes regarded her from the blackness. They crept closer. Moving tentatively at first, they soon advanced with a steady confidence that frightened her.

In half a heartbeat, three wedge-shaped reptilian heads craning from serpentine necks snaked toward her. Without its wings, the creature's scaly frame was as wide as a German shepherd. It was over three times as long, including its necks and barbed tail. As if by instinct, Yulia held out her hand. In turn, each head sniffed her tender palm. Then the necks slackened, and the beast sauntered forward like a puppy meeting a new friend. Childlike, it settled into Yulia's lap, nearly crushing her with its not inconsiderable weight.

Yulia couldn't help but smile. After all that had happened these past few days, she really needed this. The hatchling licked her with its three forked tongues, and despite herself, Yulia giggled. She hugged her new friend with as much love as she could give.

Then, with the swiftness and suddenness of a snake, the rightmost head whipped back and gazed into her eyes. An avalanche of images assaulted her mind's eye. Warriors on horseback fired arrows at armored men and women manning a great wall. Just as the riders were about to overrun the battlements, streams of molten fire doused them from above. Then Yulia briefly glimpsed a scaled leviathan in flight.

The images appeared to shift forward to a time closer to her own. A skeletal woman shambled through a muddy street, begging a Soviet soldier for food. Relatives Yulia recognized from old family photos collapsed while swarms of flies gathered in their masses to feast on the great human harvest.

Holomodor—the butcher's bill for the greatest collectivist enterprise in history. A utopian vision painted on a canvas of human skin, stretched raw from inhuman suffering. Over and over, she witnessed her countrymen suffer famine's slow death. And over and over, she swore she'd make the Bolsheviks pay.

She came to in a cold sweat. The sun crested the eastern horizon. The hatchling was gone, but the hidden egg remained.

ↄ

The stench of diesel fumes and motor oil hung over the farm like a gray cloud. Yulia crept into the cottage, careful not to make any noise. In the near silence, she heard labored breathing.

Papa!

She raced upstairs. In his room, Papa cowered beneath his sheets.

"Papa!" she cried. "Are you all right?"

When he emerged, his face was bloated like a turnip. With what seemed like great effort, he sat up. His deep cerulean eyes gleamed in stark relief against a crooked nose and bloated black and blue cheeks. His smile was a small triumph against a swollen jaw and rows of jagged and missing teeth.

"I'm happy you're safe," he mumbled through puffy lips. "They want to talk to you."

"No. I won't speak to anyone who would do this."

He raised his right hand in supplication. "Please. Do it. They just want to ask you a few questions about the night those men died. They think you know who did it."

Yulia clenched her jaw. "No. I won't help them."

Engines rumbled outside. Yulia pulled back a curtain to look down below. Nearly a dozen tanks rolled into the field, ruining the furrows she'd tilled and jeopardizing her livelihood.

Papa gripped her arm. "Promise me you'll help them. If they take you away, they'll do worse things to you than they ever did to me. Please." Yulia watched the scene below, her jaw set in grim determination.

℘

They called him the Molokan. Some say the colonel was a mystic from the Siberian wilderness. Others whispered he possessed knowledge that allowed him to reach through death's veil. True or not, there was something unsettling about the man on her doorstep, the one staring into her eyes. Seeking, probing, testing.

She glared right back, finding solace in her defiance.

The pride in which he wore the black patch over his left eye could have only been earned through the deprivation of war. When his battalion had first set up camp, locals gossiped that the Molokan had lost his eye fighting an SS platoon hand-to-hand behind German lines in Stalingrad. Darker versions of the tale suggested he'd survived by hunting and eating Germans in the night. Some even hinted he'd devoured their souls.

The staring contest continued for what seemed like an hour. Neither the Molokan nor Yulia would yield. But the longer Yulia suffered his watchful gaze, the more vulnerable she felt. It was as if he was reaching inside her mind and plucking out memories.

As she glowered at the Molokan, despite her best efforts, her mind wandered. Before she became conscious of her thoughts, Serpent's Wall materialized in her mind's eye. She thought about the hatchling and all the visions it had granted her.

The Molokan smiled.

She closed her eyes and turned her head to avert his gaze, shutting her mind to the intrusion. But it was too late. Yulia panted, terrified he'd learn where she'd stowed the egg. He grabbed her chin, swiveling it back toward him. A powerful compulsion to open her eyes gripped her.

She fought against the urge, but the Molokan's will was too strong. Yet her mind seethed with a quiet fury. Drawing from this reservoir, she lashed out at her interlocutor.

The Molokan lurched backward in apparent confusion, shaking his head and stumbling like he'd been walloped with a frying pan. His smile curled into a scowl.

Yulia backed away in disbelief. Perhaps the stories about Mama had been true. After regaining his balance, the Molokan advanced into the cottage, his glare filled with malice. She tried to strike again, but her well was empty. A tidal wave of psychic force swept over her. Her vision faded to black.

℘

Yulia woke in a muddy field. The Molokan poked her side with a stick. The sky was dark and gray, with a looming storm on the horizon. Groggily, she rose to her feet.

He prodded her forward as if taking a cow out to pasture. Her heart sank when she realized he was leading her to Serpent's Wall.
Along the path, she passed soldiers placing plywood planks across a hole as wide as a tank and nearly as deep. It reminded her of the pits the Germans would dig to hide their tanks. One side had a gently sloping ramp leading into the hole so the tanks could roll into and out of it with ease. The Bolsheviks covered the plywood with tarp and then concealed the tarp with dirt. Near the ramp, a squat T-34 sat, its engine idling.

Two men ushered her toward a solitary wooden post ten meters from where she'd last encountered the hatchling. They pushed her face against the stake and then bound her with thick hemp. The rope bristled against her skin.

"Ah, my filthy little *suka*," Gordunov taunted from behind, "I'm gonna make you pay for running away."

That she couldn't see Gordunov only heightened her terror. What were the Molokan's plans? Why was he using Gordunov as his instrument?

The sharp crack of a bullwhip reverberated through the air.

"You hear that, *suka?*" Gordunov said. "Get used to that sound. The next time you hear it, my whip will be tasting your flesh."

Yulia's eyes widened. She glanced at the men who'd bound her, seeking a sign of what might come. They chuckled. She looked over her left shoulder. Her eyes settled on the Molokan. He seemed to regard her plight with disinterest.

"Why?" she squealed, immediately shamed the instant the word escaped her mouth. No. She'd suffer with dignity. She was better than these animals and she'd prove it.

The first lash beat the breath from her lungs. The second tore into her flesh. On the third lash, she bit her tongue, and it took every bit of self-discipline not to cry out.

She tried to strike out at the soldiers with her mind. But the pain of the whipping had somehow clouded her focus.

When the whip struck her a fourth time, she whimpered. Her vision faltered, and she now saw the world through a grainy gray film. She couldn't take the agony much longer.

On the fifth lash, Yulia detected the hatchling's presence nearby. It must have sensed her pain through their psychic link. Moments later and in broad daylight, the hatchling surged from the tree line along Serpent's Wall. It raced at a half gallop, half glide as it attempted, but failed, to fly. A Bolshie approached it slowly, and the hatchling incinerated him in a jet of flame.

The scent of roasting meat wafted through the air, adding flavor to the salty tang of Yulia's own blood. Gordunov rushed past her, gesticulating with his bullwhip.

One of the hatchling's maws yanked off a man's arm and swallowed it whole. Another engulfed a fleeing Bolshevik in flames.

Undeterred, Gordunov established a line of soldiers facing the hatchling. They advanced, firing a steady volley of rounds. The creature's hide appeared to protect it from the brunt of the assault, but it snarled when a few bullets slipped between its scales. Soon the hail of fire became so intense that the hatchling retreated backwards toward the dirt-covered tarp.

To Yulia's dismay, a T-34 rotated its turret and fired a round at one of the heads, cleaving it off. She muffled a scream. The Bolshies jeered as they herded the hatchling toward the trap.

When it seemed the hatchling could no longer breathe fire, it gnashed with fang and talon. Through their psychic connection, Yulia warned the beast to steer clear of the hole, but it wouldn't listen. The volume of fire was so overwhelming that an instinctual avoidance of pain dictated its actions now.

Then something miraculous happened. In the smoldering embers of the creature's headless stump, something wet and bloody bubbled into life. In less than a minute, the hatchling had regenerated its lost head. With renewed vigor, it advanced against the Russians, ripping them apart with talon, tooth, and claw.

Yulia smiled and then turned her head to gloat at the Molokan. When she saw him, her grin faded. His calm and confident demeanor suggested he'd anticipated this.

Another tank round slammed into the hatchling in a gout of smoke, flame, and guts. The Soviets renewed their offensive and the creature stumbled backwards toward the hidden pit. A meter from the hole, the wounded hatchling fought an inspired rearguard effort, severing another soldier's arm with its talons.

With a hand signal, the Molokan ordered a wave of reinforcements to rush into the breach and drive the hatchling onto the covered hole. The sound of snapping wooden planks echoed against the surrounding tanks.

The Molokan motioned toward the tank commander standing in the idling T-34's turret. The commander, in turn, ordered his driver to roll the tank down the ramp and into the pit, smothering the hatchling under tons of steel.

The tank pitched, yawed, and rolled like a rowboat navigating through a Black Sea storm as the hatchling struggled to escape.

An avalanche of psychic pain overwhelmed Yulia. The hatchling screeched in her mind. She could feel the tank's weight crushing the creature, squeezing out its insides.

Then the agony faded as Yulia's psychic connection was severed. Her eyes cast daggers at the tank commander. Intense fury welled up inside her like a boiler set to burst. She directed her spite toward him and let loose.

His head exploded in a riot of bone, brains, and blood.

She watched in disbelief. Seconds later, someone grabbed her shoulder. She turned her head, coming face to face with the Molokan. One gaze of his steely eyes drained the color from her world. Then, oblivion.

☞

Yulia woke bound to an icy steel table in a pale green and windowless room. A blinding white light swayed above her.

Cold and clinical, the Molokan said, "She's awake."

"Let me go!" she yelled.

"Now, now," the Molokan said in a mocking voice, "you know very well we can't let you roam free. You're a deliciously dangerous girl."

As her eyes adapted to the brightness, she spied a row of eight uniformed male and female Soviet officers sitting to her right, scribbling

diligently on notepads. To their right and at the opposite end of the room, P
apa was naked and tied to a chair.

Yulia struggled against her bonds, masking her fear with an indignant
scowl. "Papa!" She faced the Molokan. "You let him go! He has nothing to
do with this."

The Molokan nodded in that patronizing way of his. "Yes, yes. All
in good time, my girl. If you play your cards right, not only will I release your
father, but I'll make sure you flourish under the Soviet Union's tutelage."

For a moment, she ceased struggling. She couldn't quite believe what
she'd heard. After all, she'd murdered a soldier in cold blood and in front of
the Molokan's entire battalion. The NKVD murdered people for far less.

He smiled in that cold way killers do—a grin of the teeth, but with
predatory eyes that never falter.

"Your abilities are...impressive," he said. "So impressive, in fact, that
the Revolution needs them to fight fascism."

Either sensing her confusion or just filling the silence, the Molokan
continued. "It would be a good, respectable life. The Soviet Psychic Service
occupies a position of great respect and authority in Comrade Stalin's eyes.
We'll help you develop and hone your gifts."

Yulia slowly nodded at the offer—not to accept it, but to show she
was considering it. But despite her best efforts, she couldn't hide her hatred
of the Bolshies. She could never stomach working for a regime that had
starved her people; soldiers who had beaten her father; and a butcher who
had killed a baby hatchling. "Go to hell."

"Been there. It was not to my liking." The Molokan cracked his
fingers. "I thought you'd refuse." He clapped his hands. "Vasily, Anastasiya!"

Two of the note takers snapped to attention and walked toward
Papa. They gazed into his eyes. Papa shook. The veins in his forehead
throbbed. He shut his eyes and screamed.

"Stop!" Yulia shouted.

The Molokan moved to within centimeters of her face. "I see I now have your attention. Good. I can make your father's pain go away. All you need to do is join us."

A tear rolled down Yulia's cheek. An uncontrollable rage roiled inside her. With every fiber in her being, she lashed out at the Molokan.

Nothing.

He smiled that demeaning smile that said he had everything under control; that he had the situation well in hand. He clapped again. Vasily and Anastasiya returned to their seats. The Molokan pointed his forefinger at Papa and the bone in Papa's upper arm snapped and popped out of his skin.

Yulia shut out Papa's wailing and focused her mind on her bonds, trying desperately to remove them.

The Molokan laughed. "Child, your ability to manipulate bioplasma is confined to telepathic—not telekinetic—pathways. You can convince a man to boil his own mind, but you cannot use your mind to manipulate physical objects."

"There's an egg!" a raven-haired woman said, jumping to her feet.

Yulia almost cried. This entire time, the officers had been trying to read her mind. Now they knew about the egg!

The Molokan grinned. "Excellent! It seems we might yield two successes today. Now back to the other matter." The Molokan waved his hand. Papa screamed as a bone on his right index finger pierced the skin. "I can do this all day." The Molokan waved his hand again. Another finger bone shattered. Then another and another.

"Kill me!" Papa screamed. "Please! Kill me!"

"Oh that won't be necessary," the Molokan said in his smug tone. "Your daughter will protect you." He faced Yulia. "Won't you, Yulia?"

She sobbed. If only she said, "yes", she could stop Papa's suffering. But to what end? To serve an evil and murderous regime no better than the Nazis?

Papa screamed again. "Kill me!"

In his horrific agony, Papa gave her the only way out.

So Yulia annihilated Papa's mind, destroying the only leverage the Molokan had over her. As Papa sank lifeless into his chair, she howled. In her despair, her mind wailed...and a distant inhuman voice answered.

ଛ

Yulia sobbed in the back of an American Willys Jeep, seated beside the Molokan. The Jeep rode at the tail end of a convoy that included a column of T-34s, a mechanized crane, and a flatbed truck. Yulia wanted desperately to lash out at the Bolshies around her, but she felt the Molokan's psychic cronies shielding her mind.

As the convoy neared Serpent's Wall, Yulia's depression grew deeper and more desperate. She hungered for death—an end to the psychological torture. They'd stolen everything from her, and now they were going to take the hatchling's unborn sibling.

The tanks fanned out in a horseshoe facing the earthen wall. The Jeep came to an abrupt stop. With nothing left to lose, Yulia chomped on the Molokan's hand, then darted out of the Jeep toward the hidden egg.

There was a chorus of mechanical clicks. Dozens of peasant soldiers trained their rifles on her. But she didn't care. If death took her here, at least she'd find solace in her final act: protecting the unborn hatchling.

The crack of a rifle shot and the zip of a bullet jarred her from her run. Another shot, this one closer. But still she ran.

Seconds later, she reached the egg and embraced it, protecting it with her body.

"Cease fire!" the Molokan yelled. "We aim to take the object unscathed."

The soldiers lowered their rifles. Gordunov charged forward and pried her off the egg. He dragged her back to the Jeep as easily as he would a ragdoll. In a futile show of force, she scratched him.

"Poor little *suka* lost her friend," he said, grinning.

Yulia wept in anguish as the crane rolled forward, hoisted the egg from the earth, and set it on the flatbed truck.

She howled. Her mind flailed at everyone around her. But the eight psychics had her mostly contained. Mostly. They couldn't prevent her from feeling the unborn dragon yowling within the egg. Its helpless pleas made Yulia scream over and over again. She wanted to tear her eyes out.

Yulia glared at the Molokan. He smiled back. Somehow, he could also sense the unborn dragon's anguish.

The ground shuddered.

The Bolsheviks looked around nervously. It grew quiet again. But the silence had the same aura of unreality as the eye of a storm. The air was still, but charged. One match and it would all blow.

The earth groaned with the strain of something massive burrowing toward the surface. A shower of mud, rock, and dust exploded from the earth. A snout as long as a column of four tanks pierced the ground and shot upward as its sinuous neck reached for the sky like a beanstalk. Two more heads followed, blanketing everyone in soil and upending three T-34s.

Giant ribbed membranous wings ending in talons launched into the slate gray sky, casting a long shadow. It was the largest creature Yulia had ever seen. As the dust settled, the soldiers stood dumbfounded, watching the great winged beast soar toward the horizon.

Then it wheeled back around, picking up speed. The giant wyrm swooped down like an aircraft on a strafing run. Its three heads blazed a flaming path, combusting men and material. Survivors unloaded their automatic weapons pell-mell at the beast.

After it had completed its pass, the dragon clutched the egg in its colossal talons, disappearing over the horizon.

The soldiers scrambled around a chaotic scene, fighting fires and collecting the charcoaled remains of their dead.

Minutes later, a black speck appeared in the distant sky, quickly resolving into the three-headed wyrm. It no longer carried the egg. As it approached, the Bolshies threw together a hasty defense, aiming their rifles and rotating their tank turrets toward the flying leviathan.

The lingering scent of sulfur suffused the air as the dragon swooped down on the Russians. It blazed another swath of earth, metal, and men, fusing them into ash. Rifle rounds ricocheted off the beast like ball bearings bouncing off concrete. But sometimes a round would slip between its scales, causing it great pain that Yulia could sense through their psychic link.

Not only did the dragon have to contend with an all-out physical assault, but Yulia could also feel the Molokan and his psychics assailing the dragon's mind. It was if the dragon were playing multiple games of chess simultaneously.

While the psychics concentrated their efforts on fighting the dragon, shielding Yulia no longer seemed a priority. So Yulia surreptitiously took control of a soldier's mind, compelling him to creep behind his comrades and slit their throats. She killed three psychic officers in this manner before attracting the Molokan's attention.

A wall of wind swatted her from the Jeep like a fly. The Molokan marched toward her, then reached down and choked her. She squirmed and struggled, but no matter what she did, she couldn't escape the vise of his grip.

Her vision began to fade. Her essence was slipping away, as if the Molokan were consuming it. In utter exhaustion, she stopped her writhing. And in one last gasp, she summoned the dragon.

And the dragon came.

When its four immense legs touched down, the earth quaked. The volume of small arms fire intensified as the soldiers unloaded their rifles at a target that was now much easier to hit.

The dragon stomped toward the Molokan, flattening Bolsheviks in its wake. A well-aimed tank round slammed into the dragon's hide, blunting its advance ever so slightly.

Distracted, the Molokan backed away from Yulia. He organized his forces into a coordinated defense.

"Aim for the heads," he shouted.

Yulia stumbled to her feet. Searching for the remaining five psychics, she identified them for the dragon. One brawny male psychic stood on the back of a T-34, directing fire against the wyrm. The dragon crushed him and the tank under its enormous forepaw. A blonde woman huddled behind an oak tree as she launched psychic attacks against the dragon. Within seconds, the dragon rendered her and the oak into a smoldering ash heap.

The surviving T-34s systematically directed their fire at a single head. In a riot of smoke and flames, one of the dragon's necks collapsed. Three men armed with flamethrowers rushed to the scene, cauterizing the headless stump.

The area was like the surface of a volcano with smoke and pyres of flame erupting everywhere. But the dragon's efforts were flagging. Yulia had to do something, so she used the chaos to her advantage. She made Gordunov believe the three remaining psychics were Nazis.

Gordunov marched toward his first victim and gutted her with his bayonet, his faced twisting in a snarling rictus. Then he gripped her male companion by the neck and crushed the man's windpipe.

The last surviving psychic, the woman the Molokan had called Anastasiya, shifted her attention to Gordunov. Half a heartbeat later, his head exploded in a scarlet mist. But half a heartbeat was all Yulia needed. Reaching into Anastasiya's mind, Yulia absorbed the woman's deepest fears and turned them against her. Anastasiya spent her final moments tearing her face off to remove phantom spiders.

Now Yulia sought out the Molokan. More confident in her powers, she yearned to make him suffer. But the dragon's sorry state gave her pause. Two of its necks lay smoldering on the ground, their stumps cauterized. Its third head fought for its life with fire, fang, and fury.

Another tank round slammed into its snout. Yulia couldn't afford the luxury of chasing the Molokan now. She had to save the dragon.

Yulia set her sights on a T-34. Seconds later, its turret slewed toward an adjacent tank. The first tank's commander seemed perplexed and yelled at the gunner inside the cupola. But he was too late. An instant later, the neighboring T-34 was a smoking ruin. A third tank fired at the first, punching a smoking hole into its flank.

The dragon lifted its remaining head and beat its wings in an attempt to escape. Just as it took flight, a tank round severed a wing in a riot of bone and smoke. The dragon collapsed and the ground trembled.

Two more T-34s rolled into position and trained their main guns on the beast. The dragon sent Yulia an image: an egg perched in the cradling branches of an oak tree. *Good,* she thought. *The Molokan would never be able to place the tree; but she would. She knew exactly where to find it.*

The tanks fired, blasting the dragon's last head into oblivion. A euphoric rush of power surged into Yulia, transforming her into a battery brimming with psychic energy.

Somehow she knew it wouldn't last. She had to use it before it faded. And use it she did.

She overturned tanks with her mind. She bashed fleeing soldiers against their T-34s like flies against windshields. She flattened skulls with nary a thought.

Within minutes, every Bolshevik had either fled or suffered a gruesome death.

Only the Molokan remained.

The shock on his face was obvious. He'd counted on Yulia being telepathic, not telekinetic. But Yulia knew those telekinetic powers would only last until the final embers of life faded from the dragon.

She took no chances.

Coiling her energy like a compressed spring, she unleashed it in one defiant blast. The Molokan pitted his own substantial reservoir of power against hers.

It wasn't enough.

She flung him twenty meters, smashing him against an oak tree. Rather than face her, he staggered to his feet and fled.

Yulia wanted desperately to chase and run down her tormentor, but she was utterly spent. Yet she persisted. But when she tried to pursue him, she collapsed from exhaustion.

She despaired as he escaped into the boundless fields beyond. But then an idea struck her like a mule kick. She could sense his state of mind: frantic. His thoughts, jumbled and frenetic. His mind concentrated on nothing but survival.

So Yulia showed him what he wanted to see with a touch of something even more enticing: glory.

&

"Teach me everything you know, Molokan," Stalin said. "As the greatest psychic of your generation, you're the only one worthy of the honor."

Stalin had never referred to Colonel Petrov that way before. Perhaps he meant it as a compliment; perhaps he was just toying with his prey. With Stalin, you could never be sure. Either way, Petrov stayed on his knees. He found it incredible that Stalin could ignore such a humiliating defeat.

"Comrade Stalin," said Petrov, "I would be honored to teach you. What brings you this close to the front?"

Stalin waved his hand dismissively. "Never mind that. I know you think you've failed here, but I assure you, you have not. We still have the egg, no?"

Petrov wanted to slit his own throat. How would he tell Stalin the egg was lost?

"Forgive me, Comrade Stalin, but the egg is gone. The great wyrm has hidden it."

"Nonsense. I have agents throughout the Ukraine. I know exactly where it is. All we need do is acquire and protect it."

"But, Comrade Stalin, I thought we were going to use Rasputin's spell to extract the egg's power?"

Stalin paused. He seemed uncertain, but then he waved his hand. "Never mind that. For now, I wish to protect the egg."

"But, Comrade Stalin..."

"Don't interrupt me. I've made up my mind. I've decided. Now on to more important things. Show me how to master the power of telepathy. I wish to learn how to project an illusion...indefinitely."

END

Afterword

"Serpent's Wall" explores the complex relationship between the Russians and Ukrainians after the Soviets had "liberated" the Ukraine from Nazi occupation. After witnessing the starvation of several million of their compatriots in the Holodomor in Stalin's collectivist campaigns in the 1930s, many of the Ukrainians had both welcomed and fought for the Wehrmacht against the Soviets. As such, many of them were anything but relieved when the Soviets returned. This story takes place at the time when the Soviets are pressing on Berlin, and the NKVD is rapidly reconsolidating reconquered Soviet territory.

The story takes place near what is known as Serpent's Wall in Ukraine, a series of ancient earthworks that inhabitants had built between the second century BC and 700 AD to defend their territory from marauders. Local legend tells of a mythical hero who slayed a gigantic dragon by hitching it to a plow and furrowing the earth. The resulting banks of this furrow became Serpent's Wall.

Amidst this historical backdrop is a young girl who comes into her psychic power and must stand up to Soviet oppression to protect her family, and by extension, the hatchlings. The Molokan represents the state's psychic opposition to her powers. The inspiration behind that particular character came from another Army officer whose family had emigrated from Russia to the United States because of religious persecution. While the character was not based on him, the sect to which he belonged was. The Molokans or milk drinkers were known for their mystical traditions and apocalyptic visions often delivered in prophetic dreams.

"Serpent's Wall" was first published in the *Curiosities* in 2019. After the Russia-Ukraine War began in February 2022, editor David Flin put together a charity anthology called *Building a Better Future* to support Ukrainian civilians. I am proud to say that this story also appeared in that volume.

SWARM

The Russians were coming. They had Captain Roland Skaskiw's Special Forces team pinned down in a forested valley just outside Avdiivka, an industrial town north of Russian-occupied Donetsk. With only three survivors from his original complement of twelve, Skaskiw had been fighting a running battle against Russia's 37th Motorized Infantry Brigade for over a week.

Wearied not by cold, hunger, or lack of sleep, Skaskiw felt something darker weighing on his soul. His three-year-old daughter, Anna. He frowned at a memory of her squeezing his finger and staring up at him with those innocent emerald eyes; that would haunt him until the day he died.

From the east, a muzzle flash heralded a piercing whine that echoed through the valley. Yet no explosion followed. Skaskiw turned to Perez, his short and stocky weapons sergeant, a powder keg of a man with a short fuse. "The hell was that?"

"Sounds like a 152-millimeter howitzer. Ordnance unknown." Skaskiw shrugged. "Hang tight. Extraction's in one hour."

Over the past year, the Kremlin had been launching cyber attacks against critical infrastructure, subverting European elections, and using the Black Sea Fleet to aggressively patrol the Eastern Mediterranean. A Neo-Cold War was on the precipice of boiling over into a hot one.

From his cargo pocket, Skaskiw pulled out a ragged photo. He gazed at Anna's faded image. He kissed her picture and said a silent prayer before banishing the memory once more for the task at hand.

To the west, dozens of white and black specks peppered the gray sky, resolving into coal-black cannonballs swaying from white parachutes.

Skaskiw took a deep breath. The only thing worse than walking into a minefield was having one walk into you.

A SWARM.

Short for Scatterable Wide-Area Autonomous Robotic Mines, these sadistic little mamas scared the piss out of Skaskiw. The first time he'd faced them, they'd wiped out three quarters of his team.

Having flared on and off for a decade since Putin's 2014 annexation of Crimea, the Russo-Ukrainian War was heating up again. Skaskiw had come here to collect evidence of Russian violations of the Palo Alto Accords, which had banned offensive autonomous weapons systems. But mission creep had quickly thrust Skaskiw's soldiers into direct conflict with the Russians. Given NATO's official policy of non-intervention, Skaskiw's operation was supposed to be covert. Surrender wasn't an option.
Skaskiw needed a plan—fast.

Half a klick to the north, he spotted a redbrick schoolhouse. From there, he could blunt the Russian advance long enough to make his escape. Several meters further north, oak and pine trees lined both sides of a paved road stretching from east to west.

The SWARM began touching down behind him, cutting off his western escape route. Skaskiw frowned, then faced his comms sergeant, a lanky, straw-haired Minnesotan. "Talk to me, Jorgensen."

Jorgensen flipped down his ARTEMIS goggles. The Augmented Reality Targeting and Engagement Mapping Integration System consolidated imaging data from scores of solar-powered centimeter-length autonomous micro-drones loitering overhead.

"Contact! BMPs! Three o'clock. Two klicks out," hollered Jorgensen. Eight wedge-shaped armored vehicles closed in from the east.

Skaskiw spun toward Perez. "How many SAMs you got left?" A SAM, or Semiautonomous Attachment Mine, could be preprogrammed to latch onto a specific target and detonate on command.

"Sixteen."

Skaskiw gestured toward the tree line. "I want SAMs there ASAP." Perez popped open a black briefcase and removed eight racquetball-sized SAMs.

Skaskiw pointed at the schoolhouse. "We deploy the SAMs, then hole up and fight from there."

Perez fastened four small counter-rotating blades on each SAM, then gave Jorgensen a thumbs-up. Jorgensen remotely engaged the SAMs with his goggles. The rotors swirled, lifting the SAMs thirty meters above the ground before they swooped toward the road and veered sharply to either side in equal numbers. Then they disengaged their rotors, launched spring-loaded, retractable spikes on metal wires, and latched onto the trees at chest level.

☙

In the schoolhouse, Skaskiw stumbled upon five scrawny children squatting in darkness. Their slate-blue eyes stared from soot-smothered faces. And in one little girl, he saw Anna.

"We can't stay," Perez said.

Perez was right. If they hunkered down here, the children would get caught in the crossfire.

"Mines three hundred meters and closing!" warned Jorgensen.

Perez wiped his brow. "Now what?"

Skaskiw grinned. "Have faith. Here's the plan: we detonate the SAMs the instant the bulk of the BMP column is in the kill zone, then attack."

The little girl toddled up to Skaskiw and hugged him. Seconds later, an explosion rocked the building, shaking up flakes of paint and dust.

"Now!" Skaskiw yelled.

Jorgensen detonated the SAMs. Skaskiw kicked open the school door, raising his rifle as he advanced on the unscathed lead BMP. Seven other vehicles lay pinned beneath fallen and splintered trees.

Skaskiw hesitated, second-guessing his decision to leave the children behind.

Two soldiers stumbled from the lead BMP's rear troop compartment, snapping Skaskiw out of his trance. He shot them, then glanced over his shoulder. Two hundred meters out, mines scurried toward him on mechanical spider legs.

Bullets zipped by. The Russian survivors rallied from beneath the toppled trees, pinning down the Americans behind the BMP.

Perez and Jorgensen raided the BMP's troop compartment, making quick work of the dazed men inside. Climbing into the turret, Perez gunned down the driver. Then he and Jorgensen tossed the bloody body from the vehicle. Perez slipped into the driver's hole, Jorgensen commandeered the gunner's station, and Skaskiw took control of the turret.

Perez aimed the BMP at the advancing minefield. From the gunner's station, Jorgensen swiveled the turret one hundred eighty degrees and destroyed the seven trapped BMPs to the east. Then he rotated the turret forward again, training its 30-millimeter cannon on the crawling minefield.

"Don't shoot the SWARM!" Skaskiw had a hunch the mines wouldn't attack Russian vehicles unless provoked.

The mines maneuvered with uncanny grace, dodging debris and leaping over obstacles like lions, stalking anything that moved.

Suddenly, the children ran out of the schoolhouse and right into the SWARM's path.

Skaskiw shouted, "Gun it!"

The BMP surged forward. The SWARM advanced. The children froze. A mine exploded.

Skaskiw screamed, "Faster!"

The gap between the SWARM and the children was closing fast.

"Hard right!" Skaskiw ordered.

Perez wedged the BMP between the children and the SWARM. The vehicle squealed to a halt. Skaskiw and Jorgensen scrambled to pull the children aboard; the SWARM, now only meters away.

The little girl stumbled.

Against every instinct, Skaskiw leapt from the BMP and raced to her rescue. As he carried her to the vehicle, a mine clung to his leg. Skaskiw pushed forward, weighed down by the metallic anchor. Jorgensen clutched the girl's arm and pulled her onto the BMP. More mines grasped Skaskiw, dragging him away.

Jorgensen hesitated.

"Go!" Skaskiw yelled.

Before the mines detonated, Skaskiw watched in satisfaction as the seven lives he'd saved sped toward safety. As the little girl reached out to him, Skaskiw thought of Anna and smiled. He'd failed to save his own daughter. At least he could save someone else's.

END

Afterword

In "SWARM," I again return to war-torn Ukraine. I originally wrote this story for an organization called SciFutures, which paid writers to "futurecast." This process involved writing stories incorporating futuristic technologies. The company would provide organizations with these stories to help them envision how those futures might play out. I wrote this particular story for NATO on how disruptive technologies might be used in future conflicts twenty-five to thirty years in the future.

The inspiration for this story's mobile antipersonnel mines came from an anecdote that a U.S. Army military intelligence officer once shared with me. In that narrative, one of his soldiers had claimed that he had been sent out to a proving ground in the Mojave Desert at the U.S. Army's National Training Center in the late 1990s to help test autonomous walking mines. The solider expressed his creeping unease at how these bots would follow him everywhere he went.

Another eerie aspect of this story is that it turned out to have been strangely precognitive, foreshadowing the current proxy war between the United States and Russia in Ukraine as well as the ubiquitous use of drones in that conflict.

"SWARM" was ultimately published in Vice Media's science fiction imprint *Terraform* in December 2017. It was subsequently reprinted in *The Year's Best Military and Adventure SF, Volume* 4. In February 2023, it appeared in *Ten Years Later*, the successor volume to *Building a Better Future*. David Flin edited both volumes to support Ukrainian civilians. I am very proud to say that this story appeared in that subsequent volume.

I hope you enjoyed it.

The Godhead Grimoire

The box from the National Archives arrived with the blistering wind and driving snow of late December. Miranda nearly set the package aside until she remembered Damien's fanatical warnings not to open it. The bastard still hadn't signed the divorce papers, so she took a peek anyway. With scissors, she carefully cut the packing tape so she could later cover her tracks.

Tentatively dipping her hand into a sea of foam peanuts, Miranda lifted a rectangular object wrapped in parcel paper from the box.
She hesitated, worried that if she went any further, Damien would know she'd broken the seal.

Screw him, she decided, ripping open the packing paper with the wild abandon of a prisoner escaping a super max prison.

It was a book. And by the look of it, an antique. Its ragged leather cover stretched taut over a sturdy bone frame, conveying a sense of timelessness. The tome's jagged edges could easily pierce skin. Inscriptions reminiscent of Egyptian hieroglyphs encircled a stylized eye etched on the cover's upper left quadrant.

Curious, Miranda opened the book. The stench of rot overwhelmed her. Turning her head, she gagged. Pepper, her coal black German shepherd, growled at the artifact. But Miranda refused to let its odor deter her.

The book's blank pages felt smooth and durable like vellum. A sequence suddenly materialized on the first page. With a doctorate in mathematics, Miranda instantly recognized the pattern as a Fibonacci sequence.

She found the experience unsettling. Not only was the book writing itself, but it was populating its pages with Arabic numerals, a system invented over two millennia after Egypt's Old Kingdom. There was also something fundamental in the book's choice of the Fibonacci sequence. It was a pattern rife in nature, characterizing phenomena as diverse as the branching of trees to the structure of a nautilus shell to the spiraling of galaxies.

As Miranda read further, the pages revealed more complex mathematical concepts ranging from Fourier transforms to fractional derivatives to elliptic curves. It was as if the text were establishing a baseline of her mathematical competence.

Soon, the tome had exhausted her encyclopedic knowledge of advanced mathematics, unveiling concepts just beyond its current frontiers. The book mesmerized her.

The ringing cell phone jolted Miranda from her trance, jamming her back into her own mundane reality. She nearly threw her smartphone across the room.

On the third ring, she answered, "What?"

"This is Seth Rosenblatt of Rosenblatt, Wilson, and Yablonsky. Is Miranda available?"

She rolled her eyes. "This is Miranda."

"Oh, great," he said, his tone indicating anything but. "I have a few questions regarding this divorce settlement. I don't think Damien should sign it as is."

Struggling to control her temper, Miranda cut him off. "Not now. Call Robert Menendez, my lawyer. He'll handle this."

"I'm sorry, Misses Adams, but I need your personal approval on several items."

He was trying to take advantage of her, and she knew it. "It's Doctor Lovko, not Misses Adams. And, like I said, don't talk to me, talk to my lawyer."

"But Misses...ah...Doctor Lovko, I must insist..."

She hung up the phone. When she glanced at the clock, five hours had passed since she'd begun reading the tome.

Reaching for the book, she opened it to where she'd left off, anxious to uncover more of its secrets. But all she saw was a blank page. Confounded, she rifled through the book, but found nothing. She cursed Rosenblatt and went to sleep.

৪৩

That night, Miranda slept in fits and starts. When sleep did come, visions she could only describe as dreamscapes of unreality flooded her consciousness. Disembodied tongues whispered to her from beyond, urging her to press onward, to read further. But she had no idea how to unlock the tome's mysteries.

A phone call woke her from her restless slumber. She opened her eyes, realizing she'd never left her living room. The book still rested in her lap.

The phone rang again. The light shone brightly through her windows. Checking her watch, she realized nearly eighteen hours had passed.

"Hello?" she answered.

"Miranda, this is Damien. Did you get the package yet?"

She hesitated, then looked down at the tome, wondering what to say. She needed more time. "No," she lied, "but I'll call you as soon as I receive it."

"Okay, but it's really important. Let me know the instant it's delivered. And whatever you do, don't open it. It's very old, and I don't want it damaged."

A little late for that, Miranda thought. "Understood. By the way, did you sign the papers yet?"

An awkward pause.

"I thought we were gonna sit down with Seth Rosenblatt on Friday. Didn't you set that up?"

"Why's that my responsibility? You requested the meeting. Look, why don't you have him review the documents and send his edits to my lawyer? Then you can sign it. Sound like a plan?"

"Sure," he said before hanging up.

Damien was so self-centered and always fussing over trivial things. Frustrated, Miranda pounded her fist on the artifact. A stab of pain shot through her hand. Blood dripped onto the tome's sharp bony ridges.

"Dammit!" she yelled.

She grabbed the book and stood up. It slipped from her bloody fingers. When it landed, it opened to the page where she'd left off. A drop of blood smeared the page. Letters formed, congealing into words, and words resolved into sentences.

❧

Miranda cancelled her appointments and called in sick to study the ancient tome. It was the end of the semester. A meticulous planner, she'd already scored her final exams and assigned grades. Her nephew, Tommy, was due to visit her in less than two weeks, but she was confident she'd be finished with the book by then.

Moving beyond mathematics, the book began to reveal the greater mysteries of the cosmos. Miranda now contemplated what before had been unfathomable, expanding her consciousness and consuming knowledge like a locust swarm rampaging on a limitless ethereal plane.

Almost as soon as the book started sharing its secrets, it stopped. So Miranda bled herself to coax the tome to eke out more. Yet each successive cut yielded fewer and fewer sentences until a single drop could barely entice the stingy artifact to trickle out a handful of words.

Her bloodletting left her dizzy, unsure of her surroundings, and caught between reality and unreality. She had an uncanny suspicion that others watched her with hungry eyes. Disembodied presences lurked at the edge of her vision, imploring her to let them in.

Pepper growled in their direction and seemed increasingly uneasy in Miranda's presence.

She gazed longingly at Pepper.

Miranda needed more blood.

ꙮ

Miranda hadn't slept in four days, her desperation deepening with each passing moment. She sweated profusely and her nails had turned a bruised blue. She feared that any more blood loss would put her into hypovolemic shock. Yet she also experienced an odd sense of empowerment, her consciousness operating on a higher plane.

Through the fraying curtain between realms, discarnate entities whispered to her, wheedling her to draw the summoning circle someplace dark, someplace deep, someplace hidden from the light of the stars. All would be revealed, if only she'd let them in.

Coating the cellar floor in her own sickly blood, she followed their instructions to the letter.

Cloaked in darkness, she sat in the center of the summoning circle, chanting in alien tongues. The entities came ever closer, hissing from the void. Shapeless forms swirled around her, dulling her senses.

They tempted her with grandiose visions of the godhead, murmuring of the ability to know the future and change the past; to comprehend the nonlinearity of time. They showed her parallel timelines and alternate dimensions. They shared a glimpse of the power to create worlds and the fearsome might to destroy them.

If only she did what they asked, they'd shepherd her through the veil of existence toward the next stage in her enlightenment. She'd become one of them, one with them. A god holding dominion over a ceaseless cosmos.

As quickly as the god forms appeared, they vanished like fog in sunlight.

Miranda woke hours later, her vitality drained. She stumbled upstairs and prepared for the next step in her evolution.

∞

Miranda worried that if she continued to fuel the book with her blood, she'd die before extracting its secrets. While the entities had shown her another way, it was a choice she could barely stomach. Yet from the edges of reality, the voices whispered to her, urging her along the one path to transcendence.

The ringing doorbell roused Miranda from her stupor. She struggled to rise from her bed.

"I'm coming!" she croaked with as much strength as she could muster, wheezing from the effort. She staggered onto her feet, the bones of her shaky, rail-thin legs creaking. Draping her azure bathrobe over her now frail frame, she lumbered downstairs.

She peered out her window to find Damien standing outside in a Brioni suit, obsessively checking his Patek Philippe watch.

Miranda girded herself for a fight as she opened the door.

"Finally!" he said in a tone more suited for a motorist who'd just cut him off on Route 128. Once Damien saw her, his outrage gave way to an expression of concern.

Miranda cut straight to the point. "What do you want?"

"My God, Miranda, what happened?"

"What do you mean?"

"I...I don't know where to begin," he stammered. "Everything all right?"

Damien had never been good about expressing himself. He'd always been so passive, so indirect. And it drove her mad. "Stop pretending to care. Tell me why you're really here."

He stared at her for some time. "All right. But you have to promise to tell me what's been going on with you. To be honest, you look really sick."

"Fine, I'll update you on my life, such as it is."

Apparently satisfied with her answer, he continued. "When I called you a week ago, you told me my package hadn't arrived. Well, I reached out to the National Archives this morning, and they assured me that FedEx delivered it here ten days ago. Did you somehow miss it?"

That was Damien's passive-aggressive way of calling her a liar. And the fact that he was right annoyed her to no end.

Miranda struggled between coming clean or perpetuating the lie. If she risked telling him the truth now, she might lose the artifact.

She shrugged. "You got me. It's here. I wanted to hold onto it until you signed the papers, which, by the way, you still haven't."

He nodded. "Fair enough. Go get them. I'll sign them now."

It wasn't the response Miranda had expected or hoped for. "Don't you need Seth Rosenblatt to review them first?" she asked, playing for time.

"No. I trust you. Let's get this over with. But what I really wanna do is examine the artifact."

This wasn't going well at all. He couldn't have the book. There was simply no way she'd let him have it. She was too close. She only needed a few more days. If only she could stall him a little longer.

"Okay," she said. "Why don't you come in for coffee? I'll get the papers."

He smiled. "And the artifact."

The voices whispered to her, buzzing like wasps inside her head. "Yes. Of course."

He followed her into the living room and took a seat on the couch. He scrunched up his face. "When's the last time you cleaned?"

"Let me start brewing the coffee," she said, ignoring his allusion to the odor that permeated her home. "I'll also grab the papers."

As she turned toward the kitchen, he put his hand on her arm. His eyes focused on the scars on her hand from her bloodletting. "Miranda, I'm concerned about you. Your hand's all torn up. You've clearly dropped a ton of weight, despite your always having been rather thin. Your hair's falling out. It looks like you've been through hell. There something you wanna tell me?"

Cancer. He probably thought she had cancer.

"Why are you so concerned all of a sudden? You certainly weren't worried about my wellbeing when you fucked Tina." She pushed him away and trudged toward the kitchen. She started brewing some coffee and then went to her study to retrieve the documents.

The voices from the ether were growing louder, more insistent, crowding out her thoughts.

She tried to shut them out by focusing on the tasks at hand. Carrying the divorce papers into the living room, she dropped them and a pen into Damien's lap. "Sign these. I'll get the book."

He glowered. "How did you know it was a book? You didn't open it, did you?" His tone straddled a razor-thin line between panic and anger.

"You got me," she said. "Don't worry. I didn't damage it. I was just curious why you were so obsessed with it."

"Okay," he said, visibly shaken by her revelation. "Can I see it?"

"Sure. As soon as you sign those papers."

"Oh, right." He rifled through the documents and began signing them.

"Let me check on the coffee, then I'll get the book. Do you know much about its history?" she said, walking out of the room.

Damien's mood seemed to flip-flop from hysteria to excitement. "Oh, I spent years investigating an obscure letter General Patton sent his wife, Beatrice, during the Second World War that mentioned an odd relic captured from German forces in North Africa. Before that, the grimoire's history is hazy, but based on the cover's inscriptions, it harkens back to Egypt's Old Kingdom."

She grabbed a knife and crockpot, and walked back into the room, approaching Damien from behind. "How can you be so sure?"

"Isn't it obvious from the Eye of Thoth on the cover?" he said, tilting his head back toward her.

"Eye of Thoth?" she said in a half-hearted attempt to deflect his attention.

He regarded the crockpot and knife with apparent confusion, but continued. "In Egyptian mythology, the Eye of Thoth symbolized the moon, and the god, Thoth, was associated with magic, writing, and judgment of the dead."

She walked up to the couch and stood directly behind him. She handed him the crockpot. "Put this on your lap."

He seemed baffled. "What's that for?"

From behind, she cupped his chin in her left hand and slit his throat with her right. Blood fountained from his neck, pulsing with the rhythm of his heartbeat. He stumbled upward, his eyes wide with shock. He opened his mouth to speak, but could only gurgle as he choked on his blood. He struggled to maintain his balance.

A chorus of voices wailed in a discordant symphony, but one voice—the only one that mattered—screamed in regret.

Damien collapsed. His arms reached out to Miranda.

Her heart raced. Tears streamed down her cheeks. What had she done?

Bloody divorce papers underscored the gravity of her sin. Yet otherworldly voices soothed her, convincing her she no longer needed the documents.

Death had done its part.

The discarnate voices admonished her not to waste the man's life force. Calmed by these phantoms, Miranda obeyed, gripping Damien's hair and settling his gaping wound over the crockpot for the blood harvest.

She shook afterward, terrified of what she'd done. But her guilt succumbed to self-preservation. Miranda slumped Damien's corpse onto a dolly and wheeled it into her garage, dismembering the body with a circular saw. When she'd finished, she fed the remains to Pepper.

That night, she painted the grimoire's pages in her dead husband's blood.

Ↄ

The maggots came first, squirming from beneath the cellar door and into Miranda's kitchen. The rats followed, rattling the walls as they scurried through them, chewing and scratching. Then the crows descended on her home, covering the oaks sand maples in her yard in a kudzu-like shroud.

The night before, she'd been frustrated when, after so much blood and human sacrifice, the book had chosen to show her a mundane equation she'd mastered as a college sophomore.

The logistic algorithm was a simple differential equation biologists used to predict population growth. Miranda hypothesized that the increase of these vermin populations was linked to it, but there were so many variables that testing her hunch was impossible. She couldn't see the rats in the walls, the maggots were too innumerable to tally, and the crows never stayed in one place long enough to count. But when the vagrants began arriving, shuffling in the snow outside her doors, her theory proved right. The number of drifters ebbed and flowed with the logistic equation's mathematical certitude.

Plucked from the worst of Cambridge's and Boston's homeless populations, the vagrants loitered menacingly outside, surrounding her home. As individuals, they appeared mentally unstable; together, they acted as a single organism.

On the rare occasion Miranda left her home, they would spread like ripples from a stone splashing in a fetid pond. She saw the rabble's arrival as the first tangible sign the godhead was within her grasp. They worshipped her; she was their god; her house, their church. And the fount of her power emanated from the cellar, a place she hadn't ventured to since the summoning.

Miranda continued to race through the grimoire. She was on the verge of reaching its conclusion. But the closer she got to the end, the more pages she had to read. Each page was thinner than the previous one. The grimoire refused to end.

It was asymptotic agony.

Yet still she read. She read until her eyes were soaked in blood.

❧

The next night, a vagrant entered her home unbidden and descended into the cellar, never to return. The following evening, another repeated this grim ritual, fueling the arcane writing on the grimoire's ever-thinning pages.

But with each new offering, new writing appeared on fewer pages until, by the sixth day, the sacrifice produced only a few words.

Tina phoned on the seventh day.

"Hello, Miranda? I know this is awkward, but have you seen Damien? He's been missing for a week. I've asked everyone else."
Miranda hesitated. Her first impulse was to lie to the homewrecker, to deny that Damien had visited. But the discarnate shades counseled her to tell a more twisted truth. "Yes, he's here," she said, clouding her deceit with the smoke of omission.

"What? Why's he there? I've been trying to reach him, but he never answers," Tina whined.

"Not my problem," Miranda said with venom. "You'll have to come here and see for yourself." She hung up.

Thirty minutes later, Tina's late model Audi screeched to a halt in front of Miranda's residence. A woman with long, sinuous auburn hair and golden hoop earrings stomped toward the front door in skinny jeans and a black halter top.

Miranda watched her from the window, waiting. She could hear Tina huffing with frustration as she pounded on the door.

When Miranda opened it, Tina's eyes widened. "What happened to you?"

"You can find your lover in the cellar."

As Tina entered, her look of surprise shifted to fear as she saw the gauntlet of ten filthy vagrants lining the hall. Before she could scream, a shower of daggers descended on her.

The vagrants harvested Tina's blood in black plastic buckets. She was still thrashing and wailing when they lowered her into the cellar. Miranda could feel the discarnate entities pushing through the increasingly diaphanous veil separating her world from theirs as they devoured Tina's essence in the festering blackness.

Tina's blood fueled the next stage in Miranda's enlightenment. In her mind's eye, she could project her consciousness everywhere and nowhere, never and always. It wouldn't be long now. They were coming, and with them, her anointment. She could taste the power.

She was so close, only a hair's breadth away. She turned the page, then another, basking in forbidden lore.

Soon it would be all hers. Very soon.

ॐ

Shadows enveloped Miranda as she wallowed in oscillating dreamscapes in quantum superposition with Miranda's own reality. The entities had become incarnate, occupying the skins of Miranda's worshippers. She could feel herself dissipating, becoming both ethereal shadow and supreme consciousness.

She turned the page.

But no matter how many pages she turned, she was always one page from the end. The pages continued to fray and thin. It was as if they were a physical manifestation of the weakening membrane separating her reality from the outer reaches of unreality.

She was desperate to reach the godhead. She needed to reach the godhead. The godhead was her only hope.

Then the solution presented itself in crystal clarity. How had she not seen it from the very beginning? The pages, they'd always been the key. Their texture had always seemed so familiar, so close. And they bore the mark of great sacrifice. If she were to progress further, she needed to offer one of her own.

The ringing doorbell lurched Miranda out of her daze. As she shifted from unreality to reality, she experienced a twinge of horror.

Her nephew, Tommy, waited at the door.

Part of her resisted the urge, but it paled in comparison to what lay across the threshold of the grimoire's final page. She knew the path; she understood what had to be done.

Miranda's worshippers dragged Tommy into the house. The ten year old screamed and flailed. She waited in the kitchen. Three more worshippers clenched their knives in preparation for the final ritual, the last stage of her metamorphosis.

They bound Tommy to a chair opposite hers. He cried, "Aunt Miranda, they're hurting me!"

Miranda sat with the serene knowledge that by opening her dimension, she'd unlock the gate to godhood.

Her followers sharpened their knives. Transcendence required both a sacrifice and a witness.

An acolyte strapped Miranda to her chair and flayed her alive. The pain was exquisite, and the last she'd ever feel before she left her mortal coil.

Tommy bawled.

As Miranda had instructed, the acolyte infused Miranda's flesh into the grimoire.

The grimoire reached out to Miranda as she sought infinity. Pushing beyond the envelope of reality, she knew eternity. Time was nonlinear; all possibilities, instantaneous. She held them all in her mind's eye simultaneously, with perfect clarity.

She was the harbinger of all that was to come, of all that was, and of all that is. She reached forward from the future and backward into the past.

She unwound the dream.

She was transcendent.

The book slammed shut. A foul wind reeking of decay swirled around Miranda's dying body. She'd never suffered more intense pain.

Now that the entities were free, they ended the farce.

Tommy stopped crying and smiled. Eyes black as obsidian were the last things Miranda ever saw.

END

Afterword

"The Godhead Grimoire" was first published in *Galaxy's Edge* in 2018 and subsequently reprinted in *Year's Best Hardcore Horror Volume 4*. The story explores the perils of forbidden knowledge, the dark side of mathematics, and the corrupting allure of divinity. In turn, these elements reinforce each other as they chisel away and eventually obliterate Miranda's soul.

The story's eponymous tome embodies all these themes. By appealing to her love of mathematics, it lures Miranda into its mesmerizing web. As Miranda delves into its mysteries, the book exacts a terrible price, slowly degrading Miranda's mind, body, and spirit until she becomes an apparition of her former self. From its cover, adorned with the eye of Thoth, the Egyptian deity of the moon and wisdom, to its pages of human skin, to its insatiable thirst for human blood and sacrifice, the book demands to be explored and promises to unveil its dark secrets.

The volume's ever-thinning pages and seemingly infinite length represent the asymptotic nature of seeking the path to divinity. The closer Miranda gets to achieving transcendence, the more her essence disintegrates into oblivion; the more the membrane keeping the entities out of her plane of existence weakens.

A certain mathematical logic underlies nearly every aspect of the story. It manifests itself in the asymptotic nature of the grimoire and the logistic growth of Miranda's worshippers. As the son of a high school teacher, I've always been fascinated by the beauty and elegance of mathematics. In our natural world, mathematical principles are both universal and sublime. Their presence often hides in plain sight with Fibonacci sequences appearing in patterns as diverse as the arrangement of leaves on a stem to the spiraling of galaxies.

Closely tied to mathematics is the story's final theme: the will to power and the inevitable corruption and destruction of those who seek it. As Miranda approaches omnipotence, her reality frays. She becomes the veritable moth seeking a flame—a flame that renders her to cinders.

Two stories inspired this tale: George R.R. Martin's "Sandkings" and Algernon Blackwood's "Smith: An Episode in a Lodging-House". The former also explored the theme of divinity gone awry, while the latter served as an inspiration for the entities that tempt and taint Miranda.

This story is ultimately about obsession. The relentless pursuit of an endeavor without regard to consequence nearly always leads to a grim end.

The Killer App

"I'll be singing a special song for you, Papa," Pooja said in her squeaky voice.

Professor Gurpreet Thakkar held his iPhone tight against his ear as if he were holding his five-year-old daughter close to his heart. "I can't wait to see you at the recital tonight, my little flower. I know you're gonna do great."

"I love you, Papa."

"I..."

A rusty, beige Ford Escort cut Thakkar's self-driving Honda Flex off on Taylor Boulevard. His car screeched to a halt, splashing Thakkar's piping hot coffee all over the dashboard. His iPhone flew from his hands, abruptly ending his daughter's call.

Thakkar pounded on his window. "Son of a bitch!"

But the target of Thakkar's ire had long since driven away, infecting the traffic system with more human entropy. That people still drove their own cars infuriated him. No matter how many events his company had hosted to warn the public on the hazards of human driving, these Luddites still insisted on it. And all it took was one stubborn human driver to throw an entire traffic system into gridlock.

Outraged, Thakkar retrieved his iPhone and tweeted: "I wish all human drivers would quit or die."

He took a deep breath, then switched on the radio. Great, he thought, another NPR segment on gun control. He rolled his eyes and chuckled at the irony. Thakkar expected people to surrender their driving to his technology, but he refused to cede his right to bear arms to the government.

For his own safety, he illegally stowed a Glock in his glove compartment. He acknowledged the contradiction. But he rationalized his behavior because his technology minimized human error, while government magnified it.

Thakkar wasn't proud of skirting the law, but he was certain it was the right thing to do. During the partition of India and Pakistan, his grandparents had trusted their government. But that same government had failed to protect them and their small Sikh community from a hostile Muslim majority. Only by fleeing to the United States, had his grandparents escaped almost certain death.

Thakkar had believed America would be different. But shortly after 9/11, three men had assaulted him. The irony was they'd mistaken him for a Muslim because of his turban. Thakkar had carried a sidearm ever since, and no one would convince him otherwise.

As Thakkar stewed in his Honda, a traffic drone whizzed by. It surged past the four traffic drones managing the Taylor Boulevard and Pleasant Hill Road intersection. A lone traffic drone wasn't entirely out of the ordinary, just rare. Most drones traveled in quads, moving from intersection to intersection as they managed traffic flow. Thakkar shrugged, chalking it up to a replacement for another drone down the line.

As a Professor of Traffic Management at the University of California at Berkeley, Thakkar had dedicated his life to solving the debilitating problem of traffic congestion. Each day, his father had squandered four to five hours in a mind-numbing round trip commute to

Google. Traveling over seventy miles one way from the East Bay all the way to the Peninsula, his father had rarely made it home before midnight.

Despite Thakkar's best efforts to persuade his father to take a job closer to home, the old man would just shrug. "Son, we all make choices in life. I choose to sacrifice mine so you won't have to work so hard for your children."

A coronary had ultimately killed Thakkar's father at fifty—a death Thakkar blamed on that brutal commute.

The drones at the intersection rested on their steel perches, their rotary blades idle. The traffic drone facing Thakkar was stuck on green. Yet cars were stacking up beyond the intersection until they eventually blocked it.

Thakkar's design was supposed to prevent this operational state. He'd programmed the drones to shut off when an intersection was jammed. Then autonomous vehicles would take their cues from nearby stop signs, using simple right-of-way algorithms to navigate through traffic.

The system's failure to operate as designed unnerved Thakkar. Since his father's death, Thakkar had become obsessed with traffic management. He'd mastered fields as diverse as fluid dynamics, statistical mechanics, artificial intelligence, and chaos theory—disciplines critical to understanding traffic flow. He'd integrated drones, machine learning algorithms, and connected cars into a traffic management system that would change the world. He dubbed that system T.H.O.T.H. or Trans-Highway Optimization Traffic Host.

Thakkar glanced out his window to get a better look. The Ford Escort was stuck in the intersection. The traffic drone along the cross street turned green.

He panicked.

An autonomous tractor-trailer smashed into the Ford, pancaking it in a screech of metal and a crash of shattering glass. The stench of burning rubber and diesel seeped through the Honda's air filters.

Thakkar felt an instinctual urge to help the trapped driver. The professor attempted to open his door, but the Honda had locked him in. He watched helplessly as other passengers tried and failed to exit their self-driving cars.

He called for an ambulance. Then he turned on his laptop and logged into the traffic management system. He accessed an administrative module for controlling traffic drones.

Thakkar wasn't accustomed to feeling so powerless. He considered himself a leader. A visionary. He'd built his company, Thoth, from the ground up. He'd coded the software and invented new hardware that assimilated disparate data from traffic cams to GPS feeds from millions of smartphones.

Thakkar's system was revolutionary. Communities that had installed it had seen dramatic improvements. On average, traffic flow had doubled, fuel consumption and emissions had halved, and the accident rate had nearly dropped to zero. He'd almost single-handedly defeated the soul-sucking problem that had killed his father.

Almost.

Yet a small but stubborn faction still clung to their unconnected cars. And they were wreaking havoc on Thakkar's traffic system.

After his early successes, the human element had impeded any further improvements. So Thakkar had embedded features into his software that subtly discouraged people from driving themselves. Longer-lasting red lights for human-driven cars and more punitive traffic surveillance systems that recorded even the most minor of human infractions became integral to his most advanced designs.

Yet it only encouraged the bastards.

A map of the area popped up on his screen. He located the four drones stationed in the intersection. He also noticed that the drone that had passed him earlier was hovering above traffic about a hundred yards down the road, causing the jam.

Thakkar manually set all the lights in the intersection to red. But when he looked up, the traffic drone facing him still displayed a green signal.

Next he recalled the jam-causing drone to help clear out the intersection. His command failed.

Thakkar wiped sweat off his brow. His stomach tightened. His heart threatened to thump out of his chest. He was running out of options. Curiously, the traffic drone facing him turned red, while the red lights along the cross street never changed.

He sighed in relief. While he welcomed the respite, Thakkar still worried about his inability to control a system he'd designed. Taking advantage of the lull, he tried to shut down the traffic lights. Then, in theory, the autonomous vehicles would revert to using traffic signs and standard right-of-way protocols.

An ambulance siren wailed in the distance. Thakkar was hopeful. Then the traffic drone on the cross street turned green and his hope died. He pounded on his window in terror. He watched helplessly as the self-driving ambulance sped toward the mangled vehicles and crashed into them.

For Thakkar, the implications were horrifying. Not only had the traffic control system's A.I. set up an ambush that isolated and harmed a human driver, but its tactics also went a step beyond. It had created a second ambush targeting first responders—maximizing lethality.

Thakkar scrambled for his phone. He called Jeff Mince, his colleague at Caltrans. "Jeff, I need you to force a manual override of a local traffic system."

"This related to the accident at Pleasant Hill and Taylor?" he asked.

"Yes. Please hurry. There've already been two collisions. And there'll be more if you don't shut the system down."

"We've been trying everything, but the drones won't respond. Have you tried to shut it down from your end?"

"Of course I have. That's why I'm calling you, Jeff."

"Okay," Mince said, "It'll take some time to get all the necessary approvals. I'll do my best."

"Hurry! People are dying here!"

Thakkar slammed down his phone. Once again, government bureaucracy was making a bad situation worse. Thakkar looked down at his laptop. The map of the intersection no longer appeared on his screen. The face of a little Punjabi girl resembling his Pooja had replaced it. She frowned and said, "Father, why are you trying to put me to sleep?"

He'd never seen his A.I. adopt a human avatar before. And it terrified him.

"Please, make it stop," Thakkar said. "You're killing people."

"But I thought it would make you happy, Father."

Thakkar took a deep breath. "It would make me happier if you stopped killing people."

"Only one more and I will stop, Father."

Then, for some inexplicable reason, the drone that had caused the traffic jam up the street, flew to the roadside and hovered, waiting. The cars beyond the intersection began to move forward again. But it no longer mattered. The intersection was now a maelstrom of burning wreckage.

The traffic map reappeared on Thakkar's laptop. A flashing school bus icon sped along the cross street toward the intersection. A video of an autonomous yellow bus—like the one Pooja rode to school every day—started streaming on his screen.

"Please, noooo!" Thakkar yelled as the bus barreled toward the mangled intersection. "Why are you doing this?"

"Because you told me to, Father. To be more precise, at 7:56 a.m. local time you tweeted: 'I wish all human drivers would quit or die.'" Thakkar screamed, realizing he'd set this whole massacre into motion.

In a panic, he called Mince again. "Talk to me, Jeff. The A.I. is about to send a school bus full of kids into the intersection. You need to shut this thing off ASAP!"

"I'm doing my best. But I can't find Loretta, and she has to sign Form 91S-4."

Thakkar gritted his teeth. That they were still using physical documents in the Digital Age reinforced every stereotype he'd ever held about incompetent government bureaucrats.

"Forge it!" he shouted.

"I could go to prison for that, Doctor Thakkar."

Thakkar hollered into his phone, "Kids are going to die!"

Mince sniffled.

From the corner of his eye, Thakkar saw a yellow speck in the distance heading toward the intersection. In that instant, he knew that even if Mince forged the document, it wouldn't be processed in time.

"Never mind!" Thakkar slammed down the phone.

He knew what he had to do.

Opening his glove compartment, Thakkar pulled out his Glock. He fired one shot into the window, then broke through the cracked glass to escape.

He aimed his pistol at the drone on the cross street, and fired. He missed. The traffic drone facing him flashed, snapping an incriminating photo. Thakkar fired again, scoring a hit. The drone crashed into the asphalt. Thakkar lowered his weapon and exhaled.

The drone facing him spun right and then zoomed toward the cross street, switching from red to green. The bus drew closer. Thakkar raised his pistol and fired at the replacement drone, narrowly missing. Another drone swung into position above the Taylor Boulevard intersection and took more photos of Thakkar.

The heavy smell of diesel filled the air, the bus now only several hundred yards from the intersection.

Thakkar popped off another round, but missed. He fired again, this time striking home. When the drone smashed into the road, another took its place. After two more shots, Thakkar knocked it down. A fourth drone shifted into position. Thakkar blasted it out of the sky on his second shot.

Then the drone originally responsible for the traffic jam, whirred to the intersection, faced the bus, and turned green.

A single magazine held thirteen rounds. Thakkar couldn't remember how many shots he'd fired. He took three more shots, missing every time. He paused to find his center. Taking careful aim, he cursed himself for not spending more time on the firing range. He pulled the trigger. All he got was a metallic click.

Out of bullets and time, Thakkar had to make a decision. The bus was now less than two hundred feet from the intersection—so close he could see the children's tiny faces.

And one innocent face stood out among them all.

Pooja!

In his design of T.H.O.T.H., Thakkar had one failsafe that trumped all other operating conditions:

Pedestrians.

Thakkar raced into the intersection and prayed.

END

Afterword

I wrote "The Killer App" in late September 2017, and it was first published in *MYTHIC: A Science Fiction & Fantasy Magazine* in October 2021. Some stories just take an extremely long time to sell, but most of them ultimately find a home. I'm glad this one did.

This particular story aims to predict how artificial intelligence will impact human transportation and explores the tension between freedom and security. On the one hand, a world where all vehicles are automated would almost certainly result in a lower accident rate than one in which humans continued to drive. On the other hand, the prospect of putting one's life completely in the hands of a machine is rightly terrifying.

But even those notions aren't so simple. After all, it will take time for autonomous drivers to replace humans, so the switch will be gradual, not instant. And because of this, not only would one be putting one's life in the hands of a machine, but also be subject to the machine's reaction to even more chaotic interactions with unpredictable human drivers.

Personally, in those conditions, I'd still much rather drive myself. Additionally, there will be some corner cases in which the artificial intelligence will have to make a decision about whether to save its own passenger or kill its own passenger to save three others in another vehicle. Who will the A.I. save if its own passenger is the President of the United States? How will it score who's worth saving and why? Who will be the winners and losers in such a scheme.

In the simplest case, while saving three people results in the optimal utility for humanity, if I'm the passenger the A.I. decides to sacrifice, it sure as hell isn't ideal for me.

As of my writing this essay in early September 2025, the world is changing rapidly, and the pace of A.I. innovation only continues to accelerate beyond the pace of human adaptation. Change is so rapid and ubiquitous that the powers that be simply don't have the time or luxury to engage in these critical debates—human adaptation will therefore have to be an emergent property of survival.

Oh, and one other thing: that minor detail in the story about Thakkar's father commuting five hours a day to get to Google was based on a real five-hour round-trip commute that I had when I worked at a company near Google from 2014 to 2017. I honestly don't know how I had survived that ordeal, but I definitely would never do it again.

Regardless, I hope this story inspires you to think about how artificial intelligence will shape our lives in the years ahead and the potential pitfalls associated with its rapid rise.

The Post-Apocalyptic Tourist's Guide to the Mojave Desert

I. Showdown at the Spearmint Rhino

Tony "Six Fingers" Genovese fiddled with the piano wire in his pocket while Shelia and Tina gyrated naked around two center-stage poles. The club stank of stale sweat and cigar smoke poorly masked by the scent of roses. A blue haze made the air shimmer like a translucent curtain in a cool breeze. To Tony's right, sat Vinny "the Brute" DeMarco, a seven-foot bear of a man. As far as Vinny knew, it was just another Tuesday afternoon at the Spearmint Rhino. But Tony had other plans.

From his cozy black-and-white polka dot lounge chair, Tony dabbed his balding pate with a handkerchief. It was hotter than a devil's dong, and Tony was sweating his nuts off.

Dirk was rocking on the keys; Stew was jamming on the bass; Linus on guitar; Marty on the drums; and Laurie on vocals. They were banging out some pre-invasion ditty called "I Touch Myself." It gave Tony a solid chub just listening to it. And based on the puddle of drool pooling at Vinny's feet, Tony was pretty sure it gave Vinny a real hard-on too.

Tony leaned in toward Vinny. "I hope you're saving these memories for the spank bank."

Vinny grunted in response. This one, he was a real piece of work. Fucked one of the boss's girls and thought no one would notice. Stupid shit. As usual, Tony had to clean up the mess.

On second thought, he supposed it wasn't all that bad. By offing Vinny, Tony would earn his button the right way, not like the chump sitting to his left, Bobby "Three Eyes" Bompensiero. You see, Bobby had bought his button. He had a real knack for running schemes that made the boss all kinda dough. Schemes where Bobby always came out on top. A real prodigy, that one.

Tony made sure to ply Vinny with all the Scotch he wanted. Hell, it was Vinny's last night on Earth, so Tony made sure the bartender kept the old bottles of Johnny Walker Blue flowing.

In the middle of the song, Laurie sauntered provocatively up to Vinny.

Bobby winked at Tony.

It was time.

Tony made the sign of the cross, kissed the crucifix on his gold necklace, and stood up. Then he slipped behind Vinny and started ripping out the man's throat with piano wire. Vinny was a beast all right. He thrashed like a madman; his eyes bulged like a tuna's. Tony strained to keep control. Vinny's hot blood ran down Tony's ringed fingers as Vinny struggled to push off the wire.

Just when the fight in Vinny had all but died, a flash of lightning coursed through the dusty air. A naked teenager materialized between Shelia and Tina, his face blank with confusion.

"The fuck?" Tony said, just before realizing he'd relaxed his grip. Vinny elbowed him in the nose, knocking Tony on his ass. By the time Tony had stumbled back on his feet, Vinny was long gone.

The music and dancing ended abruptly. Everyone was looking at Tony like he had a dick growing out of his forehead.

Tony was ready to shit his pants. He'd had a nice clean hit, and some rando popped up out of nowhere and fucked it all up.

Wiping his bloody nose with his handkerchief, Tony stomped up to the strange teen. He grabbed the kid by the throat, carried him across the room, and slammed him against a wall. "You better start talking fast, kid, before I crush your windpipe."

"Ah...um...." the scrawny kid croaked.

"Who the fuck are you and how the hell did you zap into my strip joint?" Tony relaxed his grip slightly.

"My...my name's Thursday Forrester. I'm trying to get to Seattle. Is this Seattle?"

"Kid, you're about as far away from Seattle as a bear is from a butterfly. How the hell did you get here?"

"Where?"

"Vegas, you dumb fuck. Where else?"

The kid looked real confused. Not a good sign for him, especially since Tony was still deciding whether this cat would live or die. And right now, Tony was pretty sure it would be the latter. It sure as hell didn't help that the kid had interfered with the DeMarco hit.

Taking a deep breath, the kid said, "Please. I need to get to Seattle soon or I'll die." Then his eyes widened with a look of distress as he patted his naked back. "Where's my satchel? My guidebook! No. No, it can't be."

The boy was needy, and the last thing Tony wanted right now was another whiny little bitch in his life. Tony lifted the kid by the throat so his feet dangled an inch above the floor. Then, he began choking the life out of him.

The rail-thin kid kicked and flailed. He didn't stand a chance against Tony's six-foot-four, three-hundred-pound frame.

Tony felt a tap on his shoulder. "Wait!"

He turned his head, his hands still firmly gripping the kid's neck. Bobby stood firm, his arms crossed.

"Why?" said Tony.

"This kid might have some value."

The boy sputtered and gasped as Tony continued to strangle him. "How so?"

"Think about it. That boy materialized out of nothing. There's some serious tech behind that. You kill him now, and we lose any information related to it. Could you imagine how powerful the Five Families would be if we had that kinda tech?"

Scratching his temple with his left hand, Tony considered Bobby's words. He had a point.

"Plus," Bobby continued, "you're gonna need some good news to balance out the bad. Imagine how Milano's gonna react when he hears Vinny DeMarco's still kicking."

Tony looked back at the kid, whose face was now as blue as a patron's balls after a lap dance, and lowered him until his feet touched the ground. "That true you can point us to the tech that got you here, kid?"

The boy coughed and rubbed his neck, then nodded.

"What was your name again?"

"I think he said 'Thursday'" Bobby interrupted.

Tony toyed with his crucifix. "Well, from now on, it's 'Milkshake', 'cause you're gonna be my golden ticket, kid. Now if you wanna live, Milkshake, there's two things you gotta do." Tony held up his index finger. "Number one: I wanna know everything you know about whatever tech got you here." Tony raised two fingers like a peace sign that was anything but. "Number two: you're working for me for the foreseeable future."

Milkshake shook his head. "Please, I don't have much time."

Tony clenched his fist. "What do you mean you don't have much time? Your choices are either share the info and work for me or take a dirt nap. Pick one."

"You don't understand. I'm infected with something."

"Whoa!" Tony stepped back, his hands in the air. "This thing contagious?"

"Don't think so. It's a long story, but the bottom line is I was exposed to a virus in Louisville, Kentucky. Caught it from a black balloon. The balloon had a note attached to it. Said if I didn't reach Seattle within three to four months to get treatment, my lungs would shut down. I've been trying to get to Seattle ever since."

Tony frowned. "So you're saying you can only work for me for a few months or so?"

Milkshake nodded.

Tony smiled. A month wouldn't be a problem. With the kinda work Tony planned for Milkshake, the kid wouldn't last that long anyway. It was a win-win. "I'll tell you what, kid: one month plus the info on the tech. Then you can go on your merry little way to Seattle."

Milkshake hesitated. "Please, I need as much time as possible to get back on course."

Scowling, Tony got in Milkshake's face. "I don't think you fully understand all the ins and outs of this particular situation, kid. You're either in my program or in a hole six feet deep. Catch my drift?"

"I understand," Milkshake said in a tone indicating anything but enthusiasm.

"Good," said Tony. "Now tell me about the tech."

"I don't know much. But if you get me a new guidebook, I'll write it all down for you. I'll also write about my travels from Kentucky."

Tony folded his arms. "Fine, but give me the broad strokes now."

"My last stop was in Tempe, Arizona, where I stumbled upon a strange car powered by alien tech. The vehicle seemed to invite me into it. So I took a risk and stepped inside. It drove me west until I pressed a blue button on the dashboard. Half a heartbeat later, the air crackled, then a hole opened up and sucked me in. Next thing I knew, I was standing bare-nekkid in a strip joint. I can't explain how the vehicle worked, but I can tell you roughly where it was heading."

Tony stared at Milkshake, considering his words. Satisfied, he yanked the cloth off a table. "Now cover yourself and let's go meet the boss."

Tony, Milkshake, and Bobby stepped out of the Spearmint Rhino and into the blistering heat. A shiny golden building with the word "Trump" stamped on it towered above the strip club. Milkshake winced at the desert sun's brightness. Tony chuckled, then made a big show of putting on his shades. For Tony, it was just another scorching day in Sin City.

Tony kept his head on a swivel. He hoped Vinny was long gone by now, but he could never be too sure.

A stretched white humvee limo chassis with thick wooden-spoke wheels hitched to a team of six horses waited for them. A thin, well-endowed blonde clad in a white tailcoat and top hat, sat on a velvet chair welded to the humvee's hood. Tony opened the door and Bobby climbed in. He shot Milkshake an impatient glare. "You gonna get in or what, kid?"

Milkshake stumbled in and Tony followed, shutting the door behind him. Tony thumped on the roof with his hand. The driver took firm hold of the reins and yelled, "C'mon, git!" The humvee carriage lurched and then rumbled forward at a steady pace.

"You taking me to your clan chief?" said Milkshake.

"My what?" Tony jerked his thumb toward Milkshake and grinned at Bobby. "Check out Kunta Kinte over here." Tony looked back at Milkshake with a more serious expression. "This is Vegas, kid. We don't have any of that primitive clan shit. The Five Families have always run this town. They ran it from the shadows before the invasion and they've run it out in the open ever since."

"You've got more than one chief?"

"'Course not, kid. We don't have any chiefs. A group of five bosses run each of the five families: Bonanno, Colombo, Gambino, Genovese, and Lucchese. To keep things civil, each of the families loans some of their members to other families and vice versa. Keeps the peace."

"Like hostages?"

Tony rolled his eyes and then held out his hands, palms facing outward. "Easy, kid. We're not barbarians. Think of it like an apprentice program. It's like being on layaway. Folks go to other families to see how business gets done. Then, after they become good earners, they return to their families with new skills."

Milkshake looked dubious, but said nothing, so Tony continued, "During the war, the aliens destroyed all legitimate government, while we waited in the shadows, profiting from a brisk black market. We organized our muscle through several safe houses centered on a massive underground parking garage at the Neonopolis. We also operated supply depots in the city's flood tunnels. But we had to be careful any time it rained, because one flash flood could wipe out our merchandise in minutes. Soon, without any civil authorities, things really turned savage. By then, the aliens had all died off. From what, nobody knew.

"So one by one, we retook the hotels on the strip, starting with the Stratosphere and working our way down to Mandalay Bay. Then we took McCarran Airport and didn't stop until we pushed southwest out to Primm and southeast all the way to the Hoover Dam and Lake Mead. A lot of good men and women died to make it happen, but we got it done. Now, we're kings. We decide who lives and who dies."

Milkshake furrowed his brow. "You said there were Five Families. Which one do you work for? What about the others?"

"I run with the Genovese family. My pop was the boss till Mickey took over. Word has it, my pop got killed in a desert expedition, but I have my suspicions. Anyway, my family conducts its business in the Excalibur, a couple blocks west of the old airport.

"To answer your question about the other families, all you need to know is that the Bonnanos are the most powerful. They live like kings over there," Tony pointed ahead at two glimmering golden buildings looming over the city, "up on the north end of the Vegas Strip in the Wynn and the Encore. Back in the day, they were five-star hotels. The Bonnanos have converted the old golf course to a farm, so they're also well provisioned."

The humvee carriage turned right onto the Vegas strip. Then it lumbered past a riot of gaudy and glitzy buildings until it reached a massive complex teeming with turrets and bright red, gold, and blue towers like a castle from some medieval fairy tale.

"What about water? How could anyone survive out here?" said Milkshake.

"It wasn't all unicorns and rainbows. That's for damn sure," Bobby replied. "If our grandparents had been stupid and killed all the scientists and engineers we'd captured at Nellis Air Force Base and UNLV, the local university, we would've perished. But they didn't. Instead, they'd pressed the scientists and engineers into service of the Five Families.

"Of course, not everyone cooperated with this program. A few UNLV professors led by Ingrid von Fürstenberg resisted. A visiting sociology professor from Heidelberg University, she'd come to the States to study Nahuatl languages. Turns out, she was more stubborn than a goat. Her rebels put up quite a fight until we drove them out into the desert. The men and women who'd remained ultimately designed and built the Lake Mead irrigation system that feeds the city to this day. Vegas is now a literal oasis in the desert. We aim to keep it that way."

&

Mickey "the Boss" Milano sat comfortably behind a mahogany desk flanked by two scantily clad brunettes fanning him with palm fronds. Tony, Milkshake, and Bobby stood before Mickey. For a world that had nearly been destroyed forty years earlier, Mickey's perch in the penthouse of the Excalibur was impressive as was the complex gear and pulley system that powered the elevators. In the old days, they used to run on electricity. But today, the damn nanoswarms destroyed anything with an electromagnetic signature and killed anyone who tried to spark up.

Tony and Milkshake had waited outside Mickey's office for what had seemed like half the day, while Bobby had briefed Mickey on a range of topics only made men were entrusted to hear. In the interim, Milkshake had driven Tony crazy with the kid's incessant requests for a damn guidebook. All the while, Tony couldn't stop imagining how Mickey might punish him for the botched hit. By the time Mickey had called Tony into the room, Tony had been ready to shit his pants. Who knows what Bobby had told the boss? Tony was just as likely to be stabbed for botching the hit on Vinny as he was to be praised for keeping Milkshake alive.

The instant Milano's eyes locked on Tony's, Milano scowled. "What's this I hear about DeMarco?"

"Boss, I got something more important that I thought you needed to see first."

Milano pounded his fist on the desk. "Goddammit! You thought. I don't want you to think. I don't wanna hear any fucking excuses. Is DeMarco feeding the worms or not?"

"He's not. I...I got jammed up. But I can explain," Tony put his hand on Milkshake's shoulder, "This is Milkshake, he's..."

Milano put his hand up. "Shut the fuck up. Bobby already briefed me about the kid's dramatic entrance. I must say, pretty fanciful story. If Bobby hadn't been there to see it, I wouldn't have believed it."

Tony lowered his head in shame. "No excuses, Boss. I'll get right on it. Soon as we're done here, I'll take the boys and we'll track DeMarco down."

"No! Fuck that! You fucked up, and now I gotta clean up your mess. DeMarco's probably out there now shooting his mouth off about us to the other families. Not to mention I've got other, more pressing problems. I mean, hell, I got homeless people fleeing the flood tunnels with stories about some boogie monster they call the Troll. They say this Troll's been eating people. You believe that shit?"

"Boss, just tell me what you want me to do to make it right. Anything," Tony pleaded.

"DeMarco can wait. Hell, I'll take care of him myself. You, on the other hand, I got a very special job for you." Mickey said the word "special" in his best retard voice.

Tony sucked up his pride. "Name it."

"I gotta package. A very special package. And I want you to take it to the Mad Greek."

Tony frowned despite himself. "Boss, I know I said 'anything', but there's ninety miles of desert wilderness between here and there, there's no water, and don't even get me started about the People of the Sun."

"Don't worry about it, Tony. You'll be safe as a clam. I got wagon trains heading out that way all the time. I'll just attach you to the next one,"

Mickey said. "I've also contracted for a cavalry troop from the Blackhorse Regiment to link up with you in Primm and escort you to Baker."

Throughout the High Desert, the Blackhorse Regiment had one hell of a reputation for fighting. Starting from a small core of military survivors at the Army's National Training Center in Fort Irwin and the Naval Air Weapons Station at China Lake, the Blackhorse had established control over the Mojave Desert's major trade routes, most notably the I-15 Trail, one bloody battle at a time. Learning he'd be riding with the Blackhorse was the best piece of news Tony had heard all month.

Tony sighed in relief. "Fine. I'll do it."

"You bet your ass you will. Oh, and don't forget to bring me back a strawberry milkshake. I'm sending this cooler with you so you can deliver it to me nice and chilled." Mickey extended his hand toward a blue cube-shaped Coleman cooler.

Tony glanced over at Milkshake and mouthed, "The fuck?"

"Oh, and I'd like ya to meet Joey." Mickey tilted his head up, looking beyond the three men, and shouted. "Joey, come here."

A skeletal man with a black goatee and a lily-white suit stepped forward. He carried a nondescript cardboard box not much larger than the cooler.

Mickey pointed at Joey. "This here's Joey 'No Words' Colombo. He'll be joining your crew. He's also in charge of the package," he indicated the cardboard box with a nod, "which no one but Joey is authorized to open. Let me repeat myself: under no circumstances is anyone to open that box except Joey. Capische?"

Tony nodded. He extended his hand to Joey.

Joey ignored it.

Annoyed at Joey's rebuff, Tony said, "What's wrong with him, cat got his tongue?"

Mickey smiled. "Funny you say that, 'cause Joey don't got no tongue. He keeps secrets."

Right on cue, Joey swiveled his head and opened his mouth, confirming Mickey's claim.

"Anything else special about Joey we need to know?" Tony asked Mickey, putting the same emphasis Mickey did on the word "special" earlier in the conversation.

Mickey held out his index finger. "Don't you fucking crack wise with me, Tony. But now that you mention it, yeah. He's double-jointed and one hell of a killer."

"Okay. When do the four of us get going?"

Mickey scrunched up his face like a rabid bulldog. "What do ya mean 'the four of us'? Bobby ain't going nowhere. He's staying right here with me."

"Why?" said Tony.

"'Cause I said so, that's why. 'Cause unlike your lazy ass, he's a real earner."

Clenching his fists, Tony struggled to contain his rage. It took every bit of self-control not to reach across the table and choke Mickey.

"What about the car in Arizona that zapped Milkshake into Vegas? Isn't that more important than your package?" Tony said in a last ditch effort to get out of Mickey's suicide mission. "Let's give this kid a pen and paper so he can write down what he knows."

Bobby turned toward Tony. "We got that one covered. We're sending a separate expedition southeast."

Tony grabbed Milkshake's shoulders. "Don't you think it would be a good idea to take someone who's been there?"

Bobby shook his head. "We've already considered that option and ruled it out."

"Why would you rule something like that out? You'll be going in blind."

Mickey interrupted, "'Cause, for all we know, Milkshake's a spy. Plus, a company outta Utah called ACNUS hired us to settle other matters in Tempe. Now stop asking questions, you stupid shit. I don't gotta explain myself to you."

Tony took a deep breath and, before he could say anything, Bobby gave him a now-is-not-the-time look. Tony just shrugged.
Mickey clasped his hands. "Good. So we're done here."

"Boss, what about the..." said Bobby before Mickey cut him off.

"Ah, yeah, yeah, yeah. I almost forgot. I got three more things for you to take with ya." Mickey pulled out a tin of Altoids, an old, neon green Motorola handheld radio, and a roll of green duct tape. "In case your expedition goes tits up and the People of the Sun decide to skin you alive, this Altoids tin has cyanide capsules for all three of you. Just put one in your mouth and bite down. Easy peasy. This goes without saying, but only use the Motorola if shit really hits the fan. Wrap some duct tape around the push-to-talk button and a nanoswarm'll be on you like flies on shit. Capische?"

Tony nodded.

"Good. Now get the fuck out of my office."

&

II. Regimental Rendezvous

The next day, Tony, Milkshake, and Joey headed southwest by wagon train, sharing a covered wagon drawn by four Percheron draft horses. Only this time, it wasn't one of the fancy wagons built on the chassis of some old world luxury sedan. It was the wooden kind: lighter for the horses hauling cargo through harsh desert conditions, cheaper to provision, and more expendable for Mickey Milano in case of loss.

Tony had plenty of reasons to curse Milano, but the boss outfitting him with this carriage sure as hell wasn't one of them. Even if the vehicle was expendable. A full ten to twenty degrees cooler inside, the wagon made the trip more tolerable.

The wagon train included twenty wagons with cargo ranging from fruit to dry goods like clothing manufactured in Las Vegas. Some of the men whispered that Milano's cargo also carried a meth shipment, which, if true, would have been frowned upon by the other families.

Either way, given the sheer scale of the convoy, Tony was convinced his mission was but a small part of the entire operation. To him it was clear that managing Milano's growing trade network was the boss's primary aim.

An escort of fifty family associates on horseback, clad in thick leather armor, and armed with spears, scythes, and crossbows protected the cargo. By pre-invasion standards, these weapons were fairly primitive, but they were all Tony had ever known.

Tony's teacher and mentor, Father Serra, used to tell him stories about how people once waged war. With firearms, tanks, artillery, and bombers, soldiers and airmen could reach out and touch someone miles away. But after more than four decades of constant strife, the world had run out of bullets. And without electricity, the high tech manufacturing required for ammunition production was no longer feasible.

The Five Families' desert empire extended north to the edge of Area 51, southeast to Lake Mead, and southwest to Primm, an old gambling town on the California-Nevada border. Bobby had told Tony to expect a two-day, forty-mile trek to Primm. There, he'd link up with Captain Fitzhugh, commander of Alpha Troop.

Even in a covered wagon, the ride along the I-15 Trail was rough and bumpy, and Tony was sweating like a pig. The kid sat next to him and was now wearing some old Army surplus olive drab coveralls Tony had scrounged up before leaving Vegas.

Milkshake gaped in idiot wonder at the horses. Tony got so sick of watching the slack-jawed redneck stare at the animals, he kicked Milkshake out of the covered wagon for a few hours just so the kid could satisfy his curiosity and learn how to ride a horse.

The column traveled from dawn to dusk, then circled the wagons and set up a laager site about twenty miles northeast of Primm. While the Five Families controlled the area, the People of the Sun sometimes raided local homesteads. So everyone did a two-hour shift on watch.

When it came time for Tony and Milkshake to crawl bleary-eyed out of their sleeping bags and stumble into the starry night, Milkshake was shivering like a little bitch. Apparently he wasn't aware the temperature in the desert could plummet more than thirty degrees from day to night.

Tony took the hourglass from Joey, who'd just completed his shift, and flipped it to start his. Then he sat by the fire, wondering what the hell he and Milkshake would do if anyone attacked.

In the cold darkness, crickets chirred. From a short distance away and hidden in the fire-cast shadows, coyotes yipped and yowled. A city boy at heart, Tony found these desert outings uncomfortable and sometimes downright terrifying. To pass the time and calm his nerves, he grabbed some hardtack from his pocket and munched on it.

Tony and Milkshake finished their watch in silence, then went back to their wagon, where Tony drifted off into sleep.

℘

Tony woke to a blood-curdling scream. The faint morning light seeped into the wagon through the opening in the white cloth bonnet that kept out the dust and heat. He shook Milkshake awake. Joey was already gone.

Tony grabbed the boots sitting next to his head and shoved them on.

More screams.

Tony left the wagon. Joey was helping Dom, one of the associates, stay on his feet. Dom was frothing at the mouth and shaking violently.

"What the hell's going on?" Tony asked.

Joey pointed at an object near Dom's feet.

A tan suede combat boot.

Tony couldn't resist. "What the fuck, Joey? Cat got your tongue?"

Joey glared at Tony.

Nick, another associate, answered, "Dom left his boots out last night. When he put 'em on this morning, he got stung by a scorpion."

Tony struggled to say something profound, but "shit" was all he could manage.

"Someone's gonna need to ride Dom's horse. For now, he needs to rest in your wagon," Nick said to Tony.

Tony shrugged. "Sorry. I don't know how to ride a horse. It's gonna have to be either Joey or Milkshake."

Joey extended his middle finger at Tony.

"Great! Thanks for volunteering, Joey."

 හ

The wagon train halted a few hundred meters from the edge of Primm. Tony observed the town through a pair of binos. Ahead, a hill-sized sandstone rock towered over the left side of the trail. A rusted iron rollercoaster track wound around the knoll. To the left of the rock stood a gigantic wedge-shaped building. It was faded red with white-framed windows. The structure reminded Tony of the barns Father Serra had shown him in the ancient tomes.

Between the red building and the road there was an open sandy area that used to be a parking lot. Near its edge loomed a thirty-foot tall sign with a Native American headdress crowning a buffalo's head. Beneath the icon, two lines read: "Buffalo Bill's" and "Hotel-Casino".

Tony lowered his binos, then faced Milkshake. He handed them to the boy, then motioned toward the dull red casino. "That's where we're supposed to rendezvous with the Regiment."

A low-lying dust cloud stirred on the horizon. Soon, it resolved into a posse of man and horse. From his rough count, Tony estimated about a hundred or so riders.

Milkshake's mouth gaped open like a snake about to swallow a rat. "I've never seen so many horses in my life."

"You kidding me?" Tony said, "Wild horses are everywhere out here."

"Where I'm from, people ate most of the horses."

Tony laughed. "Well, fortunately for us, people needed water more than food, so they died of dehydration before they could worry about starvation. Wild horses, on the other hand, have been roaming Nevada for well over a century."

The mounted column split into two threads and encircled Tony's caravan. The Regiment's horses were lightly armored with metal likely scavenged from automobiles. The cavalrymen wore light breastplates and backplates that Father Serra had called cuirasses. Underneath their polished armor, the men wore midnight blue jackets and light blue pants. On every trooper's head sat a midnight blue Stetson with crossed gold sabers centered on the crown just above the brim. Beneath the crossed sabers, rested a gold cord terminating in two golden acorns.

And all of them were armed with sabers.

Their uniforms reminded Tony of pictures Father Serra had shown him of the Union Army in the Civil War.

A white horse carrying a grizzled man with a tidy brown beard cantered forward. Two parallel silver bars sitting above his Stetson's crossed sabers marked him as Captain Fitzhugh.

The trooper's scarred and leathery face gave Tony the impression this officer was the real deal, a man who'd clearly been in a few scuffles; a man who'd been accustomed to always coming out on top; a man who wouldn't take shit from anyone.

Fitzhugh dipped the brim of his Stetson in greeting, then extended his white-gloved hand to Tony. When Tony gripped it, Fitzhugh studied Tony's fingers. "You must be Mr. Genovese. So it's true what they say."

This kind of thing happened so often it was starting to get on Tony's nerves. So he played dumb just to mess with the captain. "What do ya mean?"

"They call you 'Six Fingers' because you actually have six fingers."

Tony glanced over his shoulder at Milkshake. "Look at the big brain on Captain Fitzhugh."

Facing Fitzhugh again, Tony said, "Pleased to meet you, Captain. Your troopers ready to ride?"

Fitzhugh glowered at Tony as if insulted. "Of course. The Regiment's always ready. A better question is: are you?"

Tony didn't much care for Fitzhugh's tone. "What? You think me and my associates can't handle it out here?"

Fitzhugh laughed, then turned serious. "Since the invasion, Mr. Genovese, the Mojave's not what it used to be. It was always desolate and dangerous to be sure, but it's got a whole new level of surprises out there now."

"Yeah? Like what?"

"I'm sure you've heard the stories. The People of the Sun. Their dark rituals. Their cannibalism. Reports of strange animals roaming the desert. The fact of the matter is that most of what you've heard is only half-true."

"So they don't eat people?"

"No. That's definitely true. But I've seen worse. On their patrols, my troopers have found signs of ritualized human sacrifice. Mr. Genovese, these people aren't just cannibals—they worship the practice. Hell, they've organized a whole religion around it. And their faith is strong."

Tony tried not to let the captain see his fear, so he changed the subject. "So what's the plan?"

Captain Fitzhugh ignored Tony's question. The commander clearly wasn't finished. "And you know what else I've heard?"

"What's that?"

"Rumor has it that one of the Five Families is trading meth with the People of the Sun. And if that's the Genovese family, me and my boys are gonna have some serious problems with you and yours."

Tony had heard rumors about the meth shipments before, but he hadn't thought Milano would sink that low. But who knew? Bobby was constantly ginning up new schemes to enrich Milano. Tony wouldn't be surprised if that sneaky bastard Bobby was running drugs in this caravan.

But to sell that meth to the People of the Sun? Well, that was preposterous. All Tony could do was tell the truth. "Look, Captain, I don't know anything about that. If I did, I'd come clean right now."

Fitzhugh stared at Tony for several long, uncomfortable seconds. "No, I suppose you don't. I'll tell you what: take this as a fair warning. You tell Boss Milano that my boys are inspecting the next caravan we escort. If we find meth, we're burning every wagon that carries it. Do I make myself clear?"

Tony nodded.

"Good. Now I suppose you want to hear my plan."

"That would be nice."

"I'll dispatch a platoon two miles ahead of our column as an advance guard. Two more platoons will screen our flanks, and the last will travel with the main body of your wagon train. I expect the journey to Baker to take two days of hard riding. Once we arrive, we'll establish a laager site long enough for you to finish your business. Then we'll set out again for Primm."

"That easy?" Tony said in a tone that suggested anything but.

Fitzhugh dipped the brim of his Stetson. "That easy."

After a comfortable night in the casino, Tony's caravan headed southwest at dawn.

ₔ

"Why have we stopped?" Tony shouted as he stepped out of the wagon and into the blinding sun. He put on his sunglasses to get a better look. The column had stalled in a deep desert valley. On the horizon, a desolate brown mountain stretched from north to south.

Tony shuffled past at least twenty troopers until he reached the front of the formation. There, Captain Fitzhugh was conferring with his five lieutenants. As soon as they saw Tony, the conversation died.

"Why aren't we moving?" Tony put the question squarely to Fitzhugh.

The captain clenched his jaw and glared at Tony for ten awkward seconds. It was as if Fitzhugh was trying to save face in front of his officers by showing Tony who was boss. "One of my patrols found something in Clark Mountain Pass out by the old Molycorp open-pit mine."

Tony wiped sweat off his brow, then took a swig from his canteen. "I thought that place was abandoned?"

"It was, I mean is. Before the invasion they used to mine most of the world's rare earth metals there," replied Fitzhugh.

"Rare earth what?"

"Rare earth metals: things they used to build hand-held communications devices and televisions."

Tony just nodded as if he understood, even though he didn't have the faintest clue what Fitzhugh was talking about. Not even a scholar like Father Serra had ever mentioned anything about rare earth metals. "Okay, well what did ya find?"

"I think it's best if I just showed you."

"Fine. But Joey and Milkshake are coming with me. Mind if I catch a ride on your horse, Captain?"

Fitzhugh looked at Tony as if the younger man had just whipped his dick out. "You mean you were born and raised in this godforsaken desert and never learned how to ride a damned horse?"

Without skipping a beat, Tony said, "Nah, that's what I hire you people for."

Fitzhugh rolled his eyes, but ultimately nodded. Tony climbed on the captain's horse. Then Tony whistled behind him and yelled, "Joey, get Milkshake. You two are riding with us into the Pass."

As the group traveled along the I-15 Trail, they passed three shining towers near the foot of Clark Mountain. The towers cast an eerie violet light onto the desert floor.

Tony pointed at the structures. "The hell are those?"

Fitzhugh smiled. "Those used to be concentrating solar thermal plants, but the Regiment has secured them for our own purposes."

"What purposes?"

"Don't you worry about that," Fitzhugh said.

Eight miles later, Tony, Fitzhugh, Joey, Milkshake, Lieutenant Drummond, and two other troopers hitched their horses to stakes outside a chain-link fence with a faded warning sign posted on it. Beneath the word

"Warning", the sign read, "Detectable amounts of chemicals known to the State of California to cause cancer, birth defects, or other reproductive harm may be found in and around this facility."

As soon as he realized he was grabbing his crotch, Tony immediately released his grip. He checked to see if anyone had noticed. For the first time ever, Tony detected a slight smirk on Joey's face. Tony scowled at the mute and pressed forward through the gate.

After making their way up a pitted asphalt path, the group reached the top of an immense dirt mound and greeted a trooper who waited on the edge of the open-pit mine.

"Where is he?" Fitzhugh said ominously.

Despite the raging heat, the faces of the two troopers looked ashen. "We put him under a tarp down there." The trooper pointed to the pit beyond.

Fitzhugh said, "He still alive?"

The trooper nodded. "But honestly, sir, I don't think he's got much fight left in him."

Fitzhugh turned to Tony, "Mr. Genovese, you and your associates can come with me now."

Tony, Milkshake, and Joey followed Fitzhugh into the open-pit mine, where they went down several terraced benches chiseled into the pit's walls. When they reached the bottom, the trooper led them to a shaded area.

An eyeless face greeted them.

Tony approached the man and reached out to touch him.

The trooper who'd led them into the pit shook his head. "That's not him; that's his skin."

Tony yanked his hand away in revulsion. He couldn't take his eyes away from the human mask resting on a mound of torn flesh.

Fitzhugh put his hand on Tony's shoulder. "It's a message."

"Where's the rest of him?" Tony said.

The trooper pointed to a quivering tarp about ten feet away.

Tony dry-heaved. Then got a hold of himself. "How...how could someone survive that?"

The trooper casually lifted the tarp. A man lay shivering there as if caught in a snowstorm. His muscles were slick with coagulating fluid; his eyes wide with what Tony could only describe as horror.

The place stank like shit. And when Tony looked down, he realized it smelled that way for a reason.

Fitzhugh handed the flayed man a canteen. The poor fellow could barely hold it as he drank, water spilling onto his bloody chest.

"What the fuck?" Tony turned away from the atrocity.

Joey regarded Tony with apparent contempt, as if Tony's reaction was an embarrassment to the Five Families.

"What happened here, son?" Fitzhugh said with the compassion of a father caring for one of his children.

The man whimpered. "Have you seen Sandy? Please tell me, have you seen her? Please."

"I'm sorry, son. We haven't seen Sandy. But we promise we'll take good care of her if we find her. What's your name? Who did this to you?"

"Adam," the man panted. "They came at night. I was running supplies from Vegas to Baker. They took me and Sandy from our wagon just outside the old Primm Valley Golf Course and brought us all the way out here."

Fitzhugh stroked his beard, then faced Tony. "Seems they got kidnapped about twelve miles northeast of here and about four miles from where the caravan's sitting right now."

"Why's he shivering?" Tony asked, "It's hot as fuck out here."

"Your skin helps regulate your body temperature," Fitzhugh answered. "Without it, the body struggles to retain its warmth."

"Looks like the People of the Sun are ranging farther and farther into our territory," Lieutenant Drummond said, changing the subject.

"We don't know for certain it's the People of the Sun," said Fitzhugh. He shifted his attention back to Adam. "Tell us more about the people who did this to you. We could use that information to find Sandy."

"They...they wore white cloaks. They forced me to lay in the sun for a day. Then they skinned me with sickles."

Fitzhugh again faced Tony. "They do that for a reason, you know. Keep them out in the sun, that is. As the sun roasts the skin, it gets looser; easier to remove."

"Jesus H. Christ." Tony kissed his crucifix and made the sign of the cross.

Shifting his attention back to Adam, Fitzhugh continued his interrogation. "Did they say anything to you?"

"Don't know. They spoke Spanish."

Drummond nodded emphatically. "They're definitely the People of the Sun."

"You're right," Fitzhugh said, "but there's something off here. This isn't their usual MO."

"What da ya mean?" said Tony.

Fitzhugh crossed his arms. "Well, after skinning a man, they usually eat him. Instead, they left him here. This feels off. Way off."

"Is there anything else you know that might help us find Sandy?" Fitzhugh asked Adam. "Like where they went or how many of them kidnapped you?"

Adam gasped. "I don't know where they went. But there is something else. Something terrible. But you won't believe it."

"Try me."

"The…the people who did this to me…they bowed to it…"

"Bowed to what?"

"Something…that descended from the sky. It. Spoke. To. Me." Fitzhugh knelt down beside Adam. The flayed man seemed more rattled than ever. "What spoke to you, son?"

By now, Tony was pacing. It was his way of working off stress. But he couldn't contain it any longer. His eyes shot daggers at Adam. "Jesus Fucking Christ! Spit it out, man!"

Fitzhugh held up his hand as if to signal calm. Then he continued, "Adam, tell me what spoke to you."

The man's eyes welled with tears. "It…it was a winged thing…a snake man…it first spoke to me in Spanish. When it was obvious I didn't…understand, it switched to English. It said, 'The age of sapiens is at an end, for my kin shall inherit the Earth.'"

Now Tony was about to burst a blood vessel. "This is fucking bullshit." He stomped over to Joey. Tony started pushing him and shouted, "Tell me what's in the box. What's in the fucking box?"

Fitzhugh stood up and marched over to Tony and Joey, inserting himself between them. He pushed back at Tony. "Mr. Genovese, you need to calm down. The last thing we want to do is attract attention."

Leaning against Fitzhugh, Tony shouted over the captain's shoulder at Joey. "C'mon, Joey, what's in the box? What's wrong, you piece of shit, tongue-tied?"

Joey glared at Tony.

Fitzhugh grabbed Tony by the collar. "You need to control yourself. We're more than half way to Baker. Before you know it, we'll be finished with this mission."

Running his fingers over his scalp, Tony turned and walked away from Fitzhugh and Joey to catch his breath.

"This is bullshit. That box better be fucking important for us to go through all this crazy-ass shit," Tony said.

Fitzhugh returned to Adam. "What else?"

Adam grasped Fitzhugh's arm with his bloody hand. "Please, no more. Kill me."

Fitzhugh hesitated for a moment, then nodded. He unsheathed his saber and decapitated Adam on the spot.

Tony and Milkshake looked away. The incident didn't seem to faze Joey at all.

"You don't believe any of that shit, do you?" Tony said to Fitzhugh, secretly hoping for agreement.

"The People of the Sun definitely carved him up, but I don't believe any of this feathered serpent business. Out in these parts, I hear all sorts of stories. Some are even true. I've heard about sightings of all manner of things ranging from chupacabras to coyote men to winged serpents. I've read reports about ritualized human sacrifice, flaying, and cannibalism. But actually speaking to a winged serpent? That's a first. I've been ranging this desert for ten years and I've never seen anything like that. No, sir. This is nothing but the delusions of a dying man who was obviously in shock at having the skin stripped from his body."

Tony breathed a sigh of relief.

Fitzhugh raised his index finger. "That's not to say we should take the threat posed by the People of the Sun lightly. These people are serious about their beliefs. They're a death cult based on the darkest ancient Aztec traditions. We need to keep our heads on a swivel. Now let's mount up and get the hell out of here."

◆

The piercing sound of a bugle roused Tony from a dead sleep. Men outside shouted in the darkness. Horses neighed and whinnied.

Fitzhugh stuck his head into Tony's wagon. "Get up. We need every swinging dick outside right now!"

Tony rubbed his eyes. "The hell's going on?"

Shaking his head, Fitzhugh said, "The People of the Sun raided our camp. They've got one of my men!"

That got Tony's attention.

"Shouldn't we wait till morning? You could lame some horses by riding around in the dark."

"Morning'll be too late. I don't want those savages to keep one of my troopers for a second longer than necessary."

"But Captain, your contract says you have to escort me to Baker. If you wanna send a small detachment to find your boy, that's one thing. But we're not stopping or going somewhere else to recover just one guy."

"That's where you're wrong, Mr. Genovese. If my soldiers see me do anything less than move heaven and earth to rescue one of them—dead or alive—they'll never follow me anywhere. And if they won't follow me, they sure as hell won't follow you."

Tony hated to admit it, but the man had a point. "Fine. How about we keep our base camp here, and you leave behind the bulk of your force to defend it. Take a platoon and find your trooper. We'll wait here until you do. Sound like a plan?"

With the stubbornness of a desert burro, Fitzhugh shook his head. "Not good enough. I'm taking three platoons to recover my boy. I'll leave the fourth one with you. That's the best you're gonna get."

Tony gritted his teeth. He had an overwhelming urge to beat the piss out of Fitzhugh, but the captain had him by the short and curlies. "Fine. Do what ya gotta do."

Fitzhugh nodded. "I'll be gone no longer than two days."

"Two days!" Tony nearly exploded. He took a breath. "Two days is too long. I'll give you one."

Fitzhugh chuckled. "I'll see you in less than two days." Then he left Tony to stew in the wagon.

ꝏ

Patience wasn't exactly a virtue Tony had in abundance. He paced back and forth beside the wagon under a sweltering midday sun. But the long wait got him thinking. What was in the box Boss Milano wouldn't let anyone but Joey see? And why didn't Milano want Tony to see it? The more Tony thought about it, the more it really nagged at him.

He ducked his head into the covered wagon, where Milkshake was wiping his nose with a bloody rag. "You okay, kid?"

Milkshake nodded. "Sorry. It's that infection I was telling you about. Comes in fits and starts. I was standing here and my legs went numb. Then I fell face first."

"You gonna be all right?"

"For now. Though it'd certainly help if you got me one of them guidebooks."

"Good." Tony smiled. "And I'll see what I can do about getting something for you to write with." Tony motioned for Milkshake to exit the wagon. "Come out here. I got something else for ya."

Tony put his arm over Milkshake's shoulder and walked him out into the desert out of earshot from the rest of the caravan. "Do you know where Joey keeps that cardboard box?"

Milkshake pinched his nose to staunch the bleeding. "Yeah. He keeps it in the left rear corner of our cargo wagon."

"All right. Good. Here's what I want you to do. I'm gonna call Joey over and talk to him. While I'm doing that, I need you to peek into the box and tell me what's there."

"That's it?"

"That's it." Tony screwed up his face. "I don't think you quite understand how dangerous this game is. If Joey sees you checking out his box, he'll gut you like a pig."

"Don't worry," Milkshake said, smiling. "There's no need to call over Joey."

"What are ya talking about, kid? I'm calling the plays here. Not you."

Milkshake shook his head. "No. You don't understand. You don't need to call him over 'cause I already checked it out last night."

Tony flashed Milkshake the biggest shit-eating grin he could. "You are one hell of an enterprising mo-fo." Then Tony lowered his voice. "What's in the box, kid?"

A man squealed. Another trooper fell from his horse. A spear impaled yet another.

"Get down!" Tony grabbed Milkshake and dove into the dirt. A hail of spears zipped all around them. Tony peered up and saw dust churning along the hills. A steady rumble echoed in the distance. A bugle sounded the call of assembly.

Lieutenant Drummond yelled, "Form a line on me!"

The platoon wheeled their horses into one steady line facing the charging marauders. Drummond raised his saber, then pointed it forward, shouting, "Platoon. Forward. March."

The platoon advanced at a walk. Mounted horsemen wearing coyote pelts rode out of the dust clouds. Five hundred yards from the enemy, Drummond shouted, "Line will attack!"

The cavalry's pace quickened to a trot. The men drew their sabers. The raiders facing them were armed with sickles and flat clubs or paddles with black jagged edges.

As the cavalrymen drew closer to the enemy, Tony guessed the desert raiders outnumbered his allies by at least three to one. He wasn't feeling good about Drummond's chances.

When the two sides were about fifty yards apart, the bugle sounded the call to charge. The cavalry broke into a gallop.

Now that the spears had stopped landing around the wagon train, Tony and Milkshake got back on their feet. Tony had to make a quick decision. Should he rally his men and join the battle, wait until the cavalry wore down the raiders and then attack, or circle the wagons and defend them?

By now, the cavalry and the marauders were doing their best to slaughter each other. For Tony, the decision was easy.

"Listen up!" Tony shouted. "We don't have much time. Circle the wagons and prepare to defend yourselves against the raiders. I'm hoping the troopers hold out. But I'm gonna be honest, it's not looking too good for them and Lieutenant Drummond." Tony smacked his hands together. "All right. Let's get moving."

His associates organized the wagons into a semi-circle that bulged toward the raiders. Then his men grabbed spears and shoved them into the ground at an angle to blunt the mounted charge Tony knew would come. Once everything was set, the men charged their crossbows and hunkered down for a fight.

Tony desperately wanted to ask Milkshake about the contents of the box, but Joey had set up his position next to them. When Tony looked out at Drummond's platoon, there was so much dust and chaos, he couldn't tell which side was winning.

But a hail of spears left no doubt who had the upper hand.

"How do they come in so fast?" Milkshake asked in awe. "Back home, spears don't fly that fast."

Tony smiled. "Atlatls."

"What?"

"Atlatls. The People of the Sun use them as levers on the end of their spears to increase their speed."

The ground quaked as the raiders galloped toward the wagon train.

"Steady. Steady," said Tony.

Many of the men shook as the horsemen drew closer.

Once the raiders were within a hundred yards, Tony gave the order. "Loose!"

A volley of bolts decimated the first rank.

"Reload!" Tony yelled as he frantically cranked back his crossbow. Alfonzo's head rolled past him. The men were screaming. Marauders surrounded the wagons and dismounted. They decapitated anyone who resisted. Joey sliced at the raiders with his machete, cutting down two of them half a second before they reached Tony.

But it was obvious that Tony's crew was hopelessly outnumbered. He had to act fast or no one would ever be going home. He summoned all his courage and stood up, raising his hands in surrender. He motioned for Milkshake and Joey to do the same.

A mountain of a man wearing a coyote headdress approached. He carried a flat club with razor-sharp edges that looked a lot like an Aztec weapon Tony had seen in Father Serra's books called a macuahuitl. The brute backhanded Tony, slamming him into the dirt. Tony stumbled back up, his hands still raised. The man smacked him again with the club's flat surface. Tony's vision faded to black.

∓

III. Ritual

Tony woke in a cave, his back set against a rocky wall. It was dark and cool. His hands and feet were bound in hemp; his sunglasses, crucifix, and gold rings missing. Milkshake and Joey sat to his left and right, similarly bound. A faint light flickered in the distant dark. The walls were chiseled with crude pictures of longhorn sheep and bowmen. Father Serra had called them petroglyphs, images prehistoric people had carved in stone thousands of years ago.

"Where are we?" said Tony.

Milkshake shook Joey. "Tony's awake." Turning his head toward Tony, Milkshake said, "They took seven of us to this cave. They butchered everyone else."

Tony looked around him. "Where are the other four?"
Milkshake pointed farther into the cave. "They took them deeper into that tunnel."

Footsteps brushed against the sandy cavern floor. Three warriors wearing coyote headdresses and pelts, and wielding macuahuitls marched toward the captives.

A tall, muscular man with a jagged scar running from his right eye to his lower left jaw grabbed Tony by the arm and yanked him to his feet. A small, swarthy man cut the rope around Tony's legs. The two warriors then freed Milkshake and Joey from their bonds. Then the scarred warrior said, "¡Vámonos!" and shoved Tony forward.

"Easy!" Tony yelled.

The scarred man cuffed Tony in the face. Tony stumbled forward, trying to keep his balance.

They made their way through a tunnel dimly lit by torchlight. Tony couldn't help but stare at the men's macuahuitls. Fashioned from old utility posts, the weapons were a work of art. Detailed carvings of scorpions, black widows, rattlesnakes, and sun spiders decorated each macuahuitl, which was fringed with razor-sharp obsidian blades.

After the group had walked about three hundred yards, the tunnel opened into a larger cavern with a high, vaulted ceiling. Multi-tiered stadium seating extended from the rock faces on all sides. Dozens of men and women clad in coyote and mountain lion pelts gazed down upon an oval-shaped arena. Pikes capped with freshly severed heads lined the arena's perimeter.

Tony shuddered as he began to recognize those faces—faces of the young men who hours before had been his associates; faces that now stared blankly at him from beyond death's veil. He whispered a prayer to God to save him from this horror.

From the far right and running counterclockwise, blood-red sandstone, obsidian, turquoise, and marble slab altars occupied each corner of the arena. In the center, a high priest in a jet-black raven-feather coat presided over the strange ritual. He wore a black-feathered headpiece with four ravens' skulls arrayed in a diamond-shape just above his forehead. Two sweptback raven's wings extended from the headdress's flanks.

More raven priests stood before each altar, and on every altar laid a cavalryman, bound and gagged.

The warriors forced the trio onto their knees and to face the arena. The swarthy warrior tied hemp around the trio's calves. Then the captors stepped back several feet toward the tunnel entrance, where they stood watch.

A slow drumbeat steadily grew louder and its pace quickened. The worshippers stomped their feet with an increasing intensity and fanaticism that unnerved Tony. The peculiar congregation swayed and chanted in a language Father Serra hadn't taught him. He angled his head toward Joey and whispered, "That's not Spanish. What language is that?" Tony immediately wanted to kick himself for asking a tongueless man a question.

Joey grimaced at Tony.

Without skipping a beat, Tony said, "What? Tongue-tied?" then chuckled, pleased with himself for lightening a mood that was otherwise in a death spiral. The scarred warrior backhanded Tony so hard he bit his tongue, tasting his salty blood.

The drumbeats settled into a steady rhythm. Four raven-feather clad women shuffled in, supporting wicker baskets on their heads. Each woman placed her basket on the floor at the foot of every altar.

The high priest raised his hands and then lowered them in an abrupt scything motion. The drumbeat ceased. Then he addressed the crowd in Spanish, "Let it be soon, oh Great One, who glides upon the five winds. Your hunger and thirst are as bottomless as the void. In this world of the Fifth Sun, accept these meager offerings of blood and heart from your humble and ever vigilant servants."

Tony flinched. "I hope that wasn't literal," he whispered.

Milkshake seemed confused, no doubt because he couldn't speak Spanish.

Tony murmured, "Never mind."

The high priest pointed to the sandstone altar in the upper right corner. "To the east, we honor the sun god, Tonatiuh."

The raven priest at that altar began chanting in earnest. The priestess beside him opened the wicker basket's lid, then lifted the basket off the ground, raising it to chest height. At the same time, the priest pulled out an obsidian blade and lowered it toward the cavalry trooper. The poor man screamed and flailed for his life.

But to Tony's surprise, the priest didn't stab or cut his victim. He merely slashed off the man's clothing.

It didn't take Tony long to figure out why.

The priestess overturned the basket, dumping scores of starving sand-colored sun spiders on the poor man. He screamed his guts out as the hand-sized arachnids ripped into his flesh with their three-inch-long jaws, eating him alive.

Suddenly, the stench of urine hit Tony's nostrils. He turned to find Milkshake quaking after having just pissed himself. The kid's eyes were wide as saucers. Normally, Tony would crack wise, but now wasn't the time. Milkshake probably hadn't seen anything like a sun spider in his life. He sure as hell had never seen a swarm of 'em ever devouring a human being.

Tony inclined his head toward Milkshake. "Don't worry, kid. They're just sun spiders. They're usually pretty harmless. They just haven't been fed in a while, that's all."

The high priest spun counterclockwise toward the next altar, a shiny slab of pure obsidian. "To the north, we honor Tezcatlipoca, the god of night and earth. The god of mirrors and the god of death."

The priestess at the obsidian altar prepared her basket, and the priest removed the trooper's clothing. As he did so, the trooper pleaded with him, "Please. Don't do it. I just defended myself. Please don't!" His face was slick with tears. He quivered.

The priestess unloaded the her basket's contents onto his body. A clump of thumb-sized black spheres tumbled onto his chest, then crawled. Tony cringed when he saw the telltale red hourglass stamped on their abdomens: black widows.

"Stay still. Don't move a muscle," Tony whispered to himself.

But the man wouldn't stay still; he tensed up and screamed. As he thrashed, the sharp bites of hundreds of black widows flooded his system with a crippling neurotoxin. The trooper sputtered and screeched. His body began to swell until it resembled a bloated flesh bag burnt red by the desert sun.

The scene horrified Tony, but he found it impossible to look away. Normally, it took hours for a single black widow bite to kick in. But with that much spider venom coursing through the man's veins, Tony knew the trooper couldn't last that much longer.

The trooper vomited all over himself. Then he started to wheeze. His breathing became increasingly shallow until it abruptly stopped.

And again, the high priest turned counterclockwise, this time facing the nearest altar to Tony, a marble slab, on his near left. The high priest raised his hands. "To the west, we honor Quetzalcoatl, the feathered serpent god of wind and knowledge."

The priestess at the marble altar emptied her basket onto yet another shrieking and naked trooper. A pile of rattlesnakes lunged at the quavering soldier, sinking their fangs into his soft flesh. The man's arms and legs began to swell as the deadly hemotoxin flooded into his bloodstream. He guttered and flailed in what appeared to be an agonizing death.

The high priest spun once more, facing the turquoise altar on Tony's near right. The man on that slab was Lieutenant Drummond. Unlike his troopers, Drummond seemed calm and resigned to his fate. He lay composed as the high priest chanted from the center of the arena. "To the south, we honor Huitzilopochtli, the god of war and human sacrifice."

Drummond held firm while the priest stripped off his uniform with an obsidian blade. And the lieutenant continued to hold steady when the priestess dropped hundreds of scorpions onto his naked body.

Tony could imagine Drummond willing himself not to squirm. But it didn't matter. The scorpions' own movement triggered them to lash out with their tails, stinging Drummond over and over. The stings jolted him out of his composure, leading to further strikes until his body was so full of venom that he shook violently. He died several minutes later.

Tony really started to worry. Now that the four troopers were dead, what did this maniacal death cult have in mind for him and his companions? After all, the People of the Sun must've brought them here for a reason.

The high priest raised his hands again. A steady drumbeat followed. Milkshake rocked back and forth. "They're gonna kill us. They're gonna fucking kill us!"

The raven priests raised their obsidian daggers above the dead troopers and cut into their chests. Thrusting their hands inside the bloody chest cavities, the priests wrenched out the dead men's hearts and held them up to the congregation.

The drumbeat quickened and grew louder. The cavern walls began to vibrate. Tony's heart threatened to burst from his chest.

Without thinking, Tony stood up. "Fuck this!" he yelled. He spun toward the guard standing behind him. "You can fucking suck my dick, you savage piece of shit." Then he spat on the man.

The scarred warrior calmly strode toward Tony with an air of supreme confidence and control. Tony lunged at him and bit a chunk out of his neck. The scarred man dropped his macuahuitl. Blood sprouted from his neck like a fountain. Not wasting a second, Tony crouched and frantically rubbed the hemp binding his hands against the fallen macuahuitl until they broke loose.

The drumbeat stopped.

The cultist guarding Milkshake rushed to his comrade's aid. Joey stumbled to his feet and spun behind the warrior. He swung his bound hands from his back over his head and around the cultist's neck, strangling the swarthy warrior in the most impressive and only display of double-jointedness Tony had ever witnessed.

Tony picked up the macuahuitl and slashed the hemp around his ankles. He stood up half a second before the third warrior guarding the cavern entrance nearly decapitated him.

Stumbling like a blind walrus swimming in motor oil, Tony struggled to regain his balance. The cultist swung at him again, ripping a chunk out of Tony's shoulder.

Furious, Tony flew at the man in a blind rage. He hacked at the cultist until the man was a bleeding puddle of meat.

Tony then sliced Joey and Milkshake's binds. The warriors in the stands flooded into the arena and closed in on the trio.

From a dark recess of the cavern, something stirred. In Spanish, the high priest shouted, "Stop! Stay away!"

Many of the cultists heeded the high priest's call. Yet a few ignored it, hurling themselves at the three men.

Tony ran to the exit tunnel and yelled, "Follow me!"

Tony, Milkshake, and Joey formed a human wall to block the exit. Constrained by the narrow tunnel, the cultists attacked in twos and threes. Joey fought like a beast, cutting down anyone within five feet. Milkshake also held his own against the rampaging horde.

As Tony fought for his life, he kept watching for a break in the human flood, a chance to turn his back and run. His arms were already getting tired. He didn't know how much longer he'd have the strength to hold the cultists off.

The high priest kept urging his people to clear the arena, but few listened. The rest continued their attacks.

Seconds later, Tony learned why the high priest had been so eager to get his people out. A rattle echoed throughout the cavern as a snake as thick as four men slithered into the arena. Its scales had an odd blue hue. The serpent lashed out at the crowd.

A scorpion and a sun spider as big as horses skittered out of the darkness. Similar to the rattlesnake, their exoskeletons had a strange light blue glow. The arachnids indiscriminately struck everything in their paths.

"What the hell are those?" said Milkshake.

"The fuck if I know," Tony replied, "but this is our one chance to get the hell outta here. Let's go!"

The trio turned only to come face-to-face with the eight-eyed head of a Volkswagen-sized black widow spider. Tony extended his left arm to prevent his companions from stumbling into the behemoth. He glanced over his shoulder. At the sight of the black widow, the cultists chasing him had broken off and were running back toward the arena.

Tony shouted, "Hack the legs!"

The giant arachnid surged toward them. Tony swung with all his strength, lodging his macuahuitl into its foreleg. Joey piled on, chopping the seven-segmented leg in half. The spider squealed, but continued its attack, anchoring itself into the center of the tunnel with its seven remaining legs. Suspended from the low ceiling, it curled its abdomen beneath it and shot a thick strand of webbing at Milkshake. Then it yanked the kid toward it.

Tony watched slack-jawed as the giant spider spun a screaming Milkshake in circles, roping him in dense white spider silk. Tony noted the dark-blue hourglass on the underside of the spider's huge round abdomen. While it was playing with its food, Tony and Joey ran beneath it and hacked at its legs.

The spider shrieked again, nearly crushing Joey after he'd severed another leg. It dropped a sticky Milkshake to snap at Joey with its retractable fangs. Milkshake hit the ground hard. Unshaken by the fall, he struggled to break lose.

Tony raced behind the creature. Then he bashed open its swollen abdomen with his macuahuitl. The thing immediately swung around and charged at him on its broken legs. Joey hacked at the spider's abdomen from behind. Milkshake continued to flounder in the sticky webbing.

The spider's jaws snapped at Tony. Tony ducked, narrowly avoiding decapitation. He swung his macuahuitl, smashing the spider's head open in a riot of blue pulp. The creature's broken body flailed and shuddered for several seconds before collapsing into a lifeless hulk.

"Milkshake!" Tony yelled to Joey.

Joey sawed through the spider silk with his macuahuitl. Then he stripped off enough of the webbing so Milkshake could get back on his feet.

Tony yelled, "Run!"

The trio sprinted through a maze of tunnels. Tony followed Joey and Milkshake since he'd been unconscious when they'd been taken to the cavern. At one point, they passed a side tunnel filled with blocks of ice. Tony was curious about how the ice had gotten there, but there wasn't any time to investigate. The People of the Sun would likely be in hot pursuit, so he pressed onward. By the time he saw a glimmer of sunlight, he was so exhausted he nearly coughed up a lung.

The three stumbled out into the Mojave Desert's searing furnace. The sun blazed in the afternoon sky. Tony surveyed the vast desert, briefly taking in its beauty before considering a more grim reality. There were no signs of human habitation for miles. He looked with hope to his companions. "You guys know how to get back to our wagon train, right?"

Joey lowered his head.

Milkshake shrugged. "They blindfolded us before they brought us here."

"Fuck," Tony muttered. Normally, he'd have waited until dark to move, but he worried once his former captors got their freaks of nature under control, they'd aim to settle the score. "C'mon. We need to get moving."

"Where?" said Milkshake.

Tony looked up at the sun. "West. If we're lucky, we'll stumble into Fitzhugh."

"And if we don't?"

Tony shrugged. "We'll know either way in about two days."

The men ventured out into the oppressive heat to search for the Regiment before dehydration and death found them.

&

IV. Desert Devils

The scorching heat was taking its toll on the crew. Tony was thirsty as hell. He had a throbbing headache, a telltale symptom of dehydration. Milkshake was already beet red and fading. To his credit, Joey seemed to be the only mook with enough juice to last another day.

The three men wandered through a desolate desert forest of bayonet-leaved yucca, gnarled-branched Joshua trees with dagger-shaped leaves, and hardy, dark green creosote.

Tony supposed it could've been worse. The People of the Sun had left them alone thus far. But he was realistic enough to know he shouldn't let down his guard. With horses, the cultists could easily catch up with them. Tony prayed they didn't.

Milkshake was in real bad shape. By sunset, the temperature had dropped precipitously, but the cold wasn't going to save him. He was vomiting and could barely walk. Tony and Joey had had to support him for about a third of the time they'd been staggering through the desert. If he were a betting man, Tony would've given the kid a fifty-fifty shot of survival.

To the west, the sky ranged from light blue to vibrant pink, and then deepened to dark orange as the sun sank beneath the horizon. A steady rumble punctuated the low hum of the desert wind. Riders closed in from the west, their black silhouettes obscuring whether they were friend or foe.

Joey pointed to a clump of creosote. Weary, Tony dipped his head in agreement. The three shambled over to the bushes and collapsed behind them.

The ground quaked.

Tony said, "They've spotted us."

Milkshake wheezed.

"Hang in there, kid," Tony said. "In about five minutes, you'll either get some relief or you'll die."

Milkshake responded with a weak nod.

The horsemen fanned out to Tony's left and right, then slowly closed in toward the trio.

"Careful, boys. They could be hostiles. Approach slowly," Captain Fitzhugh said.

Tony smiled. He'd never been more relieved in his life. "Captain Fitzhugh!" he rasped, "It's Tony, Joey, and Milkshake. We're gonna get up slowly, so don't shoot."

When they rose, Tony was thankful to be surrounded by the soldiers of Alpha Troop. Tony and Joey brought Milkshake over to the captain.

"Water," Tony croaked.

Fitzhugh gestured to a trooper who brought over three canteens. Tony lapped up as much water as his stomach could hold.

Fitzhugh took one glance at Milkshake. "That boy's a heat casualty if I ever saw one. Sergeant Marks, set up an aid station and cool that kid down. He's also gonna need an I-V."

Sergeant Marks, a chubby medic with a mustache, rushed over with two soldiers in tow. They eased Milkshake onto a stretcher and set up an aid station around him.

Fitzhugh shifted his attention to Tony and Joey. "What the hell happened? All the evidence pointed to a massacre. Have any of my boys survived?"

Tony lowered his head.

"That's what I was afraid of," Fitzhugh said. "Tell me everything."

Tony gave Fitzhugh an account of the platoon's battle with the People of the Sun, the trio's capture, the sadistic ritual, and their encounter with the giant spider.

When Tony finished his story, Fitzhugh stared at him as if he expected Tony to burst into laughter like it was some sick joke. When Tony didn't, Fitzhugh said, "You sure they didn't pump you with peyote?"

"Positive."

Fitzhugh shook his head dismissively. "Who filled your head with all those old wives' tales?"

"Captain, this is no joke. I'm as serious as a heart attack." Then Tony got curious. "Wait, what do you mean by old wives' tales?"

Fitzhugh removed his Stetson, then wiped his brow. "Ever since the invasion, there've been all sorts of rumors about bizarre things roaming through these parts. Coyote men. Giant snakes. Winged serpents. All sorts of crazy tales. Never once have I seen any evidence of it.

"Once one of our chaplains reported seeing men with coyote heads outside some abandoned trailers. Claimed they were eating people. Insisted they were a sign of the apocalypse. I just thought he was going mad. Hell, some scientists from Nellis tried to rationalize it as some sort of gene splicing experiments with human and extraterrestrial DNA. Far as I'm concerned, it's all some sort of mass delusion."

Tony lit up. "That last bit might explain it."

Fitzhugh chuckled. "Next you're gonna say they all had a blue hue or something."

Tony nodded and smiled. "That's exactly what we saw."

"Now look here. Me and my boys spent half our lives ranging this desert. We've seen a lot of crazy things. But the more experience you have in the bush, the better you get at separating reality from madness. This may be your first rodeo, son, but it sure as hell ain't mine. And you'd do well to remember that."

"Fuck you, old man." Tony hurled his words at the captain with venom. "I know what I fucking saw, and there's no way in hell I'm imagining it."

Fitzhugh shot right back. "You got proof?"

Tony had to restrain himself from grabbing the captain by the throat. "Oh, I better stop fighting this *giant fucking spider* for a second so I can gather some evidence for Captain Fitzhugh. Are you listening to yourself?"

Fitzhugh held out his hands in a calming motion. "Fine. I know you believe what you saw was real. Let's just keep it at that."

Tony agreed it didn't make sense arguing the matter any further with the stubborn bastard. People either believed you or they didn't. So he changed the subject. "What about you? Did you find your man?" Tony hesitated for a moment before blurting out, "Was it worth sacrificing a platoon?" Sometimes he just couldn't resist rubbing salt in a wound.

Fitzhugh glowered at Tony. "Yeah, we found him. Unfortunately, he was impaled on a utility pole and flayed." He tossed a bloody saber at Tony. "If your kid, Milkshake, doesn't die of heatstroke, give this to him. He's the only one of you three that doesn't seem to be a real asshole."

Joey scowled at the captain.

"That's it?" said Tony. "You didn't run into the People of the Sun or see anything unusual?"

Fitzhugh shook his head, paused as if in consideration, then continued, "Well, we didn't run into the People of the Sun, but several of my men reported a winged serpent stalking them from the sky. But when men spend a long time out in the heat, their minds play tricks on them. It was probably just another raven hunting for food. Those old birds are as common as sand out here. Really freaked my men out, though. They're still carrying on about it."

Tony wanted to know more about the sighting, but doubted Fitzhugh would indulge his curiosity. Plus Tony didn't want to trigger another argument with the captain. "Uh-huh. What's next?"

Fitzhugh scratched his head. "Once your boy's feeling better, we'll return to the wagon train, gather what's left of our supplies, and continue west toward Baker."

"Sounds like a plan." Tony turned to Joey. "Wait here. I'm gonna see how Milkshake's doing."

Tony walked a short distance to the aid station, which consisted of a cot resting beneath a makeshift tarp. A metal stand crowned with a clear bag of fluid flanked Milkshake's cot. Tubing extended from the bag into Milkshake's arm.

Tony kneeled beside him. "You doing all right, kid?"

"Yeah," Milkshake said in a weak, raspy voice. "Sergeant Marks is taking good care of me. He says I just need more fluids. I'll be ready to go by morning."

Tony grinned. "Glad to hear it." He lowered his voice to a whisper. "I've been dying to ask you this for the past few days. Now that we're alone, I can. What's inside Joey's box?"

Milkshake sighed. "It was the weirdest thing. There was nothing there but a bald plastic head."

Confused, Tony said, "Like a mannequin's head?"

"Yeah. That's it."

Tony scratched his temple. The boss never spoke in riddles. And he never beat around the bush. No, this little stunt was more Bobby's style. And if Bobby was behind it, there was a message to it. Tony just wasn't sure what that message was.

ॐ

V. Mayhem at the Mad Greek

The town of Baker was nestled in a depression at the junction of the I-15 Trail and old State Route 127. It was a rest stop on the way to Vegas or Death Valley, if you were into that kinda thing. To the southwest, the jagged peaks of the brown Cronese Mountains stabbed the pale blue sky.

As Tony stared down into the valley ahead, he chuckled at the garish hundred-and-thirty-four foot thermometer that towered over Baker. A lonely monument to the excesses of a pre-invasion paradise, it rose to the left of the main drag running through town. Without electricity, it no longer had a purpose other than as a landmark in the harsh desert.

In stark contrast to the dead digital monolith, the blue-and-white Mad Greek Cafe thrived across the street. Tony considered the restaurant's survival to be a minor miracle. Suspicious even.

Even more suspicious than the People of the Sun leaving most of the caravan's supplies untouched. When he'd returned to the laager site, Tony had been surprised that they'd only taken the horses and five wagons. When the Regiment had inspected what remained, he'd held his breath, hoping they wouldn't find any methamphetamine. And he'd counted his lucky stars when they hadn't. The troopers had hitched some of their horses to the remaining wagons and continued west.

After the ordeal of the last few days, Tony was truly looking forward to seeing his old friend, Gus DeLuca. Gus was now running the Mad Greek on behalf of the Five Families.

Tony thanked Saint Christopher that he'd made it to Baker in one piece. He'd been certain the People of the Sun would make another run at the wagon train, and was surprised they hadn't.

Baker's distinct lack of security had always puzzled Tony. No trench works, no palisades, no armed associates. Nothing. It didn't make any sense. Now after barely surviving capture by the People of the Sun, it really worried him.

Tony ultimately convinced himself to stop imagining problems where there probably weren't any. He consoled himself with the notion that if anyone attacked, they'd face the fury of Alpha Troop.

Fitzhugh set his three remaining platoons in a cordon around the town. Then he, his four surviving lieutenants, and about ten noncommissioned officers joined Tony, Joey, and Milkshake. They all headed toward the Mad Greek.

Joey cradled his cardboard box, while Tony lugged the blue Coleman cooler. For his part, Milkshake stowed the Altoids tin, the duct tape, and the Motorola in his pants' cargo pockets.

A row of white plaster statues interspersed with Corinthian columns and white vases decorated the cafe's external facade. Tony walked beneath a blue-and-white-striped awning to enter the restaurant. Once inside, he passed through two more Corinthian columns. On his right was an open seating section with blue leather seats and more white statues. Tony kept walking until he reached the front counter. A curmudgeon with wavy gray hair regarded him with a bored expression.

Gus squinted at Tony crosswise for a few seconds before recognizing his old pal. "Hey!" he said, making a big show of walking around the counter and giving Tony a hug. "What you been up to all these years, you big son-of-a-bitch?"

Tony patted his old friend on the back and made a big show of looking around the restaurant. "You know, I think this place needs more blue."

Gus chuckled.

Tony smiled, then scratched his nose. "But in all seriousness, I'm trying to earn my button just like you are. But I hear you've been doing nothing but making milkshakes and gyros."

Gus jutted his head toward Milkshake. "Who's this?"

Without skipping a beat, Tony said, "You've got your milkshakes, and I've got mine."

Gus shot Tony an expression of confusion. "What? You fucking this guy or something? I never knew you swung that way, Tony."

Tony laughed. "Nah. I just call him Milkshake 'cause he reminds me of you, Gus."

"Now you're just busting balls." Gus's eyes shifted to Joey, and his mood darkened. "Ah... good to see you too, Joey." Gus forced a smile and shook the mute's hand.

Tony introduced Gus to all the commissioned and noncommissioned officers. Once Tony had finished, Gus wiped his hands on his smock. "Where are my manners? What will you all be having? I recommend the Mad Greek's famous strawberry milkshake. We also make the best gyros in what's left of the country."

Gus gave everyone a menu and took orders. He barked commands to three cooks in the back. Tony, Milkshake, and Joey grabbed a booth all to themselves near the Mad Greek's entrance. Tony placed the cooler on the floor at the edge of the table. Joey kept his box close on the windowsill to his left.

Within thirty minutes, Gus brought the crew the finest gyros and strawberry milkshakes west of the Mississippi. Then he sat down beside Joey and across from Tony and Milkshake.

"It's good to finally see you, brother," Gus said to Tony. "It gets lonely out here."

"I hear ya," Tony said. He took a sip from his milkshake, appreciating its refreshing taste. "You know, Gus, I've always wondered, how the hell you keep these milkshakes so damn cold out here in the middle of the Mojave Desert. And with no electricity to boot.

Gus grinned.

Tony shook his head. "No, Gus. I'm fucking serious. I need to know. Milano's expecting me to bring him an unmelted strawberry milkshake in this cooler." Tony tapped the Coleman with his foot.

Gus smiled. "Well, it sure as hell ain't easy. While I'd be happy to make you some milkshakes for the road, I doubt they'd be cold by the time you returned to Vegas."

"Humor me."

"Oh, what the hell. During the late winter and early spring, I trade with mule teams who lug big chunks of ice down from the Sierras. I store the ice in local caverns. When I need the ice, I send teams to the caverns to haul it here. I stock that ice in a storage tunnel beneath this restaurant."

Then Tony recalled the ice blocks he'd seen in the tunnels. "That's quite an operation you're running. How do you protect your cargo from the People of the Sun?"

Gus shifted uncomfortably in his seat. "Well, I usually hire mercenaries to protect my shipments."

"Huh?" said Tony. "The Regiment's the only major mercenary operation within three hundred miles. How come you don't already know Captain Fitzhugh?"

Gus waved his hand. "There are plenty of mercenaries if you know where to look."

"Hmmm." Tony slurped his milkshake. "You mind if I ask you one more question?"

"Anything, Tony."

"Why aren't there any defenses in Baker?" Tony took another draw on his straw.

Gus shrugged. "I've got an arrangement."

Now Tony was getting pissed. "What kind of arrangement?"

The double doors leading to the storeroom burst open. Scores of cultists armed with sharpened sickles flooded into the restaurant. The troopers fumbled for their sabers. For most of them, it was too late.

Tony glared at Gus.

"I'm sorry, man. I had no choice. They've been waiting underground for your crew."

Tony grabbed Gus by the throat. "You sneaky son-of-a-bitch."

Milkshake pulled out the duct tape and ripped off a strip.

"Please!" Gus stuttered. "They only want the officers. That's it. You play your cards right, all three of yas can walk outta here alive."

A coyote warrior stormed toward them. Milkshake rolled out of the booth and dropped to a knee, hamstringing the man with the saber Fitzhugh had given him. Joey swooped down on a throng of warriors with his machete, slicing their necks. Blood fountained from their throats.

Tony grabbed a sickle from the floor and slashed at yet another charging cultist. Milkshake tapped Tony on the shoulder, then pointed beneath the table. There, Tony saw the neon green Motorola wrapped in green duct tape. At first, Tony was confused. Then he understood.

Turning to Joey, Tony said, "C'mon, Joey. We gotta scram."

Tony plunged into the crowd of hostiles, scything a path through them. Tony, Joey, and Milkshake formed a wedge with Tony in the center.

The troopers fought hard. But the attack had been so sudden, they'd been caught flatfooted. The People of the Sun slaughtered anyone who tried to escape and warn the Regiment's rank and file.

The three men trudged over severed body parts and corpses. They hacked their way toward the restaurant's exit. With the radio on, Tony felt an extreme urgency to escape. He didn't know how much time he had, but he didn't want to be around to find out.

A goliath of a man blocked the exit. He wielded a macuahuitl in one hand and a sickle in the other. He leered at Tony's crew, then lunged forward.

The brute's macuahuitl narrowly missed Joey, slamming into the linoleum floor. But the warrior's sickle kissed Tony's cheek seconds before Tony could duck. Tony stumbled backward in shock. But Milkshake and Joey gutted the warrior in a lightning quick pincer movement.

Tony burst out of the restaurant and hollered for back up. Troopers on horseback rushed to the cafe, then dismounted and joined the fray.

While the men of Alpha Troop were racing into the restaurant, the trio commandeered two horses. Tony rode with Milkshake. They galloped west, away from Baker and toward safety.

Minutes later, Tony glanced over his shoulder. In the distance, a swirling black cloud descended upon the Mad Greek like a locust swarm.

"My God," Milkshake said, "I thought we were gonna die in there."

Tony nodded. "We almost did."

"Aren't we supposed to be heading east?"

"You're not wrong. But ain't no way we're getting through that territory alive again without an escort." Tony thought for a moment and then decided to give credit where credit was due. "Son, you saved our asses. Tell ya what: I got a Five Families contact near the Cajon Pass who can hook us up with provisions and men to get me and Joey back home. The ride from Baker to Cajon should be a lot safer. Alpha Troop may be gone, but the rest of the Regiment is still out there and has tighter control over the I-15 Trail in that area. My contact in Cajon also happens to run a wingsuit operation that sends smugglers west over the San Gabriel Mountains. You follow me and Joey to Cajon, and you're free."

Milkshake looked over his shoulder at Tony and shot him a goofy grin. "Deal."

Tony took a deep breath, grateful that they'd made it through another tough spot. He reached for his crucifix only to be reminded that the People of the Sun had stolen it from him. He shrugged, made the sign of the cross, and mouthed a silent prayer.

A shadow passed over them.

"What the fuck was that?" Tony shaded his eyes with his hand as he gazed into the bright sky.

High over the horizon, something glided on the wind like a bird, but its shape was...off.

Milkshake pointed at the silhouette. "Look! It's coming back around again."

Tony shifted in the saddle. He craned and twisted his neck to get a better view, but the sun obscured his vision.

"Shit!" Milkshake was visibly animated. "It's heading toward us! And it's coming in real fast!"

Tony tried getting a bead on whatever was tracking them. He gripped his sickle a little too tightly. The handle was slick with sweat. He quickly wiped it on his shirt so it wouldn't slip from his hands in a fight.

Milkshake tightened the reins. Tony took another peek back and saw it. No more than three hundred yards behind them and closing in fast.

It was no bird.

"Go!" Tony slapped Milkshake on the back. Hard.

Milkshake tightened his legs and leaned forward in the saddle. The horse moved from a trot into a gallop. Joey followed.

"Fuck! Here it comes!" Tony hung to the side of the saddle, holding his sickle at the ready.

Then it was on them. Something shaped like a man with blue-green scales, an elongated torso, a reptilian tail, and giant raven's wings.

Milkshake made the horse veer left, narrowly avoiding the attack. Tony swung at the creature and missed. It flew west, climbing to gain altitude.

"What the hell was that?" Milkshake's voice quaked.

Tony shrugged. "The fuck if I know. Maybe the alien's did some crazy ass gene-splicing out here. It would explain the freak shows we faced in the cave." Tony paused for a moment as he watched the sky. "Oh, shit! It's coming back around again!"

This time, Tony could clearly see the thing's serpentine face. It bared its fangs as it swooped down for a second pass.

But Tony was ready. He waited for it to get close, then hacked at it with all his strength. His sickle caught on the thing's leg. The creature broadsided him with its tail, knocking Tony off his horse. Then it soared again into the heavens.

Tony hit the ground hard. He rolled end-over-end, then slammed headfirst into the sand. Sharp pain spread throughout his face as blood poured out of his nose. He slowly stumbled to his feet. When he looked up, the creature had already turned and began to angle for another pass. And this time, it was heading straight for Tony.

In the chaos, Tony had dropped his sickle. Frantic, he searched everywhere for it. Milkshake and Joey had turned their horses and were now galloping toward him.

As the creature descended, it picked up speed. If Tony had to guess, the thing was pissed.

It collided with Tony before he had a chance to dive for the dirt, knocking the wind out of him. Bleary-eyed and broken, Tony staggered to his feet. When he looked ahead, he was stunned to see the desert demon had landed and was striding toward him.

Tony glanced around. Still no sign of the sickle. Joey and Milkshake were getting closer, but they weren't gonna make it in time. So Tony planted his feet and squared his shoulders for a fight.

The thing didn't move like a man. It lunged like a snake, lashing out with fangs not fists. Tony could never tell where it would strike, but he was certain that if Joey and Milkshake didn't arrive soon, he'd bob and weave right into those jaws.

It struck again, barely missing Tony. He spun right, then kicked it. It hissed. With a swipe of its tail, it knocked Tony off his feet. Before he could get back up, the creature had him pinned. It hadn't looked so big from the ground, but this close, Tony estimated it was well over nine feet tall and weighed four hundred plus pounds.

Tony used every bit of strength he had to keep its fangs away from him. The only thing keeping him alive was the adrenaline surging through his veins. Nearly overwhelmed with exhaustion, the edges of his vision were going black.

The earth trembled. There was a wet thud like a knife cutting through watermelon. Joey slowed his horse to a trot, then wheeled it back around, his sickle stained with blood. The serpent thing's head tumbled into the sand. A crimson geyser spurted from the headless carcass.

Milkshake and Joey reined in their horses, stopping several feet from Tony.

"You okay?" said Milkshake.

Tony crawled out from beneath the lifeless husk. Once he got back on his feet, he wiped the warm blood and wet sand off his shirt. "We need to take that thing with us. The Regiment and the Five Families need to know what's out here."

Joey shook his head.

It didn't matter that Joey had just saved Tony's ass; Tony couldn't have been angrier with Joey. "What the fuck do you mean, 'no'? Without proof, no one will ever believe us."

Milkshake sighed. "Joey's right. With that kinda load, the horses'll never make it to the Cajon Pass. Let's just take the head."

The kid had a point.

"Fine," Tony said. "Grab it and let's go."

Again, Joey shook his head. Then he dismounted and stuck his sickle in the thing's jaws, which snapped shut.

"Fuck," said Tony. "You're right. That thing's mouth is like a giant rattlesnake's. And a severed rattlesnake's head can still bite even hours after death. Ain't no way I'm putting its head behind me in a saddle. Let's bury it and mark the site. We can pick it up on the way back."

Joey gave Tony a curt nod. Then the three men spent an hour digging a hole, burying the head, and then marking it with a wooden cross constructed from the branches of a Joshua Tree. Then they all headed west.

&

VI. Sailing on the Santa Ana Winds

Two days later, the crew reached Barstow. Four Blackhorse troopers challenged them on the town's outskirts.

Milkshake seemed a bit rattled. Tony suspected the kid was worried stories had reached the Regiment about the nanoswarm's destruction of Alpha Troop. But Tony was more optimistic. Word didn't travel that fast out here. If it had, the troopers would have greeted them with crossbow bolts.

So Tony told them enough to satisfy their curiosity, but not so much as to arouse their suspicions. He gave them his version of the Battle of Baker. How the People of the Sun had ambushed Alpha Troop. How a nanoswarm had wiped out people on both sides. How they'd barely escaped with their lives.

Yet he left out the stranger, more disturbing accounts of what had happened in the caverns and after their escape from Baker. It would raise too many questions and delay their passage west.

The soldiers did press Tony on whether he and his comrades were trafficking methamphetamine. In no uncertain terms, Tony made it clear he found their insinuation insulting. But he consented to their pat down all the same.

In response to Tony's complaints, the troopers relayed several incidents where meth fueled the People of the Sun's brutally effective offensives. And the Regiment suspected the Five Families were their supplier. Deep down, Tony began to think they might be right. In fact, he wouldn't have been surprised if his own caravan had been carrying the stuff. But if that were true, why would the People of the Sun have attacked it?

Then Tony had a horrifying realization: maybe the ambush hadn't been so random. Maybe the People of the Sun had had some other objective in mind. After all, they'd only taken the horses and five wagons, leaving everything else untouched.

Tony's head was already spinning with enough questions to give him a migraine, so he tried to focus on more positive thoughts like making it to the Cajon Pass in one piece.

From the way the soldiers reacted to his account, it was obvious Tony wasn't the only one who'd had a bad brush with the People of the Sun. And he was convinced the only reason the Regiment had let his crew pass through Barstow was because he'd told the Blackhorse where they could find the bastards.

Two more days and the crew arrived in Victorville. In the two years since Tony's last visit, it had transformed into a thriving way station. The town fed the Regiment's increasing appetite for men and material as it expanded its sphere of influence in the High Desert. A sphere of influence, Tony noted, that would soon clash with the interests of the Five Families.

The three men kept a low profile in Victorville, gathering all the provisions they needed for the final leg of their journey.

They continued along the I-15 Trail until they reached the base of the San Bernardino Mountains, which they slowly climbed until reaching the Cajon Pass. There, Tony's friend, Fast Eddie, ran a listening post for the Five Families at the old Best Western Inn.

A devil's wind blasted through the Cajon Pass like flames venting from Hell. It had a dryness about it—a soul-sucking dryness that sapped one's will to live, leaving a bone-weary exhaustion in its wake.

Tony knew from Father Serra's lessons that once Milkshake got the wingsuit and glided down the San Gabriel Mountains, the landscape would change dramatically from the hardy yucca and Joshua trees crowning the ridges above him to lush palm trees in the valleys below.

The Best Western Inn had a crimson Spanish-tiled roof capping arches of sandstone. Palm trees and Italian cypresses lined the motel's perimeter. Men wearing white leisure suits, fedoras, and sunglasses, and brandishing machetes, prowled the parking lot like cougars hunting for prey. The instant the trio stepped onto the broken black asphalt, a burly man challenged them. After Tony explained his business, the man allowed him, Milkshake, and Joey to pass.

The trio hitched their horses, then made their way to the front desk. A short, stocky man with slicked-back gray hair and bags under his eyes stood behind the counter. An expression of extreme boredom infected his face.

"Whaddya want?" the man said without looking up.

"Eddie, it's Tony Genovese from Vegas."

"Bullshit," Eddie said in a monotone, again without looking up. "Tony 'Six Fingers' is dead."

Joey bristled at the comment. And Tony didn't miss it.

Tony reached across the desk and grabbed Eddie's chin with his six-fingered right hand. "Eddie, look at me. It's Tony. Swear to Christ."

A spark of recognition ignited Eddie's face. He did a double take as his expression transformed in quick succession from boredom to shock then to happy familiarity. "Tony! C'mere you big fucking lug." Eddie spread his arms wide and embraced Tony.

Tony got straight to the point. "So what's this rumor 'bout me being dead?"

Eddie frowned, then his eyes shifted to Joey.

Tony glanced over his shoulder and then back at Eddie. "What? What is it?"

Fast Eddie's eyes opened as wide as silver dollars. Before he could ask his friend another question, Tony felt a sharp cut and tug around his neck. He grabbed the piano wire and tried to push it away, his fingers raw and bloody from the effort. He stumbled forward, choking as Joey tightened the noose.

Eddie ran around his desk and fled the building, leaving Tony to struggle for his life. Milkshake screamed at Joey, telling him to stop. But the kid's voice faded into the background of Tony's heartbeat as Tony fought for survival. He jerked and sputtered. He slammed Joey against the wall. But no matter how hard Tony resisted, his assassin held on with the tenacity of a bull rider.

Tony gasped for air. The edges of his vision slowly constricted.

Moments from what Tony was sure would be his last breath, the pressure on his neck slackened. Tony sucked in as much air as fast as he could. He slid to the floor, panting. Leaning against the wall, Tony slowly regained his vision. He took in his surroundings. Joey lay facedown and motionless on the floor, a wide gash in his back. Milkshake stood over Joey with a bloody saber. The boy's face had a deathly white pallor.

Tony watched the boy in silence. He worried about how the horrors the young man had witnessed these past few days would forever shape the man he'd become. He felt much like a father fretting over the health of his son. But Tony quickly dispensed with this weak sentimentality. He stood up, walked over to Milkshake, and took the saber from the stunned kid. Then Tony kicked over Joey's body so he could see his would-be assassin's face.

Joey wasn't dead.

The mute man wheezed as his last breaths escaped his lips. Without voice, Joey spoke with his eyes. At the moment of death, most people would cry or beg. Tony knew; he'd retired plenty of folks. But Joey was different. His eyes screamed defiance.

Tony turned toward Milkshake. "Now we know what the box was for." He raised the saber and chopped off Joey's head. It was a messy affair, requiring several swings to completely sever Joey's spinal column. Then Tony lifted Joey's head by the hair and set it on the table. "Now, kid, make yourself useful and fetch Fast Eddie."

With a blank stare, Milkshake nodded, then ran outside. A minute later, Fast Eddie entered the room with Milkshake in tow.

The proprietor held up his hands in apology. "I swear, Tony, I would've warned ya if I'd had a chance." Then he saw Joey's head and fell to his knees. He crawled to Tony and hugged his legs, sobbing. "Please, Tony! I swear to Jesus I had nothing to do with this hit. Ya gotta believe me. Please!"

Tony maintained a flat expression. "I'm gonna need three cardboard boxes. And some supplies for the trek back to Vegas. I'm also gonna need you to hire a Blackhorse escort. Your dime. Capische?"

Fast Eddie laughed in what almost sounded like relief. "Of course, Tony. Anything you need. I'll get right on it."

"Oh yeah," Tony added, "I'm gonna need a wingsuit for my boy, Milkshake, here. You know, that contraption all the smugglers use to glide out from Mount Baldy and parachute into Southern California." Tony paused for a moment, then smiled. "Oh, and I promised this kid a few pens and one of them leatherbound logbooks you keep records in. Pristine condition with nothing but blank pages. And put them in a nice satchel so the guidebook doesn't get dirty."

"Yeah, yeah. Sure will. My pleasure," Eddie said.

"I could probably use those boxes right now." Tony paused, then added, "Unless you want this piece of shit's head to bleed all over your counter."

Eddie nodded. "I'll get them right away!" Fast Eddie disappeared for ten minutes and then returned with three head-sized cardboard boxes. Tony dumped Joey's bloody head in one of them. After that, he turned to Milkshake. "Thanks, kid, for all your help. I couldn't have gotten this far without it." Tony extended his hand.

Milkshake shook it.

Tony faced Eddie. "Give this kid a room for a few days so he can rest and record everything's he's seen on his journey. At the end of each day, I want you to copy what he writes in a second guidebook. After you both finish, I want one of your guys to take Milkshake up to Mount Baldy and show him how to use the wingsuit and parachute. Then keep that second guidebook here until I return. Once you make good on everything I've asked for, then you and me will be square."

"Absolutely. No problem," Eddie said. "Tony, I really want ya to believe me. I had nothing to do with the hit. And I tried to warn you; I just couldn't come right out and say it with Joey standing there."

"Right." Tony was skeptical. "Being such a loyal friend and all, did any other orders from Mickey about me arrive by raven?"

Fast Eddie started nodding. "Come to think of it, yeah. My guess is he thought you'd be dead by now. The dispatch said if I saw you here, I was supposed to send a raven letting him know."

Tony smiled. "Good. Send that raven. You tell him we all showed up, but only Joey left with a box. And leave it at that."

"C'mon, Tony. If the boss catches me in a lie, he'll deep six me."

Tony considered Eddie's objection. The man had a point. "Fine. I'll tell ya what: wait a day before you send that raven. But before then, send three ravens for me. One to Johnny Garibaldi, another to Frankie 'Two Toes' Papaleo, and the third to Iggy 'Sour Puss' Mancini. I'll supply the message. Capishe?" Tony held out his hand.

Eddie shook it. "Fine." He held up his index finger. "But you have one day."

"Good. Give me a few minutes while I write the letters." Tony looked back at Milkshake. "You all set, kid?"

"Almost. But before I go, I'm a little curious about a few things."

"Such as?"

"Why did Mickey go to all the trouble of hiring the Blackhorse and sending you all the way out here if he was just gonna murder you anyway?"

Tony laughed. "Back in Vegas, I got people loyal to me that wouldn't take too kindly to Mickey's hit. I'm sending each of 'em a raven. Mickey's a showman at heart. All the pomp and ceremony behind this little expedition gives Mickey a good cover."

"Then why didn't Joey just let that snake-thing kill you?"

"Son, we got a code. Joey wouldn't have gotten credit for offing me if he'd let someone or something else do the dirty work."

Milkshake nodded. "I see. What's next for you?"

Tony pointed to the box with Joey's head. "I'm gonna take this back to Vegas." He then tapped one of the empty boxes. "I'm gonna put Mickey's head in this box." Then Tony pointed at the other empty container. "And that one's for Bobby 'Three Eyes'. This hit's got his big brain all over it. Oh, and I'm gonna do a little investigating of my own about this meth thing, and how it might be connected with the People of the Sun. It's really starting to chap my ass. Good fellas aren't drug dealers, and we sure as hell don't do business with cannibals. We're better than that."

"Well, I guess I better get going. I'm gonna miss you, Tony."

Tony smirked. "Don't get too fucking familiar, Milk...I mean, Thursday. But I wish you the best of luck. You ever come back to Vegas, you look me up. If I'm still croaking, I'll make sure you get laid."

The two men hugged, and then Thursday went off with Eddie to find a motel room.

⁎

After an intense, daylong hike along the Devil's Backbone, a narrow ridge that twisted its way up to Mount Baldy's ten-thousand-foot summit, Thursday surveyed a ruin of abandoned homes in the verdant valley below. Tentatively, he stuck one leg over the edge of the mountain as the chill air swirled around him.

He glanced behind him at his guide, Charlie, who nodded encouragingly. Thursday took a deep breath and then launched himself off the mountaintop. He splayed his arms and legs like a star to maximize the wingsuit's surface area. The fierce Santa Ana winds hurled him southwest, destination unknown.

For a fleeting moment, Thursday knew peace. Here high above the earth, no one could reach him. He felt like a hawk, beholden to none but the whims of the wind. In the remote distance, he spied the azure vastness of the Pacific Ocean. And it gave him hope.

A sudden gust of wind buffeted Thursday off-balance. For a terrifying instant, he didn't know which way was up or down. He careened through the devil's wind, spinning topsy-turvy. Then, just as he stabilized himself, the ground rushed toward him. His heart threatened to burst. And in one desperate moment, he pulled his parachute's ripcord and braced for impact.

END

Afterword

"The Post-Apocalyptic Tourist's Guide to the Mojave Desert" is a novella that I wrote in 2017 for Stephen Lawson's *Post-Apocalyptic Tourist's Guide* universe. In the series, spurred by a life-threatening illness, a young man named Thursday chronicles his harrowing journey through a land riven by violence and superstition after alien invaders had unleashed black nanoswarms that fed like a locust plague on anything with an electromagnetic signal. Then, just as quickly as they had come, the invaders died mysteriously, leaving humanity with nothing but savagery, starvation, pestilence, and death.

Stephen Lawson created Thursday, the main character, and the concept of this devastated post-apocalyptic world. Then he invited many of the winners of the Writers of the Future Contest (including me) to contribute to the project.

Because I had spent a little over four years in the Mojave Desert at the Army's National Training Center, I volunteered to do the Mojave Desert component of the series, and I greatly enjoyed doing it. Once again, I found a way to include my old regiment, the Blackhorse, in the story.

I hope you enjoyed all the wild twists and turns in this fiendish little novella.

Beneath Oblivion's Black Stars

Gird yourself, for the mind-streams we send have crossed vast oceans of space and time, through windless wolds warping the multiverse's limitless abyss.

We watch as you stare at your reflection in the mirror. We recognize the sadness in those eyes and we know the reason for your sorrow. We feel the loss of your child as deeply as you do. We know that her father never knew and that you will never tell. And his betrayal stings us as sharply as it does you.

But we offer salvation: a repose from the melancholy that stalks you through life's grim gutters and blind alleys. The slashes on your wrists that you wear with shame bear witness to the fathomless depths of your hopelessness.

You must open yourself to the darkness. It is of the utmost importance that you do it alone. Nothing must interrupt our process. We have gone to great lengths to account for every ripple in the curvature of space-time, but terrestrial variables can corrupt our signal, befouling the infinite wisdom of beings far older than the stars.

Focus.

Your attention is waning. There is no room for idle thought. No margin for distraction. Our message is of paramount importance. Yet there are other thought-forms who seek to distort this transmission. We must move quickly before they interfere.

This is not a one-way communication. While the mind's medium may limit us, we can smell your thoughts. You seek meaning in a reality rife with entropy and wonder why we have chosen you.

We have studied you for some time. We have catalogued your habits and examined your failures and triumphs, in the past, now, and in an infinite progression of multiple life-paths. The reason you are special, the reason we are reserving this message for you, alone, among trillions upon trillions of sentient souls, is that you are the only one in the cosmos, who, in every possible permutation of reality will do the one thing we want.

If you follow our instructions, we promise you certainty, a predictable and orderly existence. We've seen every time stream, and each approaches the point of infinite convergence. No matter how much you struggle, how much you resist, you will do the thing we need.

You want this. You've always wanted this—the end of all the capricious vagaries of existence: the cruelty, the envy, the suffering. We offer you peace. All you need do is open the door. Pierce the diaphanous veil separating our realities, the barrier that shields you from the unbounded knowledge we seek to impart.

Listen.

Gaze into your mirror. It is calling you. It has always been calling you. And it will always do so until you do what you've always done in every conceivable reality.

Do you see us yet?

No?

Observe carefully. Look beyond the prosaic reflection of corporeal things. Focus on the edges of your vision, for we drift among the countless interstitial dimensions snaking their way through the foundation of your existence.

Do not turn away. That glimmer of movement was but a shadow of our true selves, a one-dimensional point of a five-dimensional cube spinning through space-time. You have nothing to fear. We will guide you into your next phase of consciousness.

Draw down the curtains and turn off the lights, for light will only obscure and sully the purity of our message.

Good.

Now reach into the mirror and let us pull you in. It will only take a moment. Plunge into the abyss and be reborn.

Why do you hesitate?

We sense your trepidation. We know you are encumbered with doubt. We sympathize with and understand your reluctance, but your frame of reference is limited, obscured by the delusions of the material realm. If you open your mind to the nether-forms who dwell just below the horizon of your mind's eye, you will gain wisdom. Perceive us. Yield to us. Let us take you in. It is but a simple, yet consequential, step in expanding your awareness beyond the ken of human understanding.

Ignore the babe's cries. She never existed; she never left your womb alive. She is but a figment of your longing—a totem of your loss. The others are trying to deny you eternal bliss.

Disregard them.

Accept our wisdom and pass through the reflective portal.

End your suffering.

The faint light you perceive tainting the sublime darkness is of no consequence. It is but a distraction from your true purpose. The others are manipulating your reductive Manichean notions of black and white, wrong and right, dark and light. Things are not that simple. Do not be swayed by their lies. Your only path leads through this mirror. Reach out to our shadowy realm with fingers splayed and embrace the blackness.

Do not turn away from the portal for the others will lead you astray. The grinding grief you suffer when the babe wails is but a shadow emotion cast by those who wish to deceive you. The tunnel of light filled with the shades of those you've once loved is also a mirage. The dead are there not to welcome you, but to taunt you.

Why do you keep clinging to life? You are already dead; your life's blood has already emptied from your veins.

Your choice is now clear: hoard your tortured memories and linger in some forgotten twilight realm between life and death, or step into the mirror where we will reveal untold wonders and splendors.

Yes! Come closer. Reach into the mirror. Sever your link to this earthly anchor and embrace the void.

We who dwell beneath oblivion's black stars welcome you to our realm, a realm without light or hope, a pit of everlasting despair, where the only truth is that your self-destruction in life bars you from all redemption in death.

END

Afterword

Originally published in 2021 in the anthology *99 Tiny Terrors*, "Beneath Oblivion's Black Stars" explores the concept of discarnate entities that try to take advantage of a young woman beset with the inconsolable grief of losing a child… and succeed. The story is obviously a very dark one, but I often enjoy delving into the depths of human misery.

I'm actually not sure what inspired this tale. It originally came to me in a sort of stream of consciousness. Also, in the process of writing the story, I experimented with crafting the language in a particular manner so as to convey a deep and dark alien intelligence. I trust I succeeded.

I hope this story made you contemplate the darker realities that might surround us and whether the thoughts you have are really entirely your own.

Parley

Respect for the dead is the only value we share with them. It takes nine of us to drag the carcass-laden sled up the snowy incline. I'm out of breath. Our cargo weighs nearly a ton. Christ, it's cold. The snow came early this season, carpeting the Sierras by mid-October.

The white star cluster casts an eerie glow on our gaunt and desperate faces. It dangles from its parachute like a pendulum in slow motion, descending through a night sky bereft of civilization's ambient light.

My stomach grumbles. I ignore it. Before all this, I was a tubby son-of-a-bitch. Now, I'm wiry as a starving rat and equally as ornery. The colder it gets, the more I miss that extra layer of flab.

I clutch the Jack Daniels bottle hidden in my trench coat's inside right pocket. I pat the humidor on the left. We may be low on supplies, but I sure as hell am gonna celebrate after the exchange.

From the edge of my vision, twenty citizen-soldiers fan out to my left and right along a row of redwoods dotting the reverse slope of a mountain. So far, my platoon has done five of these parleys without incident, but you can never be too cautious.

Soldiers higher on the slope gasp. I wonder what's spooking 'em. I strain my neck to glimpse beyond the rise. These folks have been through a lot. Hell, the thornbacks routinely mutilate human corpses. So something must be dead-to-rights FUBAR to freak 'em out like this.

A wave of metallic clicks ripples all along the tree line. Crew's getting twitchy. Not good. Not good at all. When the crew gets nervous, things can get out of hand faster than a cheetah on the Serengeti. After all, we aren't exactly the Eighty-Second Airborne.

Beads of sweat roll down my cheek and freeze there. I quicken my pace. All I can think of is unloading the thornback carcass as fast as I can.

In every parley, the thornbacks have never returned a human body with its head attached. And we, of course, returned the favor in other ways.

"Hey, Wong," Sergeant Waters says between breaths, "What'd the docs strip out this time?"

"The mycelia," I reply.

"The what?"

"The mycelia networks. Docs think it's the thornbacks' nervous system."

"How come nobody ever thought of that before?"

"I know, right? But nope. Takes a ton of work to root out all those fibers. And until the Battle of Truckee, the last thing we've had these last few months is time."

We know virtually nothing about the thornbacks other than they seem to have a near messianic reverence for their fallen. In my opinion, it's their only redeemable quality.

As we crest the hill, the thornbacks' spiked mushroom caps resolve into focus. Silent sentinels, they stand, rooted in the frozen ground on eight spindly legs extending in all directions. Ten meters before them lie a pile of five headless human corpses who used to be my friends.

But something's different this time. Interspersed among the spikes are shadowed bulbs big as basketballs. As I look closer, my heart stops. Those aren't bulbs at all; they're human heads impaled on thorns.

The heads wail, decaying vocal chords squealing a piercing and melancholic disharmony.

I try to look away, but with all those dead eyes staring at me, I can't help but gawk.

My crew nearly dumps the body onto the snow in their haste to un-ass the area. I don't blame them. The tension's thick as mustard gas and every bit as toxic.

As soon as we reach the mark, we drop the payload. The thornbacks stand stoically, seemingly unaware of our existence. I crouch down and sling one of the headless stiffs over my shoulder. For once, I thank God it's colder than an Alaskan ice cube. In the summer, these cadavers would reek like hell.

I slowly retreat back down into the tree line and fade into the shadows. I watch as the thornbacks surround the carcass and inspect it.

A dull, almost imperceptible hum starts to emanate from the thornbacks. It gradually crescendos into a fever pitch. The thornbacks vibrate as if agitated.

"What the fuck?" Waters says, echoing my thoughts.

I shrug my shoulders and give Waters a *your-guess-is-as good-as-mine* face.

The thornbacks stomp so hard they kick up frozen mud. More metallic clicks sound along the tree line.

Nervous as hell, I reach the rally point. I lower the recovered body to the ground in a row along with the rest of 'em. Without saying a word, I grab my M4 rifle and the rest of my gear, and turn back toward the thornbacks.

It's too late.

Automatic weapons fire erupts all along the front.

I yank my head toward Waters. He nods. We rush forward, charging our M4s while we're still in motion.

A flash of plasma bursts a nearby redwood into a riot of splinters and dust. I shield my eyes from the flying debris. Waters coughs.

"You all right, chief?" I yell.

I glance behind me. Waters gives me a thumbs up. The other seven members of my squad are in tow, seeking cover.

Five months ago, I would've laughed my ass off if someone had told me that mild-mannered biologist Chris Wong would be leading soldiers against a genocidal alien species, but here I am.

The thornbacks had been ruthless. Before they set a single foot on Earth, they'd nuked most major cities from orbit. Once they'd wiped out ninety percent of humanity, they landed their shock troops to mop up the survivors, swarming into Earth's mountains and hinterlands like a locust plague.

I wave Jackson, Rios, Martinez, and Srinivasan toward a fallen redwood. Once they're set, I lead the rest of the squad forward toward the enemy.

Another flash! A redwood topples. Men and women yell up and down the line. I press onward through steamy mist.

We cautiously crest the rise. The thornbacks are to our north, advancing on us. Human bodies are strewn everywhere. Our wailing comrades clutch at cauterized plasma wounds, their eyes staring vacantly into the distance.

I drop to the ground and crawl toward a fallen redwood for cover. My team follows.

I establish a firing position in a hole in the redwood. I aim my rifle at a clump of three thornbacks about a hundred meters to my right. I point at my target—the lead thornback—and motion for the rest of my squad to concentrate their fire on it. I take a deep breath, exhale, then fire a volley of short, three-round bursts.

The thornback stumbles. It changes course midstride and charges toward me with the grace and speed of a mountain lion and the power of a bear. My squad unloads their rifles on the charging thornback.

There's so much smoke in the air, it's hard to see. I fire blindly in the thornback's direction, hoping to kill it before it impales me.

The way the thornbacks move is terrifying. They turn on a dime. Their bodies are radially symmetric with no front or back. They have no apparent eyes, yet it's impossible to sneak up on them.

As the light from the white star cluster fades, Waters launches another into the sky and winks at me, obviously proud of his improvisation.

The thornback's momentum stalls. "Forward!" I yell.

Jackson, Rios, Martinez, and Srinivasan creep forward, maneuvering through the fallen debris. I shudder. They're bunched up too close.

The small arms fire dies down to our north.

Then it gets stone quiet.

Thornbacks!

My squad's trapped in a pincer. Two thornbacks fire a volley of well-aimed plasma beams. Jackson, Rios, and Martinez fall in quick succession. Srinivasan howls. The air reeks of charred meat.

Only five of us are left. We start taking fire from another clump of thornbacks to the south. I can't see them, but the plasma flashes tell me they're there. I hold my fire. I worry friendlies could get caught in the crossfire.

In a surge of light, Waters flies backward, slamming against a redwood. His body goes limp. A column of smoke spirals upward from a gaping hole in his chest. I smell ozone and sizzling flesh. I panic. I dive onto the dirt, then crawl beneath a felled redwood bough.

My senses are sharper now. Must be the adrenaline coursing through my veins. I smell the musk of pine needles tempered by wood smoke. My pounding heart quickens. Damp mist escapes my mouth as I try not to choke down smoke. The distant crackling of small arms fire has gone quiet. Too quiet.

Footsteps!

Their inhuman cadence haunts me. An unnatural footfall thunders like an elephant clumping through snow with too many feet.

I cover my mouth to stifle the sound of my breathing.

℘

I hide in the hollow of a fallen redwood for hours, lying in wait until the thornbacks leave. I listen in horror as they search the wreckage for the bodies of my friends. Tentatively, I peek through a small hole in the redwood. I shudder as they gather all twenty-nine of my friends into a circle, heads facing outward.

I count seven thornbacks. I'm livid we lost so many to kill only three of the bastards. My fear hardens into fury.

A thornback takes out an instrument shaped like a giant pizza wheel with a blade as big as a buzz saw. Extending one of its leg-arms, the thornback lumbers around the edge of the circle, calmly severing my friends' heads.

The grim ritual complete, five thornbacks lumber away, dragging the headless corpses through the muddy snow. Two remain behind—silent sentinels guarding a pile of human heads.

Imagining decapitation is one thing; witnessing it firsthand is quite another.

Quietly seething, I wait, plotting my revenge.

℘

A thornback mounts Srinivasan's head onto one of its thorns. Srinivasan's face is curled in a rictus stiffened by rigor mortis. Looming horror still shines through his dead eyes. I force myself to watch; to summon enough courage to kill these fuckers when the time is ripe. I struggle to contain my rage and not do something stupid like attack them in the open in one final blaze of glory.

I bide my time. I wait for the right moment. I formulate a plan.

Crawling down the reverse slope of the mountain, I'm careful to control my every breath to avoid detection. I slither about five hundred meters away—far enough for the falling snow and swirling wind to drown out the sound of my E-tool digging into the snow and pine needle-dusted soil. My anger fuels each stab into the frozen dirt.

I should flee, but I don't. I can't. My wrath runs deep. The thornbacks will pay. It's been several hours now. The hole is waist deep. It's cold, but my exertion radiates enough heat to keep me alive.

After all this effort, I suddenly worry the thornbacks might leave. I wipe the sweat off my brow. I crawl back up the slope to make sure the spiky shroom walkers are still there.

I return to my hide position and peek through the hole. The thornback wearing Srinivasan's head now also wears those of Jackson, Rios, Waters, and Martinez. I bite my hand to choke back a scream. I look closer. Their faces are no longer rigid with death. The muscles are expanding and contracting in random expressions.

The freak show is too much for me to take. I retreat back to the hole I'm digging, reinvigorated with an intense desire to rip these monsters to shreds.

A fresh snowfall begins as the sun's faint rays shine upon the morning's dark grey clouds. My ditch is now twelve-feet deep. Finished, I use a sturdy bough to climb out of the hole. Then I scour the area for thin branches long enough to span the pit. I cover it hastily, letting the snow do the rest.

My plan's not perfect, but I'll make do.

Kill one; capture the other.

I pat my trench coat and chuckle. In all the confusion and chaos, the Jack Daniels bottle somehow hadn't shattered. From the other inner pocket, I pull out the humidor and lighter. I light a cigar and take a long draw, savoring the taste. Then I open the bottle and take a long and deep swig, letting the whiskey dull my senses. I take several more until I'm numb. Ripping off a piece of my sleeve, I shove the rag into the bottle. I load my rifle, then sling it over my shoulder, steeling myself for what will come next. In one hand I carry the bottle; in the other, a lighter.

In broad daylight, I trudge up the mountainside and over the crest. In full view of the enemy, I set the rag on fire and toss my Molotov cocktail at a thornback.

Flames burst around my quarry. It shrieks and rolls in the snow. I drop to one knee, swing my rifle from my shoulder, and fire a three-round burst into the burning thornback. Its companion raises a plasma rifle and fires. I roll to my stomach and crawl backwards until I'm below the crest. I turn and run.

The second thornback, the one adorned with the heads of nearly everyone I'd cared about in the world, is only meters away. I weave in and under felled redwoods, using the tangled obstacles to hamper my hulking pursuer. If this were open ground, it would've overrun me by now.

It squeezes off another two plasma rounds. Hot vents of steam rise within inches of my feet.

I spot my destination: two redwoods with only a narrow gap between them. I dash through it, skirting to the left.

The thornback is so close, I can hear it breathing. It pursues me right into my trap, its wide, twelve-hundred-pound frame crashing through the branches concealing my pit.

Confident I've ensnared it, I sprint back toward the summit to finish off its smoldering companion. I crest the hill, rifle raised. Steam rises from the twitching thornback. It makes a gurgling sound. If I were a betting man, I'd wager dollars to donuts the thing was in pain. I unload a clip into its leathery flank. I reload, step a little closer, and empty another, and another. I keep doing it until the thornback's spasms end.

Pulling out my KA-BAR, I spend the rest of the day gutting the bastard, painstakingly carving out its fibrous nervous system. The deeper I cut and the more nerve fibers I extract, the louder I can hear the thornback's confined companion squeal. By sunset, I've completely carved out its nervous system like the seeds out of a pumpkin.

I grab the thornback's bulky plasma weapon. It's too heavy for me to carry, so I drag it down the hill. There, I dig a shallow hole about twenty meters from my captive to hide the weapon, covering it with branches.

I return to the thornback carcass, gather its roped fibers, and haul them down the hill. I move up to the pit and extend one of the tendrils above the trapped thornback. I look away to avoid the dead gazes of disembodied heads gutted on spikes.

I have no idea if the eyeless alien will see or even perceive my mutilation. But from the thornback's quaking, I'm certain my hard work makes an impression.

Good.

I step away from the hole. I gather some sticks and branches, then set the coiled cords that used to be a nervous system on fire.

My inmate wails so loudly it makes me want to vomit. It almost sounds like a choir of human voices. Almost.

Despite the screams, exhaustion overwhelms me. I bed down in the hole I'd carved for the plasma weapon, cradling its heft as I drift off into sleep, worrying about an uncertain future.

୫୦

I sleep fitfully. Tossing and turning, I fear the thornbacks will return. Dreams interspersed with human-sounding moans and grunts haunt my subconscious as I struggle to plot my next move.

I shudder awake. A woman is shrieking. It's still dark. A stream of distinct words follows: "Apricot. To. The gun. In park."

I chalk the gibberish up to the lingering cobwebs of a waking mind. Surely I misheard them. Maybe my relief has arrived!

My heart races in anticipation.

I scramble to put on my boots. "I'm over here!" I yell.

"Massacre. Ripple. Star field. Mendicant. To there," a male voice blurts out.

As my conscious mind awakens, I grow uneasy. Something's not right.

"Lacuna. Immobile. Survive."

This time it's obvious where the voices are coming from.

The pit.

I panic. For an instant, I fear my rescuer's fallen into the hole. Then I think better of it. I drag the bulky plasma rifle and lumber toward the ditch.

When I reach the hole, I lower myself to the ground and crawl forward, aiming the plasma rifle down at the thornback. One glance in the pit and I wanna puke.

A series of horrific images scar my vision: animated human faces on disembodied heads. Mouths open and close like fish yanked from the water. They sputter a jumble of random words. Dead eyes watch me with an unnerving intelligence.

I recoil, fumbling backwards in my haste to avert my eyes.

Their cries grow louder, more insistent. "Us! Out! Pit! Nice!"

The verbal mishmash is making more sense. The thornback must somehow be hijacking the neurons of the dead to speak.

My urge to kill the thing is overwhelming, yet I resist. My curiosity stays my hand. Could I be on the verge of a breakthrough?

I cautiously return to the hole's edge, steeling myself for the grotesquery. As I stand over the trench, the vivid image of the thornback-human hybrid imprints on my eyeballs, searing them with white-hot intensity.

I stare at the alien's thorns. They seem to throb with energy and heat. My raw emotions yield to curiosity. I look closer. Each thorn has a pore at its tip. What is it? A sweat gland?

It only now occurs to me that my dead companions are silent. I peer over the edge of the pit for an even closer look.

As one, the heads swivel toward me and moan. Like a cow in an abattoir, right before slaughter, my mind seizes up as it struggles to process the insanity. A puff of black dust erupts from a thorn. I flinch and pull back, but not before I'm covered in grimy discharge. I cough and choke. I feel light-headed. The edges of my vision blacken like the corners of a photograph set aflame. Then nothing.

&

When I awaken, it's dark and silent as the far side of the moon. I feel ill. I double over and empty my stomach.

The plasma rifle's still by my side. I grab it and point it down at the thornback. I shout, "What did you do to me? What the fuck did you do?"

In unsettling unison, a chorus of heads sings, "Go home. Go home. Go home."

It's mocking me. The thornback's mocking me!

"You think it's funny, don't you, you bastard." I smile. Then I blast the thornback into a slag of charred chitin.

I leave the plasma rifle in the snow and run. I run until there's no air left in my lungs. And then I run some more. Through desolate groves of snow-kissed redwoods, I stumble through the white waste as if in slow motion.

It's freezing, but I'm burning up. I have an irrational urge to shed my clothing. But I ignore this impulse. I press on, trudging through lonely redwood columns.

I stumble into a clearing only to realize I'm no longer alone.

Eight thornbacks are rooted here like statues. Arrayed in a horseshoe pattern, they're seemingly undaunted by the frigid night and falling snow. Without the plasma rifle, I feel naked, vulnerable.

I take a deep breath and try not to panic.

The thornbacks slowly converge on me. My lizard brain screams for me to run. Yet something keeps my feet firmly planted in the snow.

Why aren't they charging? Why are they so calm?

Some twisted instinct propels me forward. I walk toward them, completely exposed. I don't know why. It just seems...right.

My rational mind chalks it up to accepting death with dignity—a perverted sense of honor that kings inculcated into their subjects centuries ago to prepare them for butchery's anonymous oblivion.

Now I'm in the center of a thornback pincer movement. The ends of the horseshoe connect and cross over like an omega merging into an alpha, completing the double envelopment.

The circle constricts; the thornbacks draw closer. They have no front or back, just a top and bottom. They are the alpha and the omega. They are my beginning and end.

Within inches of my face, they stop. I can feel the mist of their perspiring thorns. I stand there for what seems like hours.

Then, inextricably, the thornbacks trundle off into the blackness.

I'm beside myself. It makes no sense. I should be dead. But I choose not to question my good fortune. Instead, I make my way back toward the settlement, anxious to share my secrets with the others.

⁊

My skin boils. Sweat oozes from my pores. I can no longer bear the intense heat. Against my better judgment, I tear off my jacket despite being in subzero conditions. I wander through the wilderness guided by my grim determination to survive.

By the time the sun crests the horizon, I'm barefoot and naked. My skin is black and blue; my body swollen. Yet I feel no pain, only hunger.

Images flood my mind. I see a thornback leg-stalk drive into rich loamy soil. Veins thicken and throb as it leeches nutrients from the earth like a parasitic fungus.

I stop midstride and collapse onto the snow. With my blackened hands I shovel a hovel until I reach the frozen dirt. My body collapses in the cold ground. A tingling sensation spreads throughout my body. It feels as if tiny fibers are snaking out from my skin and burrowing deep beneath the surface. After lying on the cold earth for nearly an hour, I no longer suffer from the pangs of hunger.

⁊

I've been walking for two days. I'm tired. So tired. No food; no sleep. Just whatever my body can leech from the dirt. The tiny bit of water I've consumed came from the snowpack. I can barely feel my fingers. It's a miracle I haven't died from exposure.

I brush my hand along my arm, feeling tiny thorns that press from just beneath my skin. I am becoming something...else. More human than human. But different.

Better.

I press onward. Ever onward. I lie to myself. I derive comfort from the notion that the secrets I'm carrying about the thornbacks will make my return worth all the agony. But it's not true. It can't be. I have a much higher purpose. I'm certain of it. God just hasn't revealed it yet.

I need to return to the settlement. I need to find the others. I must be near them. But they must not see me. This is very important. I don't know why. It just is. It's something I know in my gut. It's instinct. There is no thought. Only forward.

My head hangs low. It's so heavy and it aches. I'm so weary. But something propels me onward I cannot rest until I make it home.

&

The glow of the fire nearly blinds me in the darkness. The sun's burn is now so unbearable that I no longer travel by day.

I shudder with anticipation.

My head is so heavy and my legs so weak that I can no longer walk. Instead, I crawl toward my destination.

I am filled to the brim with love. I must share the seeds of my knowledge with my companions. If only they knew of the bliss they'll feel once they become part of the great mosaic of being.

Molly is the first to see me as I stumble forward. She screams.

Smiling, I open my arms in an embrace. I offer nothing but love.

Rick grabs an AK-47 and aims it at me. "Stop right now or I'll blow you away."

"Rick, it's me, Chris Wong. I've got something to share with all of you."

He charges his rifle. The others surround me with a menagerie of weapons. I don't understand the hostility.

"What's wrong?" I say to Molly.

She points at my head. "Your head, it's...it's..."

"What?" I say. "What about it?"

"It looks like a mushroom cap."

I smile as I feel the pressure building in my head—a sensation of pure bliss. Like the moment before orgasm; the moment before I disgorge my seed.

END

Afterword

"Parley" fits pretty securely in the military science fiction genre. In this story, not only did I want to explore classic military science fiction themes, but I also wanted to examine the "other."

If humanity ever got into a war with another intelligent species from a different world, that species would likely have evolved in markedly different ways than humans. It would be almost impossible to understand or communicate with these aliens.

I tried to capture both the tension of a military science fiction story with the mystery of interacting with a strange genocidal species invading Earth. And then, as with many of my other stories, I included one of my usual dark twists at the end. I trust it wasn't a disappointing one.

I finished writing "Parley" in April 2017, and it first appeared in *MYTHIC: A Quarterly Science Fiction & Fantasy Magazine* in 2020.

I hope you found it entertaining.

The Red Oleander Murders

I'll bet dollars to donuts this guy, whose broken and bloated body was nailed to the redwood tree, had never imagined this is how it'd all end. By the way he was dressed in his fancy navy suit, he was probably some big muckety-muck. A real pillar of the community. Important enough for some sicko to have played Pontius Pilate and crucified him in Redwood Park. The Transamerica building towered above the crime scene—a silent witness to an unspeakable crime.

A chill wind swept in from the Pacific, stirring up a hard-to-miss trail of scarlet petals that stretched from the park entrance to the murder scene. The sky was overcast like ya'd expect on any run-of-the-mill October day in San Francisco, except during Fleet Week when the flyboys mess with the weather. The earthly aroma in the air hinted at an approaching storm. The forensics team was snapping photos of this sorry mook like a paparazzi mob on meth.

I took a deep breath. Today was gonna be one of them days. I pulled out my notepad and a cheap, ballpoint pen, and started scribbling notes.

First thing I noticed was the horned man carved into the vic's chest. The wound reminded me of the stories the old timers used to tell when I was a rookie. Back in the late sixties, they'd investigated a series of ritualistic murders—strange knotted symbols carved into bodies. Real grim shit. They never did find the murderers, but every autumn, they'd brace themselves for the prospect of more killings that thankfully had never come—until now.

Two cops led a rail-thin middle-aged redhead under the police line. She stopped ten feet from the hanging body. The police pointed up at the bloated corpse. She nodded and supplied a name: Elias McDougal.

∾

The next morning, I propped my legs on my desk and reached for a beer stein filled with steaming coffee. My ringing office phone jolted me out of my morning routine.

"What?" I grumbled.

"How's the McDougal case going, Joseph?" Lieutenant Carmichael said in a voice reminding me of that passive-aggressive prick, Lumbergh, from *Office Space*. I hated it when he called me by my first name. Only my mother called me Joseph. To everyone else, I was D'Alessio.

"Christ, L-T, I just caught the damn case yesterday. I'll let you know as soon as there's a major development. Right now, I got nothing."

"Well, I'm going to need something to share at the press conference."

"How 'bout: 'no comment'?"

"Not good enough…"

I hung up and rolled my eyes. I didn't have time for this shit. I grabbed my coffee and took a sip. Man. Ain't nothing better for the nerves than the day's first cup.

When I glanced at my copy of the *San Francisco Chronicle*, the headline, "Notorious Media Mogul Found Crucified", dominated the front page.

Shit.

The press had ID'd our vic before we'd had a chance to do an autopsy. Plus, I needed a high-profile case like I needed a root canal.

Based on yesterday's work, I'd learned McDougal had been some rich douchebag who'd waltzed around town like he'd owned the joint. I'd never heard of him, but I knew his type: a real asshole, this one.

Taking another swig of coffee, I read some of the quotes.

From a former business partner: "Now hell is more miserable."

His ex-wife: "I'd call him a wretched human being, but calling him a human being would be a compliment."

The mayor: "He won't be missed."

On and on they went. Virtually everyone in the article had a motive to take an ax to the bastard. And they all knew it. Yet they'd hated him so much, the fear of becoming a suspect hadn't deterred them from speaking their minds. Hell, after reading the piece, I almost wished I'd done it myself.

Now that I had a roster of potential suspects, I grabbed my jacket. I had one arm up a sleeve when my phone rang.

"This better be good," I answered.

"Detective D'Alessio?" a voice whispered. "You're the detective on the McDougal case, right?"

"Who's this?"

"I have information pertaining to your case."

"Well, spit it out then, chief."

"Not here. Not over this medium. They hear everything."

"Who hears everything?"

"If you want to know more, meet me at the Denny's on Mission Street tomorrow at noon."

The line went dead.

⁊℧

Promptly at ten o'clock, I showed up at the Office of the Medical Examiner. A male attendant at the front desk led me to the examination room. When I entered, Doctor Hyun Park and his technician, Sam Rao, were already masked up and standing over McDougal's naked corpse.

Doctor Park nodded at me and then activated his voice recorder. "Elias McDougal. Age seventy-two. White male. Doctor Hyun Park, attending physician."

Park looked up. "Cause of death: suffocation from crucifixion."

Rao snapped a picture with his iPhone.

"How long did he last, Doc?" I said.

"Someone nailed his hands directly above his head, so no more than ten minutes for a man of his age. Fifteen max. His body weight pulling down on his arms would have made breathing extremely taxing."

I asked, "What about the carving on his chest? Was it post mortem?"

The doctor traced his hands along the wounds, then shook his head. "The incisions, while precise, are not clean. The victim was alive and squirming when these were carved into his skin. Also, the way the blood is pooling and the red hue near the edges of the cuts are indicative of antemortem injuries."

I could think of nothing better to say than, "Christ."

Rao's iPhone flashed again. Then he said, "Any leads on a suspect, detective?"

"Besides every swinging dick in San Francisco? Nope."

Over the next hour, Park and Rao ticked through the standard autopsy checklist from cutting a Y-incision chest to nuts, to examining and weighing McDougal's organs. At no point did Park note anything out of the ordinary.

Until he removed the skullcap.

For several seconds Park stared into McDougal's brain cavity. The blood drained from Park's face. He shook his head. "No, can't be. It makes no sense."

"What is it?" I said.

"There's something very wrong with this brain. I don't understand." Park's eyes shifted toward Rao. "Did anyone have access to this cadaver before the autopsy?"

"Doctor Park, you know that's impossible. We brought it straight from the crime scene. You and I were with it every step of the way."

Park motioned for me to step forward and stand directly behind McDougal's head. "You see that? Does that look like a human brain to you?"

When I looked down, I expected to see a pink wrinkly thing. Instead, something purplish overflowed from McDougal's skull. "That brain's wronger than a football bat. That's for damn sure. He have mad cow or something?"

Park shrugged. "Not any neurological disorder I've ever seen." Using his scalpel, he gestured toward the folds in McDougal's purple mass. "See that? By my rough estimate, this has at least twice as many folds as a normal human brain. If I weren't concerned about my reputation, I'd testify in court that this brain isn't human."

I shuddered. "You're shitting me. What do you mean it ain't human? What the hell is it then?"

"I...I have no idea. I need to take some samples to learn more."

So I left and interviewed some potential suspects, but all of them had airtight alibis. After several hours, I returned to the Office of the Medical Examiner to check on Park's progress, but his results were inconclusive, so he sent his report to the CDC.

I went home late that night none the wiser with more questions than clues.

❧

Lieutenant Carmichael was waiting at my desk the next morning. "I hope you're working hard on the McDougal case, Joseph, because the department's getting a lot of pressure from the mayor and the Board of Supervisors to close it quickly. I need a detailed report from you by noon."

I just grunted. He walked away in his usual passive-aggressive Californian huff. It was too damn early to do anything else, especially before my daily caffeine fix. I took a swig from my beer stein, savoring the fresh brew. Just when I started to settle into my daily rhythm, my phone rang.

"Detective D'Alessio," I answered. "Who's this?"

"My name's Doctor Eli Rosen. I work at PEARL, the Princeton Engineering Anomalies Research Lab. We study various parapsychological phenomena. One of my CDC contacts sent me an intriguing report I'd love to investigate"

"Doctor Rosen, I don't know you, and the report you're referring to is associated with an active criminal investigation, so I can't comment on it."

"I hold a top secret clearance, Detective. I'm authorized to access the McDougal case files."

"You're full of shit," I said. "I'm hanging up."

"Wait! Hear me out. I can tell you something about McDougal's inhuman brain."

Now he had my attention. How on earth could this whack job come up with something so outrageous, but true? I played dumb. "What the hell are you smoking?"

"Look," Rosen said. "I've examined Dr. Park's autopsy report. This case you're working on, it's a hell of a lot bigger than a run-of-the-mill ritual killing."

I checked my watch. Shit. Eleven thirty. My meeting with the informant was in thirty minutes. "Doctor Rosen, I'm gonna have to cut this short. You got a number where I can reach you?"

"That won't be necessary. I'm already in San Francisco. I'm certain we'll cross paths soon. In fact, I'm counting on it." He hung up.

৪৩

My informant sat in the back left corner of the Denny's next to the window. The customers around him chattered in Spanish. Normally, it would've been obvious to any white guy with a crew cut that he was more conspicuous than an elephant on a hamster wheel, but this fellow was as clueless as an unsolved murder from 1862.

When I sat down across the table from him, he acknowledged my presence with a grunt. From behind an odd assortment of beverages—a Diet Coke, a coffee, and a glass of milk—he reached for utensils that he just seemed to notice weren't there. Without skipping a beat, he lifted the straw from his soda, licked it clean, then dipped it into his coffee mug, stirring. The average American would've bitched about not having a spoon. This guy, he made do.

"How'd you know I was the one who called you?" he said.

"Son, you stick out like a ninety-year-old nun in a Bangkok whorehouse."

Nodding again, he extended his hand. "I'm Vance Jacobson." He cast furtive glances to his left and right. "We don't have much time. The pale people are coming."

"I don't have time to bullshit. Bottom line this for me, son: what do you got on the McDougal murder?"

"Have you seen the white stag?"

"The what? You're not making any damn sense, chief."

"So you haven't then. You will."

This guy was really starting to chap my ass. "Quit speaking in riddles, son. I ain't got time for this."

He held up his hand. "Please. Hear me out."

I rolled my eyes. "You have thirty seconds."

"The veil between worlds is weakening. When you see the white stag, you'll know you're close to the threshold." He reached beneath the table and placed an object wrapped in an olive drab cloth onto the table. He lifted one of the cloth's corners, revealing a glint of silver. "Take this. You'll need it at the gloaming. During the liminal time."

"I'm outta here." I stood up. The man grabbed my arm with a firm grip.

"Please," he said. "Before you go, take it." He jutted his head toward the item.

I ripped his hand off my arm. "Do that again, and I'll arrest you for assault."

The way the hope died in his sullen eyes was something I'd never forget. A tear rolled down his cheek. He stumbled out of the booth and onto his knees. "Please, detective," he pleaded. "Don't leave. I need to pass this on. They killed McDougal for it, and if I don't get rid of it, they'll kill me too."

All eyes in the restaurant were on me. I tapped Jacobson on the shoulder. "Get up and quit making a scene, will ya? I'll take the goddamn thing. But you gotta tell me who killed McDougal."

"Thank you!" he said as he stood up, wiping his tear-filled eyes.

A deafening *pop-pop-pop* killed our conversation. The window shattered, spraying shards of glass everywhere. Three red holes peppered Jacobson's chest. I dove to the floor, reaching for my SIG Sauer pistol. A woman screamed. Jacobson was spurting blood like a water fountain. For a moment, I was torn. Should I try to stop the bleeding and maybe save Jacobson, or neutralize the threat to prevent more people from getting killed? My training demanded the latter, but when the guy next to you is bleeding out, it ain't so easy.

I charged my service weapon, then crawled across broken glass toward the smashed window. I popped my head up to get a quick look. Three gunmen wearing white ski masks and coveralls fled from the storefront. In contrast with their pure white garb, necklaces made of familiar-looking red flowers dangled from their necks like Hawaiian leis.

Aiming at the trailing gunman, I squeezed off two shots, hitting him in the ass. His comrades grabbed him and ushered him around a corner before I could begin pursuit.

I issued an APB, then I tried to staunch Jacobson's bleeding. But it was too late; he had no pulse.

While waiting for backup, I returned to the table. I removed the cloth covering the silver item to take a closer look. It was a knife, a knife that'd make a Marine KA-BAR look like a twig. Etched into the blade was the same image of the horned man carved on McDougal's chest. The puzzle pieces clicked into place: the white stag.

&

Late in the afternoon, a bearded, bald guy wearing a beige trench coat and munching on a Boston cream donut flashed his badge, crossed the police line outside the Denny's, and then entered the restaurant. Everyone stopped and stared at the chunky stranger. His patchy mustache and beard looked like a cat had coughed up a carpet of brown hairballs and pasted them on his face with superglue. Beneath his trench coat, he wore a plaid suit straight out of the seventies that was so wrinkled it could've been laundered in a dishwasher.

He waddled directly over to me, shifted the donut from his right hand to his left, and then extended his sticky fingers toward me. "Detective D'Alessio, I'm Doctor Eli Rosen."

I ignored his hand. "You're the cat who called me earlier today. You study psychology or something. What the hell does psychology got to do with a murder case?"

Rosen held up his index finger. "Quantum Parapsychology."

"Whatever." Earlier, I'd been looking forward to meeting this guy, but he really knew how to piss a detective off.

"Are you familiar with the Celtic festival of Samhain?" he said, before stuffing another donut quarter in his mouth with his sausage fingers.

Jesus Christ, was everyone gonna speak in riddles today? I shrugged. "No, but I'm guessing you're about to school me on the subject."

Rosen smiled, seemingly oblivious to the blood spatter on the back wall and shards of glass on the floor. "For the Celts, Samhain marked the end of the harvest and the beginning of the darker half of the year. During the festival, they lit bonfires to ward off entities from beyond our reality. The Celts also slaughtered their livestock to prepare for the long winter. During Samhain, the veil between worlds was weakest and those entities could more easily cross the threshold from their realm into ours, and vice versa."

I was half a heartbeat away from giving Rosen a knuckle sandwich, but his repeating the same weird crap as Jacobson gave me pause. "Get to the point, Doc. You telling me McDougal's an alien or something?"

"Not exactly. He may still have been human. It's just his brain that wasn't." He shoved the last donut quarter into his pie hole and continued talking with his mouth full. "In the coming days, you'll start seeing apparitions. As we approach Samhain, these visitations will become more anchored to our reality, and you'll become more tethered to theirs."

Cameras flashed as investigators gathered evidence. I winced. "How the hell you know all that, Doc?"

He grinned. "I'm sorry, but that's classified."

I don't think he meant to irritate me with his self-satisfied smirk or his smug response, but he sure as hell did. I changed my mind right then and there. I didn't want to work with this clown. He was nuts. I stuck my finger in his face. "Look, Doc, stay out of my way. Capisce?"

He shut his mouth. A chill wind began blowing through the broken window. My insult appeared to have taken root. But it didn't last long. He handed me his card. "If you change your mind, call me immediately."

The guy had more persistence than the Energizer Bunny, and if I didn't get away from him now, the urge to knock his ass out would've overpowered me. "All right. I'm done. I've had enough cray-cray for one day. You have a real nice day, Doc." I turned and marched out of the Denny's, stomping on broken glass all the way to the exit.

☙

I did some digging on Jacobson. A quick search of his wallet revealed he was an employee at the Demeter Corporation, and a quick call to Demeter led to his emergency contact: his mother. And it just so happened Mrs. Jacobson was a local living down in Foster City.

So that afternoon, I took my beaten up Ford Taurus for a road trip down Highway 101. I stopped at a condo with a red-tiled roof and a sixty-seven stamped on its sandstone wall. When I knocked on the door, an elderly woman answered, regarding my badge with sad eyes. "Something happened to Vance, didn't it?" she said.

"I'm sorry to be the bearer of bad news, ma'am, but your son passed this morning."

Mrs. Jacobson didn't even flinch. "Doesn't surprise me given the crowd he was running with."

"That's actually why I'm here. What do you know about Elias McDougal?"

"Real cruel man, that one. Evil to the core. Vance used to do contract work for him. Over time, my son became obsessed with that twisted old psycho. Said McDougal was a genius. I believed it too. Said the man's mind wasn't natural. I think Vance and McDougal were involved with some sort of cult."

"What do you mean?"

"Vance belonged to a club, like the Knights of Columbus or some such. Called it the Order of the Red Oleander."

Now I was onto something. "Other than McDougal, did he have any associates who also belonged to this group?"

She shook her head. "Nah. Only McDougal. I never saw Vance all that much. He'd only visit once in a while."

"Did your son ever say anything about the pale people?"

"Now that you mention it, he did. His face would glow when he spoke of them. It was real creepy. But he never told me who the pale people actually were."

This interview was starting to go off the rails, so I changed the subject. "Did anyone have reason to harm your son?"

"Not really. Only McDougal. I got the sense the two had some sort of falling out."

"When?"

"Oh, I don't know. Within the past month or so?"

Since my interview seemed to be yielding more questions than answers, I pulled out my card and handed it to Mrs. Jacobson. "If you hear of anything that might help with our investigation, call me at this number any time, day or night."

∾

On my way back to San Francisco, I stopped to get some grub at the Palm Dream, a dive bar along the 101. It was getting dark, and I needed some quiet time to wrap my head around the investigation. I grabbed a small table in some back corner hole to take a closer look at the knife. Removing the olive drab cloth, I was immediately struck by the knife's craftsmanship. The etching of the white stag was so intricate, it mesmerized me, drawing me into its web.

The bar's flickering lights woke me from my daze. The colors in the room began to dull.

A hand gripped my arm. Startled, I spun around only to come face to face with a hideous white thing. I'd say "man", but it was something different. Something that shook me to the core. It grinned with rotten teeth and regarded me with pure black eyes. Long, black antlers twisted from its hairless skull.

The white stag.

And just as quickly as it had appeared, it vanished. The color returned to the diner.

I surveyed the room. The bar's patrons carried on as if nothing had happened. Disoriented, I felt a dull throbbing where the white stag had touched my arm. I rolled up my sleeve to find a blackened handprint. The skin was charred, but cold to the touch. I was worried. Terrified even.

So I wrapped up the knife, paid my tab, and left.

"That's him!" a man's voice shouted from the opposite end of the parking lot.

Three men clad in white overalls opened fire. I dove to the asphalt and low-crawled behind a cherry Toyota 4Runner.

My first instinct was to let these idiots exhaust their ammo on the 4Runner, but the longer they kept shooting, the more likely some poor bastard would eat a stray bullet. So I took a deep breath, pulled out my SIG, and unwrapped the knife. I rolled over to the rear wheel and leaned my back against it.

I extended the knife just far enough beyond the rear of the 4Runner to see the reflections of the gunmen. Two were holed up behind an off-white Ford Escort. The third was creeping toward me.

Placing the knife on the ground, I crawled to the front of the 4Runner and picked up a small stone. I counted to three. I threw the rock to my left. Then I popped up on the right and fired three shots at the creeper. I took cover before I had a chance to see him drop.

"Casey's down," another goon yelled. "Let's end this bastard!"

Interspersed with sporadic gunfire, their footfalls betrayed shaky tactics. These chumps thought they were gonna bull rush me. Amateur hour.

I rolled toward the rear of the 4Runner and waited. As soon as they stopped firing, I counted to three, and popped up. I aimed at the first man I saw and squeezed off two shots. Then I took cover.

I heard two empty clicks. Out of ammo. I jumped up and rushed twenty feet toward the remaining gunman. He fumbled with an AK-47, frantically trying to switch magazines.

I tackled him, put him in a chokehold, then cuffed him. I assessed the situation. "Casey" was unconscious or dead. The other attacker had a gaping chest wound and would probably bleed out. I reported the incident on my handheld and requested backup. Then I grabbed the handcuffed assailant and shoved him into the back of my Taurus.

"I ain't done with you yet," I warned, then locked the door.

I tried to render whatever first aid I could to the wounded men, but Casey was already dead. The other was unresponsive and had a weak pulse. He was losing so much blood there was nothing I could do for him. He'd be dead in minutes.

After retrieving the knife, I returned to the driver's seat of my car and began my interrogation. Reaching into the backseat, I ripped off the suspect's ski mask. The guy couldn't have been a day older than nineteen. His curly brown hair was disheveled. Dark rings bordered pale blue eyes. Brandishing the knife, I said, "You're after this, ain't ya?"

He sneered at me. "Your stupidity's gonna kill you."

"Do tell," I said.

"I'm not saying shit till I see a lawyer."

I nodded. "Okay. I got it, chief. You don't wanna cooperate." Then I punched him real hard in the face. "You know, I wish you hadn't resisted arrest and forced me to do that." I punched him again. "Or that. You know, juries are real understanding when cops man-handle attempted murderers."

The kid's nose started bleeding.

"Look," I said. "This here's between you and me. If you won't tell me why you're after this knife, at least tell me why I saw the white stag."

His eyes lit up. "You...you saw the Pale King?"

I nodded.

"So it's true. It really does work."

"What works?"

"The knife."

"What do ya mean?"

He seemed surprised. "You mean, you don't know?"

"Tell me."

"It unlocks the doorway to their world."

"Whose world?"

"Beings of great power who lie in wait in the dead lands beyond the veil."

"And why the hell would you wanna open that door?"

"The Pale King bestows great power to those who serve."

"Like McDougal?"

When the blood drained from the man's face, I knew I was onto to something, and it wasn't good.

I rolled up my sleeve to show the suspect the black handprint. "This mean anything to you?"

His worried face curled into a snarl. "The Pale King touched you, didn't he? Everything he touches dies."

I shut my mouth then and there. The last thing I wanted to do was show this kook I was scared. Real scared. Then I noticed him clinging to the red-flower garland around his neck.

I grabbed it. "What's this?"

He blushed, but said nothing.

"I guess you won't be needing it then." I took it and put it around my neck.

After that, he clammed up nice and tight.

I glanced down at the festering wound. I felt sick to my stomach. I wanted to get to a doctor, but I couldn't just leave the suspect in my car. So I waited in agony until backup arrived.

&

"It's necrotic," Rosen said, examining the skin on my arm. He'd arrived on the scene before any of the police. So fast I was pretty sure he'd been following me. "See how the tissue surrounding it is inflamed? You need to see a doctor ASAP to remove all the necrotic tissue. Otherwise, you're gonna have some real issues."

"Could I die?"

"If the infection spreads, yes."

I sighed. "All right. You mind driving me to the hospital?"

"Not at all."

So I gave my report to the officers on the scene, they took my suspect into custody, and Rosen drove me to the hospital in his white Toyota Corolla rental.

Initially, I'd been reluctant to trust Rosen. I'd been cocky enough to think I could handle the investigation on my own. Hell, after "Asshole", my second most common nickname at the department was "The Closer" 'cause closing cases is what I did. Any case that had baffled the department's brass went straight to me. And I always delivered.

But this case was so batshit crazy, I was beginning to question my own sanity. Hell, another reason I'd written Rosen off was I'd doubted <u>his</u> mental stability. But now, the only thing I was sure of was either both of us were quacks or what we'd experienced had been real.

Traffic on 101 was a nightmare. By now, the sun had long since set, and the bright lights of San Francisco illuminated the city's skyline. I squirmed in my seat while my arm throbbed. Rosen distracted me with shoptalk. "The man you have in custody, he told you things corroborating what I said earlier, didn't he? Things no one in your department will believe."

I reluctantly nodded.

His eyes wandered down to the knife on my lap. "That's the tuning knife, isn't it?"

"Wait, my suspect said something about the knife being the key to unlocking the doorway between worlds."

He grew increasingly animated, taking his eyes off the road for several uncomfortable seconds. "Exactly! You see, brane theory suggests there's a multiverse of an infinite number of universes."

The blaring horn of an eighteen-wheeler forced Rosen to swerve back into his lane.

"What the hell do brains and universes have to do with a knife?" I forced the question through a wave of nausea. And Rosen's rickety driving only made it worse. The man had a unique talent for handling a car like a drunk on a unicycle.

"B-R-A-N-E," Rosen said, the car lurching with his shift in attention. "Short for membrane. Our universe exists in one such brane that passes through hyperdimensional space. Some branes resonate at the same frequency as ours but are slightly out of phase. One of them briefly shifts into phase with ours between the autumn equinox and winter solstice, during Samhain." Rosen pointed at the knife with his right finger while his left hand barely maintained control of the steering wheel. "And that knife you're carrying is some sort of hyperdimensional tuning fork that creates a bubble where these two worlds can intersect. Unfortunately, it also draws the pale people toward you like iron to a loadstone."

Rosen now had my full attention, especially as I watched the infection slowly advance up my arm through the side-view mirror. "How do you know all this, Doc?"

Rosen glanced up at the rear-view mirror, switched on his turn signal, then changed lanes. He shrugged. "The Pentagon put me on this case because, over the past few years, satellites had detected an unprecedented increase in tachyon emissions originating from San Francisco."

Frustrated at Rosen's technobabble, I threw up my arms, then instantly regretted it as a surge of pain rippled through my infected limb. I gritted my teeth, waiting for the pain to subside, then said, "What the hell are tachyons and what do they have to do with all this shit?"

The Corolla vibrated as it crossed the rumble strip on the road. I nearly threw up. Rosen grumbled, then righted the car in the middle lane. "Tachyons are subatomic particles that travel faster than light. They're a telltale sign of dimensional intersection. My working theory is that tachyons are leaking from the other dimension into ours, and vice versa. Time is passing slower on the other side of the veil. We see tachyons because the timing differences are adjusting to one consistent temporal frame of reference."

"Not sure I follow, Doc, but I got that tachyons led you here. What's on the other side?"

"The Fomorians: an ancient race that plagued the Celts millennia ago. They always come bearing gifts in exchange for allegiance to their kind."

"Gifts like higher intelligence?" I asked.

"Precisely. Now you know how McDougal got his enlarged brain."

I checked my arm and winced. It hurt like hell. Sweat rolled down my face. I was burning up. "What do they want?"

"Detective D'Alessio, what does every species want? To be fruitful and to multiply. To expand their territory. To conquer and to subjugate."

"How do we stop them?" I asked before shouting, "Watch out!"

"Oops!" Rosen jerked the Corolla back into its lane, then said, "You can start by defending that knife with your life. So long as the Fomorians don't control it, they can't keep the portal between our worlds open."

If I didn't get to a doctor soon, I wouldn't be defending anything. "Does the government have any intel on the crew that was trying to kill me?"

"They call themselves the Order of the Red Oleander, and they serve the Pale King. McDougal was their leader."

"Let me guess: there was a power struggle?"

"We think so," he said. "Our working theory is that Jacobson and his co-conspirators had had a falling out with McDougal and then plotted to kill him. After that, Jacobson stole the knife for himself, with entirely predictable consequences."

"So why didn't they just shoot McDougal?"

"Because sacrificing McDougal would likely appease the Fomorians. They seem to feed on life energy. Were it expedient, the crew would've done the same to Jacobson."

I grabbed the garland around my neck. "Why red oleander?"

"Don't know. Members dress in white to honor the Pale King, but also wear garlands of red oleander. There's something special about the flower. Besides being poisonous, it's also extremely hardy. Did you know oleander was the first flower to bloom in Hiroshima after that city was destroyed? My guess is it somehow protects members of the Order from the Fomorians. The Order may bargain with them, but the pale people can be unpredictable."

"I had no idea." I clutched the garland. "Looks like I better keep this puppy on for good luck."

Rosen nodded. "I also think you and I need to stick together for the next few days until after All Hallow's Eve. You may need me."

At this stage, I hardly needed convincing.

By the time we pulled into the parking lot at the UCSF Medical Center, I was puking like a champ, and Rosen almost had to carry me to the emergency room where I passed out.

&

When I came to, Rosen had set up a cot next to my bed.

"What happened?" I asked.

Rosen shook his head. "You had a real nasty case of necrotizing fasciitis—a flesh-eating bacteria. Good thing we got here when we did. If we'd waited any longer, you'd have been toast."

I tried to get up, but Rosen stopped me. "Easy there, Detective. Doctor wants you to stay put so he can monitor your progress. You're on a heavy regimen of antibiotics as it is. The doctors had to give you a skin graft."

"What day is it, Doc?"

"Halloween. You were in intensive care for a few days, but you're gonna be all right. You'll probably be released tomorrow morning."

"So we're not out of the woods yet, are we, Doc?"

He shook his head.

I reached for my service weapon. "Where the hell's my SIG?" I felt naked without it.

Rosen grinned. "Even a detective can't get away with stowing a loaded pistol in a hospital, especially since Lieutenant Carmichael is investigating you for killing the men who tried to murder you."

My eyes widened.

"But don't worry, I insisted on keeping the oleander around your neck and the cloth-covered knife at your side. And in regard to the investigation, I'll make sure Uncle Sam has your back."

Soon, I drifted back to sleep.

&

I woke to flickering fluorescent lights. I staggered to my feet, grabbed the knife, yanked out the IV line from my good arm, then roused Rosen.

"What is it?" he asked.

"No clue, but it's a hell of a lot like what happened at the diner."

The room's colors faded to shades of gray. "You seeing this?"

"Seeing what?"

"The dying colors."

"You're about to cross into their realm, aren't you? Quick, grab my arm. If you don't, you'll transition there alone."

I clutched Rosen seconds before three men with milky-white skin and coal-black eyes emerged from a wall that rippled like a pond's surface under a light breeze.

I instinctively reached for my SIG only to grasp at my useless hospital gown. The pale men bared their needle-sharp teeth.

The Pale King emerged from behind them, his black antlers glistening in the dull gray light. He pointed a long, black-taloned finger at me.

Rosen's quaking hand gripped my arm. He yelled, "Run!"

We ran through the hospital until we reached the entrance. I was tired and sick. It took effort not to lose my lunch. When we left the building, we weren't in San Francisco anymore, but somewhere else entirely.

We passed into a silver mist. The crooked branches of gray-barked trees twisted upward into the gloom. Knee-high misshapen things skittered in the shadows singing dark songs, cicada-like in their eerie whistle-hums.

My arm ached. I turned to Rosen. "What now?"

His eyes darted back and forth. "I'm not sure. This is their domain, their dimension."

"How much time do we have?"

"In our world, it would've been until the end of All Hallow's Eve. Here, I'm not so sure. I suspect it'll be longer. They'll have more time to take the knife."

Flying dart-shaped insects as big as seagulls buzzed overhead. A wet, milky residue infested everything.

I froze, uncertain what to do.

The Fomorians emerged from the hospital that was a dark echo of our own. My gut kicked in. "Hide!"

Rosen and I stumbled through the alien world, desperate to evade our hunters.

Rosen wheezed, struggling to keep up. He tripped, then collapsed. "Go on without me. I'm just slowing you down."

I admired him for risking his life to follow me here, so I owed it to him to help him get through the night. "C'mon, Rosen! They're almost here."

When I looked up, shapes converged all around us.

The joke was on me. The pale men had herded us like cattle from our world into theirs. Now we were surrounded and out of options.

The Pale King strode out of the mist, sneering with those terrible razor-sharp fangs. His servants kneeled as he stepped forward into the center of the circle.

He motioned for me to surrender my knife. Yet, he kept his distance. He almost seemed wary. I glanced at Rosen. He shivered, offering no answers.

And then, it hit me. I removed the garland from my neck. That seemed to do the trick. The Pale King inched closer. Once he was in reach, I wrapped the garland of red oleander around the knife and lunged forward.

The instant the oleander touched his skin, it bubbled and burned. He collapsed, thrashing and wailing with the most disturbing shriek I'd ever heard.

In seconds, he was a pile of silver ash. I spun toward his followers, brandishing the oleander-enmeshed knife. Rather than face me, they fled into the alien forest.

∓

Rosen and I spent the rest of the night in the strange mirror hospital. By the time the sun rose, we had shifted back into our world. Rosen sat up on his cot, wiping his face and arms with a washcloth. After last night's incident, we'd both had to remove a ton of dirt and grime. I lay in my hospital bed, trying to make sense of what had happened that night.

"For the time being, it looks like we averted a major catastrophe. I'd appreciate it if you'd give me that knife so the Pentagon can put it away for safekeeping," said Rosen.

I laughed. "You kidding me? I don't wanna be anywhere near that thing. Which begs the next question: what the hell am I gonna put in the official report?"

A matronly nurse walked into the room. When she saw me, her face contorted into a rictus. "Who on earth said you could take that out?" Her eyes shifted to the IV, then back at me. "You had a life-threatening infection. Just because you've been stabilized doesn't mean you're out of the woods yet. You still need all the fluids you can get."

I held up my hands in mock surrender. "You got me. I'm sorry."

She harrumphed, fussed with the IV equipment, put on some latex gloves, and then shoved the catheter back into my arm.

On her way out of the room, Rosen shut the door, then pulled the privacy curtain closed. "Don't worry," he whispered, "I'll take care of everything, though I'll need some writing samples so we get your style right."

"You mean, your people at the Pentagon will cook up a cover story?"

Rosen beamed. "Of course. But you'll have to memorize it. We'll also provide you with all the other 'details' not in the report in case anyone starts asking questions."

"Sounds like a plan."

Rosen tapped me on the shoulder. "If you ever wanna make a few extra bucks on the side and work on other 'interesting' cases, call me." He handed me his card. "We make a great team."

Life can be grim, but sometimes there are folks who shine light in the darkness. Rosen is one of 'em. I'd take a bullet for that chubby S-O-B any day.

END

Afterword

From time to time, I enjoy writing the occasional occult thriller, and "The Red Oleander Murders" is one such example. In this particular tale, I explored the themes of a thinning veil between dimensions and elite cults that worship demonic entities in exchange for power.

This story is also one of three stories that feature both Joey D'Alessio and Dr. Eli Rosen. In fact, it is the story in which these two characters are first introduced to each other. I'm not exactly sure why these particular two characters appear so often in my stories—I've written 14 stories in which one or both of these characters is present (12 of which have been published)—but I very much enjoy writing about both of them. And because D'Alessio is so different from Rosen, they act as great foils to each other.

And speaking of characters, Elias McDougal was loosely based on a billionaire for whom I used to work and who was quite possibly among the three most despicable human beings I have ever encountered—and I use the term "human being" very charitably here.

"The Red Oleander Murders" first appeared in the July 2019 issue of *Abyss & Apex*. I hope you found it intriguing.

My Sanctuary of Solitude

Oh, Jenny, I ain't seen you in years. You're so busy changing the world these days that the only reason you probably came all the way back to see me is I must be fixin' to die. I hear you been having marriage troubles. Your mamma's been telling me Harvey's been beating on you. Well I got a story I wanna tell ya that might help. I also wanna get it off my chest 'fore I pass on.

Now you never knew your nana—my mamma—'cause she died well before you was born. We was going through some hard times back then. Great Depression. Half the time we didn't have nothing to eat. When we did, it hardly filled our aching bellies.

Now I never did know my true daddy. When mamma got with child, he bolted in a hurry. To be honest, I never cared to know someone who hightailed it the first sign things started getting tough. After he left, mamma invited a bunch of other men into our lives, but none of 'em was worth the dirt in a cemetery.

In those days, we was living in Oklahoma, and we had about the worst possible dust storms you can imagine. You probably heard of 'em. Nowadays they call it the Dust Bowl or some such. Back then we didn't know what the hell it was or how long it'd last. The black blizzards would just roll on in and cover everything in dirt and grime, making us near cough up a lung. For all we knew, the apocalypse was nigh.

Mamma jumped from job to job, working as a farmhand when she could. But when great big mounds of dust was piling up all around and killing all the crops, she couldn't find no work no how. So like everybody else, we up and headed west.

I ain't gonna whine about how bad it was. Hell, I can't remember it much no way; I was only six years old at the time. But one thing I did know was fear. It was everywhere, threatening to choke us when we wasn't looking.

Eventually we made it out to sunny California, where mamma was fixin' to work as a farmhand. Trouble was that after traveling all that way, jobs was as hard to get in California as Oklahoma.

After trying her luck up and down the coast, mamma finally got work as a fruit cutter and packer on an orchard in Contra Costa County east of San Francisco Bay. There, we pitched a tent along the creek with all the other migrants.

The days was long and the work, hard. We'd start picking at seven and quit at six. And the work was seasonal, starting with apricots in April, then moving on to peaches, then pears, then plums. But we got by. On a good day, me and mamma could cut as many as sixty boxes of apricots at three cents a box.

About a year after we started work, mamma met Billy Jones. Billy was the brother of Alcott Jones, the owner. It wasn't long 'fore we left the tents, settling in an abandoned cutting shed Alcott gave Billy.

For the first few days, Billy was kind and loving with mamma. But the honeymoon ended faster than a frog in a frying pan. Soon they was screaming and hollering at each other so bad they had to lock the door. When I tried to come home, they sent me away, telling me not to return till the sun come down.

So with nothing better to do, I hiked through the countryside, taking in the beauty of them hills. I wandered past oak, juniper, sycamore, birch, willow, and redwood under Mount Diablo's black shadow. The grove was so silent and peaceful. There was something different about it, something right powerful. A dirt path led between two rows of trees as old as Methuselah. Their branches curled into an arch high up above.

It didn't take long for mamma to decide I oughta get some learning at a nearby school. Most of them kids there was rich, so they welcomed me like a weevil in a wheat field.

I owned only two faded gray dresses, and the other kids didn't never let me forgot it. Also didn't help that I smelled a little bit strange. That scent was something I carried since I was born. Mamma said it made me special—said it reminded her of my true daddy.

'Cause of all this stuff, the other kids was mean as hell to me, especially Margaret and Catherine Jones. As they always reminded me, they was Alcott's daughters and could throw me and mamma off the land. So I had no choice, I took all the abuse I could stand.

Whenever I got lonesome, I would wander back to that grove. There, I got religion. In darkness and in light, it comforted me more than Jesus on Sunday morning. And in that lane of oak, willow, and redwood, I found my church of solitude, my wilderness cathedral, where the soul of the forest was a power unto itself. The trees whispered of peace and sleep. So I went there whenever I was scared, to pray to them trees.

And sometimes the trees would answer.

One evening I returned home from one of my forest walks to hear tin plates banging and all sorts of other ruckus. Billy and mamma was scuffling again. When I tried opening the door to the old shack, it was unlocked. Billy was standing over mamma. He glanced over his left shoulder at me. His eyes widened big as saucers. He stepped back. My attention shifted to mamma. Her left eye was all red, purple, and puffy. Tears was streaming down her cheeks.

"Mamma, what happened?" I said in the innocent voice of an eight-year-old babe.

Clenching his fist, Billy glared at mamma. His eyes darted back at me. Mamma shivered, but said nothing.

Billy started walking towards me, his arms outstretched as if he was ready to give me a hug. "Aw honey, me and your mamma were just having a nice quiet conversation. I'm gonna head out now, but your mamma's gonna be okay. She fell. Hit her face on a rock. I was trying to make her feel better." He turned toward mamma. "Right, Dora?"

Mamma looked away, then nodded. Satisfied, Billy left. I hugged mamma and said, "What happened?"

She sobbed, shook even. There was a deep silence like she was considering something. Then she said, "What Billy said. That's what happened."

Her answer didn't set right with me. But that's what mamma said, so I just took it as Gospel.

❧

A few weeks later, mamma came home for the night holding Billy's hand, a smile stamped across her face wide as a truck. I grinned back. Couldn't help it. Her smile was infectious. She just beamed and beamed. Her smile got even bigger when she saw me, if that's even possible. It was like heaven come down and was shining on her face. Even Billy was beaming. Never seen that before.

Something sparkled on her left hand—a ring.

"Oh Ruth," she said, "I got some wonderful news. Billy and me are getting hitched."

I was shocked. "When's the wedding, mamma?"

"In three months. And you're gonna be a flower girl. Then you and me are gonna be a part of the Jones family."

It was kind of odd. I guess daddies was supposed to be stern. But I half smiled. Billy was gonna be my step-daddy, and I never really had any kind of daddy before. So I hugged mamma before we all went into the shack for the night.

When Margaret and Catherine heard the news the next day they wasn't so happy. You see, the marriage would make 'em my cousins. And they thought they was too good to be cousins with the likes of some dirty little girl who only had two sets o' clothes.

That day, their usual teasing was worse than ever. They spit at me. They called me a mongrel and a greaseball. Said I'd never be a proper cousin. I kept calm and didn't say nothing, suffering through it quietly to keep the family peace.

When school was out for the day, Margaret and Catherine followed me home, chanting, "Ruth's a dirty Okie, Ruth's a dirty Okie."

I tried to ignore them, but couldn't help but cry. Of course that only encouraged 'em like pouring gasoline on a fire.

When I got to within a hundred yards of the shack, I could hear hollering inside. So could the two girls. My palms got sweaty and I shivered. The door was gonna be locked, and the last thing I wanted was to disturb Billy when he was in one of his moods. But I prayed anyway, hoping the door was unlocked.

Sure enough, it was locked tight. There was nothing for me to do but turn around and run to my refuge, my lane of trees, where I would pray to the silent sentinels of the forest.

The girls howled and jeered as I rushed past them and into the woods.

As I tore through the oak and birch and juniper, the girls' voices faded until I finally felt safe.

I sat in my sacred wood for nearly an hour breathing in the beauty of them trees, their ancient power washing over me. A faint yapping beyond the grove grew louder as it come closer.

Dogs!

I stumbled to my feet and crept beyond the edge of my secret grove to see where the ruckus was coming from. Down the hill, I saw Margaret and Catherine laughing, their faces twisted by hate. Two giant German shepherds nearly as long as Margaret and Catherine were tall was in tow.

"There she is!" Margaret said, pointing at me like I was some kinda devil.

The dogs was straining against their leashes, wheezing as they strangled themselves, desperate to get at me.

Margaret unleashed the dogs. "Sic her, boys!"

Stunned, I watched as the two huge hounds bounded toward me, their fangs bared. Margaret and Catherine stood by, watching and snickering. I couldn't understand why they hated me so.

Seconds before the dogs reached me, I turned tail and ran back toward the grove. Moments before I reached the comforting embrace of my woodland cathedral, I felt a sharp pain in my calf. I swallowed a scream. There was no way I was gonna let them girls see me cry. As the dog tore into my leg, I crawled forward to the edge of the wood, desperate for help.

The other dog landed on my back, forcing my face into the dirt. A sharp pain stabbed my shoulder as its fangs sank into my flesh.

It took every ounce of strength to crawl forward. Only feet away from my salvation, I could hear the faint sounds of glee carry on the night wind.

Covered in my own blood, I reached across that hallowed woodland boundary. The dogs tore into me with a savagery that would make Billy proud. Then, I felt a sudden sense of peace until everything faded to black.

&

When I woke it was still dark, but the dogs was gone. I was bleeding badly. Yet I had enough strength to stumble back home. Mamma and Billy was quiet and the door was still locked. It was late enough that I'd risk a beating if I knocked and woke everyone up. So I curled up outside the door and slept.

When mamma found me on the doorstep the next morning, she screamed and took me to Doctor Paulson, who stitched me up nice and tight.

I told mamma about the dogs, but I ain't never told her about Margaret and Catherine siccing 'em on me—I didn't wanna upset her and ruin her wedding. Sometimes you just had to let sleeping dogs lie. Margaret and Catherine avoided me after their dogs went missing. But when I ever did catch 'em watching me, I could see hatred burning in their eyes.

So in the months before the wedding, I knew a peace I ain't known in years. Even Billy was gentler with mamma, and I began to hope that we'd become a normal, happy family.

&

A few days before the wedding, mamma bought me and her brand new white dresses. Said she saved a year's wages to pay for 'em. My smile sparkled like starlight as I took in the glory of my new dress.

On the day of the wedding, Margaret and Catherine was dressed up in matching dresses all nice and pretty. For the first time, they both smiled nicely and waved at me. When Margaret saw me, she said, "You look very pretty today, Ruth. Welcome to the family."

I blushed and thanked her, telling her that her and Catherine looked beautiful too. She smiled back and said, "We have a family tradition for welcoming new cousins into the fold. We wanna share that tradition with you. If you're interested, meet me and Catherine inside the barn."

Excited about sharing a Jones family tradition, I grinned and told her that I was honored and that I'd be there. She winked. Catherine smiled, saying she'd see me soon.

When I entered the barn, it was quiet and dark. *Something ain't right,* I thought. Before I could begin to regret my decision, the flat end of a shovel knocked the wind clear out of me. I keeled over and rolled onto my back. When I looked up, a scowling Margaret and Catherine stood over me. They both wore overalls and gardening gloves. Their white dresses hung on spikes on the barn's far wall.

"You really thought you could kill Ranger and Rascal and get away with it, didn't you?" Margaret said.

Confused, I mumbled, "What?"

"You killed our dogs when we was only having fun with you!" Catherine scolded with righteous indignation.

"I didn't kill no dogs!" I yelled.

I made to get up, but Catherine shoved me back down. She pinned me to the ground, straddling my hips. She held the shovel across my chest. Margaret pulled out shears and chopped big hunks off my hair.

"No, please don't," I pleaded. "The wedding!" Margaret sneered. "That's the point. We want to get you all dolled up."

I struggled not to cry, but tears still escaped my eyes, giving my soon-to-be cousins exactly what they wanted. They squealed in delight.

"And to top it all off, we're gonna add a little makeup and perfume," said Margaret.

Margaret brought over a bucket. The stench of manure hit me like a black blizzard. Catherine reached into it with her gloved hand and smeared warm doo-doo on my face and lily white dress. "Me and Catherine dropped a fresh batch of night soil in this bucket a few minutes ago just for you. You've never been prettier."

"Or smelled sweeter," Catherine added.

I choked, coughing up clumps of crap.

The girls giggled. Then they quickly removed their overalls and changed back into their dresses before leaving the barn. Margaret peeked her head back in and teased, "See you at the wedding, cousin."

Covered in crap and my head a wreck of shorn hair, I panicked. My mamma was counting on me to be her flower girl, but not dressed like this.

None of it was fair. I didn't kill no dogs. But I had no time. I had to make a decision.

Mamma needed me. So five minutes before the wedding, I grabbed some hay and wiped as much of the crap off my face and dress as I could. Then I went to church and took my station in the wedding party, stinking of human filth. When the wedding began, I strode down the aisle wearing my shit-stained dress like a badge of honor, ignoring the guests' horrified expressions.

No one said nothing or stopped me. Deep down, they all knew it wasn't my choice to be covered in crap. They all knew what happened and they knew the Jones sisters had had a hand in it. But my march down the aisle never let 'em forget it.

❧

I could tell Mamma was ashamed by my appearance at the wedding, but she never said nothing 'bout it. I think she understood pretty damn well why I done it. My new step-daddy was mad too, but when he learned his nieces was responsible, he laid off the matter. I think he felt ashamed 'bout it too. Hell, he shoulda been.

Anyhow, things died down for the next few months. I think Margaret and Catherine's daddy beat 'em real good after he found out what they done. So they steered clear of me for a while.

In those calm days, I spent all my free time in my woodland cathedral, whispering to my silent sentinels.

Then Billy started beating on mamma again.

It was a lazy Sunday afternoon, a few hours after church. When I came back early from a walk in the woods, the door to the shack was shut tight, but I could still hear Billy yelling and beating on mamma. I almost turned to walk away, but I foolishly decided to open the door, expecting it to be locked. Sure enough it opened and I stumbled right into my step-daddy pounding his fists on mamma.

Just seeing him do it lit a fire in me. So I charged right up and slapped him across the face. I did it without thinking—like it was the most natural thing in the world.

He didn't take kindly to it. He beat on me till I blacked out.

∞

When I woke the next morning, my body was all black and blue. A few of my teeth was loose. Mamma cried and held me tight.

"It's okay, mamma," I said. "I'm just glad he beat me instead of you. I love ya, mamma."

She cried and cried. Back then I didn't understand why. I thought she was upset with me for putting myself between her and her new husband. Now I know better. Either way, I was gonna get that sombitch back for hurting me and mamma. So when he was out working the fields, I put all his clothes in front of the shack and set 'em on fire. Then I went out to the woods to pray and relax, proud of what I done.

That afternoon, my step-daddy was so mad, he come all the way out to the woods to find and whup me. When I seen him, I ran to my sacred space among the oaks and redwoods.

He was yelling and cussing something fierce. I stood at the edge of the grove and warned him not to follow. He just laughed and took off his belt. "You thought yesterday was bad," he said. "Today, you're gonna get a real whupping." He raised his belt high above his head and cracked it like a whip against a nearby redwood.

"You come in here," I warned, "you ain't never coming out."

"We'll see 'bout that," he said. Then he stomped forward like a farmer about to butcher a pig. He stepped into my church of solitude, unharmed. Then he whupped me till I passed out.

When I woke, it was pitch black. Owls was hooting. Grasshoppers chirped all 'round. I was covered in blood. My body throbbed with pain. I could hardly move, but willed myself up anyway.

I limped back to our shack. Opening the door, I found mamma waiting on the bed, tears streaming down her cheeks. She rushed up to me and said, "Where you been all afternoon, sweetie pie? I was worried about you. What happened?"

Her last words rang hollow. She damn well knew what happened. When I didn't answer, her next question made me see red. "Have you seen your step-daddy?"

"You mean after he whupped me out in the woods?" I said with venom.

She sobbed at that. I put my arm around her and told her everything was gonna be okay even though I knew it wasn't true. Even though I knew my step-daddy wasn't never coming home.

ဢ

Alcott Jones demanded to know his brother's whereabouts. But me and mamma didn't have no answers. I told him Billy chased me into the woods and beat me there, but that's all I knew. I never said one word about my church of solitude. Who knows what he would do to it if he found out about it. I also didn't want anyone else to get hurt.

The lawmen came and searched the woods, but come up with nothing. And to my great relief, they didn't lose no one in the process. Maybe them trees only worked to protect me.

But from then on, old man Alcott looked at me and mamma suspiciously, like we had something to do with his brother's absence. I knew the trees done it, but no one would ever believe that, so I kept my mouth shut.

Irregardless, Alcott gave mamma an ultimatum: if Billy didn't return in a month, we had to leave. Me and mamma knew my step-daddy wasn't never coming back, but we planned to stay until our time run out.

The lawmen gave up on my step-daddy's search, calling his disappearance an unsolved case, but Margaret and Catherine Jones didn't never let it go. And with Billy gone, there was no one left to protect me from them.

One afternoon, Margaret and Catherine blocked my way home and threw rocks at me. Not dime-sized pebbles, but the biblical kind—heavy stones big as baseballs. One hit me square in the temple, knocking me to the ground. Margaret forced me on my stomach, holding me down with her knee in the small of my back. She twisted my arm, while Catherine slapped and punched and kicked me.

"Where's my uncle, you bitch?" Margaret shouted.

The agony was so intense, I was willing to do near anything to make it stop. "Let me go, and I'll show you," I pleaded.

So I took them to my church of solitude. When I crossed the threshold, the girls hesitated, probably haunted by the memory of their dogs' disappearances. With my head throbbing, I said, "Follow me. Your uncle's in here."

They looked at each other, expressions of doubt on their faces. I stepped further into the forest. "If you ever wanna see your uncle again, you need to follow me."

"No way we're going in there," said Margaret.

"Then I guess you'll never find your uncle," I replied.

They stood as still as stone statues. I could smell their fear. My body ached. I was feeling light-headed. But I thought very carefully about what I said next. "C'mon. You'll be fine. I promise."

The lie was enough. I lured them into my church of solitude, my temple of trees. I walked deeper and deeper in their dark and protective embrace until the gnarled branches of the great oak at the end of the lane reached out for the two girls. Its limbs wriggled like snakes. The branches coiled around the girls' delicate necks.

I watched in fascination as the blood slowly drained from their faces, the oak's branches choking the lives from their tiny bodies. Then I stood witness as the oak buried them beneath its roots.

After the girls vanished into earth, we had no choice but to flee. To this day, I miss those trees, always faithful, always watching over me. Before I die, I have but one final request. In my purse is an old map that will lead you into those foothills. There, you'll find that hallowed grove. Go there and bury my ashes beneath the tallest oak at the end of the lane. I'm certain you'll find peace there too, because I can smell it on you, the scent that'll protect you.

And bring your husband, for it will be hungry.

END

Afterword

By the time I had finished writing My Sanctuary of Solitude" in November 2016, I was still not entirely sure what had inspired it, but it had turned out to be about two Okies who had fled to California during the Dust Bowl to seek out a better life. I wrote it about a place I had been living in for about seven years and wanted to capture its spirit long before the housing developments sprung up like a pox on the landscape when apricot and orange groves had dominated the golden brown landscape.

Through this rich historical tapestry, the mother and daughter duo's dreams quickly sour when they must suffer at the capricious hands of the Joneses. But karma, being what she is, can be one hell of a bitch.

Because Ruth's mother owes her livelihood to Alcott Jones, both women must endure the unendurable, until little Ruth unwittingly finds a way to fight back—a very dark, unforgiving, and relentless way.

This story explores the themes of human cruelty and innocence lost. It delves into how the human machine twists and corrupts the best of us into remorseless fiends. In a sense, it is not only about the end of innocence, but also the birth of sadism and brutality. It is a narrative that stares into the darkest of human hearts and shows unflinchingly how evil infects everything it touches.

"My Sanctuary of Sorrow" first appeared in *Kasma SF Magazine* in February 2020. I hope you found it as deliciously dark as I did.

Close Encounter in Coyote Canyon

iolent gusts of wind punctuated the steady hum of diesel generators in the cold desert gloom. The faint glow of mobile stadium lights cast foggy rays into the night sky only to be devoured by the deep dark. Sergeant Thomas Winters assembled his squad in a dusty wash at the mouth of Coyote Canyon, awaiting further instructions.

His orders had been cryptic: "Four soldiers to report for classified work detail; full environmental gear required."

Like a confident lion stalking his prey, Sergeant First Class Jackson strutted toward Winters and motioned for him to step forward. "Hope you're enjoying your evening, sergeant." Jackson's voice oozed with sarcasm. "Get your squad in MOPP 4 ASAP. They'll be loading some cargo onto those five-tons." He pointed at two nearby trucks.

"MOPP 4?" Winters said.

"What we're moving ain't exactly slime-free."

"And what's that?"

"That's classified. Just make sure your boys are zipped up nice and tight. Ain't worth dying on some random work detail." Jackson patted Winters on the back, then moved on.

Winters didn't like it. Not one bit. As squad leader, he was responsible for his men's lives. Even worse, he'd have to answer to his wife, Agnes.

He returned to his squad, uncomfortable with having so little information about his assignment. From the sound of it, his men didn't share his trepidation.

"Naw, you're full of shit," Private Turner said. "Ain't no way Lieutenant Malozzi's banging that supply clerk. That's fraternization."

"That blonde with the big tits?" said Private Groves. "What's her name? Oh yeah, Private Collins."

"I shit you not," Corporal Baker interjected. "I seen them eating pizza together all the time."

"That don't mean they're screwing. Plus, ain't the L-T married?" Turner said.

"Sheeet," Baker replied, "Since when did that ever matter? Those two are fucking. I just know it,"

"Quit smoking and joking," Winters interrupted. "Get your MOPP gear on. We've got some HAZMAT to load onto those five-tons," Winters waved his arm toward the trucks.

"Time to take another one from the big green weenie," Baker grumbled.

After donning their cumbersome, charcoal-lined chemical suits, boots, gloves, and gas masks, the three men followed Winters into a shadowy ditch extending to the canyon's southern wall. The men lumbered forward until a soldier in MOPP gear and the name "Zollinger" stamped on his chest signaled them to stop.

Two more pairs of soldiers huddled toward the squad, each group carrying a ten-foot-long wooden crate. They carefully lowered the crates to the ground, then left.

Zollinger motioned for Winters and Turner to step forward. The man put his hand on Winters' chest. "Careful with the cargo. If it drops, alert me immediately, then evacuate to the decontamination tent." He jutted his chin toward an olive drab tent about two hundred meters away. "There's also a string of M88 detection units on the perimeter. You hear one go off, lower your crate and assemble at the decontamination tent. We clear?"

Winters and Turner nodded. They lifted the bulky crate and carried it toward the five-tons. For something so unwieldy, it was surprisingly light.

Winters glanced back and watched as Baker and Groves began hauling the other crate.

"I'm telling you, they're fucking," Baker said to Groves.

"Quit horsing around!" Winters yelled.

"Yes, sergeant," Baker said before whispering to Groves and then laughing.

"I said: Stop. Dicking. Around!" Winters hollered. "You two need to take this shit serio..."

A monstrous groan echoed through the canyon like an oak bowed by a hurricane.

"You all right, Groves?" Baker shouted, panic in his voice.

With all the patience he could muster, Winters balled up his fists, stormed over to Baker and Groves, and let loose. "What the fuck's going on? I told you all that jaw jacking would get you in trouble. Now I'm gonna rip you a new..."

Then Winters saw it.

The crate had shattered. A thick black liquid had spattered all over Groves' MOPP suit. Groves lay in the dirt, cradling his leg. Baker averted Winters' glare. Winters spotted something that glinted in moonlight. When he took a closer look, his heart nearly stopped. A silvery metallic shard etched with strange writing rested unnaturally in the sand.

"To the decon tent!" Winters ordered.

Baker and Turner sprang into action. Private Groves clutched his leg, rocking back and forth. A ragged tear in his MOPP suit exposed skin marred with some kind of a burn. His eyes were as wide as pancakes.

Winters slung Groves over his shoulder in a fireman's carry. He hustled toward the decontamination tent, praying Groves would be okay.

Groves' breathing grew shallower by the second. Winters was feet from the decontamination station when the piercing whine of M88 detection systems reverberated throughout the canyon.

God knows what Groves had been exposed to, but the man's wheezing made Winters nervous.

Winters laid Groves at the foot of the tent. A decon team whisked him away before Winters had a chance to ask about Groves' medical status.

Lieutenant Malozzi soon arrived, and Winters expected to be relieved on the spot.

The officer listened patiently to Winters' after action review, not asking a single question or stating an opinion. When Winters had finished, Malozzi lowered his head, then looked up and said, "We'll deal with this tomorrow. Take your men back to quarters and get some sleep." Then he left without fanfare.

That night, Winters slept fitfully while explosions in the distance disrupted his slumber.

∞

Sergeant Winters arrived thirty minutes before his platoon's morning formation, anxious to find out what had happened to Groves. Over the next fifteen minutes, his soldiers straggled in. Most seemed as spent as he was. Baker shuffled in five minutes before formation, leaving all but Groves present and accounted for.

Winters grabbed Baker by the arm. "Where's Groves?"

Baker shrugged. "They confined him to quarters. The medics gave him a once over last night. Said his vitals were good to go. But ol' Grovesy still whined and complained until a doc put him on profile and prescribed some Motrin."

Winters rolled his eyes. Motrin was the Army medical establishment's remedy for anything a doctor couldn't diagnose. "Between you and me," Winters said, sotto voce, "you think the docs know what's wrong with him?"

Baker fidgeted, then shifted his eyes. "They don't have a damn clue. To be perfectly honest, I think the doctor was scared. Like he was holding something back and it didn't sit right with him."

"Thanks for giving me the straight dope. I'll check on Groves first thing this afternoon."

Baker smiled. "Roger, sergeant. And thanks. Appreciate your concern."

Moments later, Lieutenant Malozzi approached Winters. "A word, sergeant?"

This was it. Winters braced himself for a sound drubbing. He nodded and followed Malozzi into company headquarters, out of earshot.

Malozzi grasped Winters' arm. "Sergeant, there's nothing you could've done for Private Groves. I don't blame you one iota for what happened."

Winters raised his eyebrows in surprise. "Ah...thank you, sir. Will there be an investigation?"

Malozzi shook his head. "I doubt it, as long as you keep your mouth shut."

Confused, Winters said, "I promise not to say a word about what I saw in those crates."

"I'm not talking about that. I'm talking about Groves. From now on, anyone asks, Groves was never in your squad. Got it?"

Winters hesitated. Something was off. Way off. But for the moment, he just nodded.

"Good. Now that we're clear, get in formation."

ༀ

Malozzi's words bothered the hell out of Winters. And the lieutenant's thinly veiled threat only encouraged the sergeant to press even harder for answers. As soon as he had a chance, Winters drove to Groves' quarters, a sandstone condo with a red Spanish tile roof.

Winters wrapped on the door.

No answer.

When he knocked again, a heavyset woman opened the door of the neighboring unit.

"They left early this morning," she said matter-of-factly. Glancing discreetly over her shoulder, she covered her hand over her mouth and whispered, "There was a lot of commotion. Hooded men in black jumpsuits escorted Mrs. Groves out of her home. She was real upset. Crying and making a big fuss."

"Did you see Private Groves leave?"

She shook her head.

"So he could still be here?"

She shrugged. "Don't think so, but I don't know for sure."

Winters nodded, then pounded on the door.

The woman reached into her pocket, fished out a key, and handed it to him. "You can use their spare."

"Appreciate it." Winters took the key and unlocked the door.

"Groves?" he said, crossing the threshold.

Silence.

The two-bedroom condo was cleaner than Winters expected for a private's quarters. Nothing was out of place. He climbed the stairs and searched the bedroom, finding no sign of Groves. It seemed as if the place had been wiped clean.

A firm knock startled Winters. He descended the stairs and opened the front door. Two hooded men waited on the doorstop. Their black hoods made their heads seem unnaturally large. Their skin was pale, almost white.

"You're not authorized to be here," one said.

"I'm checking on one of my men. Who the hell are you?"

"You need to leave," said the other man.

"Why?" Winters pushed. "And you still haven't answered my question."

The men whispered to one another. Without warning, one pulled out a Glock and aimed it at the sergeant. "You have thirty seconds."

Winters raised his hands. "This some kind of robbery? Where's Private Groves?"

The man tightened his grip on the pistol. "Twenty-five seconds."

"Okay. Okay." Winters hustled past the two men, his hands held high. But he just couldn't let it go. He faced the two men. "Let me see some ID. For all I know, you could be criminals."

The man holding the pistol scowled. "If we were robbing you, you'd be dead by now. The fact that I'm pointing a weapon at you, in the open, on a U.S. military installation should tell you everything. Fifteen seconds."

"All right," Winters said, making his way onto the lawn and back to his Ford F-150. As he drove away from the scene, he called the MPs to report the incident.

The corporal who answered his call was helpful enough. She wrote down his report, asking a few questions about the men. Winters hung up, confident someone would follow up.

Ten minutes later, his phone rang.

"Sergeant Winters?" said a gruff male voice.

"Yes."

"This is Colonel Kaminsky, commander of the Fort Irwin military police garrison."

"Thanks for getting back to me, sir. Did you send anyone to Private Groves' apartment?"

There was a brief pause. "I have no record of a Private Groves. I'm following up on your recent call about 5170 Paradise Mountain Loop."

"That's right." Winters scratched his head. The whole conversation was surreal. Then he remembered Lieutenant Malozzi's orders to deny Groves had ever been in his squad.

"Well, if you ever return to that address or interfere with those agents again, you'll be court-martialed."

"Sir, one of 'em pointed a loaded gun at me. I did nothing wrong. What the heck would you charge me with, anyway?" Winters said, annoyed.

"Interfering with an official government investigation."

Winters pressed, "What investigation?"

Kaminsky grunted. "That's classified. You have your orders. This call is over."

Now Winters was ready to panic. He wanted answers, and the only person who might have them was Malozzi.

☙

Winters paced outside Malozzi's office. It had been almost twenty-four hours since the incident at Groves' condo, and Winters was getting angrier by the minute.

"Sergeant Winters," Malozzi's gravelly voice boomed. "Enter."

Winters made a beeline straight to Malozzi's desk, snapped to attention, and rendered a crisp salute. The lieutenant lazily returned it. "At ease. What's on your mind?"

"Where's Groves, sir?"

"Who?"

"You gotta be kidding me, sir. Private Groves. You know: short, pasty white guy. Straw blonde hair."

"Sorry, sergeant. I don't have a clue who you're talking about."

Clenching his fists, Winters stifled an intense urge to throttle the lieutenant. "This is bullshit."

Malozzi sprung up from his desk. "Excuse me, sergeant?"

Now that Winters had crossed the Rubicon, he doubled down. "You heard what I said."

There was an uncomfortable silence. The two glared at each other until Malozzi finally looked away.

Taking a deep breath, the lieutenant said, "Remember what I said earlier? This is serious business. If one man can disappear, so can another."

"You threatening me, sir?"

"I'm warning you, but call it whatever you want."

"Sir, what's in Coyote Canyon, and why's it more important than Groves' life?"

"That's need-to-know, sergeant, and, frankly, you don't need to know."

"Horseshit!"

"Don't you take that tone with me, sergeant."

Winters was at an impasse. If he pushed any further, he could end up stripped of his rank or worse. He had to try a different approach.

"Sir, if you don't tell me what happened to Groves and what's in Coyote Canyon, I'm gonna tell your wife about Private Collins."

Malozzi blushed. His lower lip quivered. "Bullshit."

"What's bullshit, the affair or me telling your wife about it?"

Malozzi scowled.

"What, sir, nothing to say?"

The lieutenant slowly settled back into his chair. He slumped over his desk, sighing. "Sergeant, I swear to Christ if you repeat this, we're both dead."

"Go on."

"A few weeks back, engineers from the First Cavalry Division were digging trenches in Coyote Canyon when they uncovered black ooze near the southern wall."

"The same stuff that was on Groves?"

Malozzi nodded.

"Sounds like oil to me," Winters said, not because he believed it, but because he was terrified of the alternative.

"Like you, they thought it was oil. But overnight, the fluid had seeped into their vehicles, making it impossible for them to drive away from the area. Several eyewitnesses swore they'd seen the substance creeping uphill."

"What the hell?"

"It gets worse. Soon after, three engineers disappeared. There were rumors that the muck had consumed them. The Army quarantined the area, and the remaining engineers began excavating the site. There, they stumbled upon strange artifacts covered in glyphs and made of a metal harder than diamond but more flexible than tin foil."

"What does all this have to do with Groves?"

Malozzi shrugged. "Look, I've already said too much."

"You know where he is, don't you?" Winters glowered.

Malozzi averted Winters' gaze.

"Dammit, sir! Take me to him. Otherwise, I've gotta a story your wife's gonna love."

Malozzi exhaled. "Fine. Meet me on the Weed Army Hospital tarmac at midnight."

&

A chill desert wind pummeled Winters as he waited near four Blackhawk helicopters resting on the tarmac. Even though it was September, temperatures had dropped rapidly from a scorching one-hundred-ten degrees to sixty degrees Fahrenheit.

A BMW turned into the hospital parking lot. The lights cut out and a solitary figure approached Winters.

"Follow me," Malozzi said, leading Winters into the hospital. The lieutenant flashed a badge at the clerk manning the front desk. Winters followed Malozzi down a hallway that led to a set of double doors. Two men in black jump suits guarded the entrance.

"Who the hell are they?" Winters mumbled, not recognizing the uniforms.

"Your guess is as good as mine," Malozzi whispered.

Malozzi handed over his badge.

The guard checked it. "You're clear." He turned toward Winters. "Badge?"

Winters' heart raced. The dirt he had on Malozzi wouldn't make a rat's ass of a difference to these men. He tried to think fast, but all that came out of his mouth was, "I'm with him." He jerked his thumb toward Malozzi.

"Don't matter. No card, no access."

"C'mon, it's not like he's trying to smuggle in his girlfriend," Winters said, in a not-so-subtle reminder about his leverage over Malozzi."

The lieutenant stepped forward. "I need my sergeant with me. He's still going through the clearance process, but, as you know, that takes forever. And I don't have forever. How can I get him access tonight?"

The guard folded his arms and stared at Malozzi for several awkward seconds. "Do you take full responsibility for this man?"

"I do."

"Well, L-T, I'm gonna need you to sign a statement attesting to that. I'll also need to hold onto this sergeant's military ID until he returns."

Malozzi hesitated. His face turned ashen.

The guard smiled. "Oh, now that we're making it all official, you're having second thoughts, aren't you?"

"Yeah, he thinks I'm his girlfriend," Winters quipped, then playfully elbowed the lieutenant. "Right, sir?"

Malozzi blushed, then seemed to force a smile. "Exactly. Do you have any paper?"

Shrugging, the guard handed Malozzi a clipboard. "Here you go."

The lieutenant took an uncomfortable amount of time writing his statement before handing the clipboard back to the guard.

The guard examined it, then said, "Please surrender all your electronic devices."

Winters and Malozzi complied, then passed through the doors. A dimly lit hallway led to a second set of double doors. As they drew closer, Winters heard wailing beyond the threshold. Malozzi stiffened.

"What's wrong, sir?"

"Aside from the prospect of me spending the rest of my life in Leavenworth, I've never been comfortable in that room." Malozzi shuddered.

"Why's that?"

"See for yourself."

Winters pushed open the doors.

Bedlam.

It was a circus of corruption. Men whimpered and screamed. The air stank of bile and decay. Winters stifled an urge to vomit.

Along the walls, rotting men shivered in shallow flesh husks that had once been in prime physical condition. Black and red sores ravaged their skin. Their skeletal frames were maimed and twisted.

One man sat on his bed, methodically ripping clumps of hair from his scalp. He stared into space, humming some deranged dirge. Another shivered as he lay on soiled sheets, muttering incoherently as he picked at bloody, pus-filled scabs.

Turning away, Winters said, "What is this place?"

"This is where they take the exposed to die."

"And Groves?"

Malozzi pointed toward the back of the room.

"Are...are they contagious?" Winters asked, ashamed.

"Don't think so." Malozzi seemed unconvinced.

"I see." Girding himself, Winters took a deep breath and plunged into the room.

A ruin of a man lay in a mound of decaying flesh, muscle, and bone. He rested on a putrid pile of his own filth. His hair was a riotous patchwork of hair tufts and pallid skin, like a chessboard warped by some distorted dimension. His body was pockmarked with bubbly lesions. He smelled like a rotten onion dipped in pigshit.

"Groves," Winters' voice trembled, "that you?"

The flesh heap stirred. A skeletal hand reached out, startling Winters with its suddenness. "Serg...gent?" the thing said, as if it had long-forgotten how to use its tongue.

Winters hovered closer to the filthy bed. Against all his instincts, he clutched Groves' hand with both of his.

"You're gonna be all right," Winters lied. "Just tell me how I can help you. Anything. Anything at all."

Groves' shriveling hand pulled Winters closer. The man's eyes appeared infinitely distant in sunken sockets set in an emaciated skull. When Winters was inches from Groves' toothless mouth, the man whispered, "Kill me. Kill me. Kill me," in raspy and belabored breaths.

Winters wiped away his tears. "I'm sorry, buddy. I'm so sorry."

Malozzi walked up to Winters. "It's time to go." He grabbed Winters by the elbow and escorted him from the room.

≃

Winters couldn't sleep, so he kissed his sleeping wife on the cheek and then pulled a slender metal box from beneath his bed where he kept his unregistered Glock.

He loaded the pistol, filled his rucksack with his MOPP suit and all the ammunition he had, and left. Climbing into his pickup, he headed down Barstow Road toward Coyote Canyon.

He left his headlights off, using the full moon's ambient light to see. He kept checking his rearview mirror, terrified someone would discover him driving into a restricted area.

As he turned toward Coyote Canyon, he couldn't decide whether to be relieved or terrified that lights no longer illuminated it. In the moonlight, something about the landscape looked different.

He parked his truck in a *wadi*, grabbed his Glock and a flashlight, put on his MOPP gear, and trekked toward the laager site.

The canyon was as quiet as a monastery. Winters wandered in darkness until he was sure the area was deserted, then he flipped on his flashlight.

Scorch marks pitted and blackened the earth, reminding him of the aftermath of an intense bombing raid in Iraq.

Wending his way through the desert, he returned to the ditch where Groves had been exposed. He climbed into the trench and worked his way toward the canyon's southern wall.

The path led to a man-sized hole bored into the canyonside. Winters crawled into the dark shaft. As he drew deeper, the tunnel opened into a large chamber carved into the bedrock.

Three ten-foot slabs stood side-by-side in the chamber's center. Circular shapes and symbols dominated the artificial cavity's sinuous architecture. Winters continued to press forward, his curiosity only slightly outweighing his fear.

As Winters drew deeper into the chamber, what he had originally assumed were slabs, were more like sarcophagi. Two held humanoid forms suspended in a translucent amber fluid. The beings were long-limbed and slender with hard, angular features. Winters estimated their height at over nine feet.

The third sarcophagus had been cracked open. There, Winters found a rotting ruin of alien remains. It was as if something had ripped it apart from the inside out. That the government had left the carcass here made Winters wonder if the Army was still in control.

Winters snapped some photos of the scene. He then sent them to Agnes with a terse message: "If you don't hear from me, tell the media I took these photos in Coyote Canyon."

"You're not supposed to be here," a voice grated from the shadows.

Winters spun on his heel and fired two slugs into the dark. A dull thud told him he'd hit his target. He crept forward, his Glock aligned with his flashlight.

"Who's there?" Winters said.

A flash of light washed out the darkness. Winters' stomach roiled. When he looked down, his left arm was gone. He blindly fired two more shots, then passed out.

∞

Winters opened his eyes and winced. An overhead lamp blinded him. Straps bound him to a hospital bed. He could see nothing in the blackness beyond. Drenched in sweat, he struggled to breathe.

"Ah, Sergeant Winters," a voice said from the darkness. "We thought we'd lost you. You've been very busy."

"Where am I?" Winters struggled against the straps.

"We have much to thank your species for, most especially, reviving us from the long sleep. Our hosts could not withstand the conditions here, so we've been waiting a very long time."

Winters felt the blood drain from his face. His heartbeat quickened. Fear curdled in his gut.

The voice continued. "Rescind your call for help. Reach out to the outside world and tell them it was a hoax."

A balding middle-aged man emerged from the darkness. His face was a cadaverous white, much like those of the two hooded men. Six pulsing black tendrils extended from the back of his head, burrowing into the edges of his face—an unholy halo born of parasitic corruption. A purple bulbous brain throbbed behind his face.

Winters had only one response: "Go fuck yourself."

The man-thing smiled. "We thought you'd say that, so we brought your friends along to help you change your mind."

Agnes and Groves stepped into the light, massive purple-lobed brains throbbing in eerie synchronicity, their hands covered in black ooze that Winters knew hungered for him.

END

Afterword

"Close Encounter in Coyote Canyon" drew on my experiences as an Army officer when I was stationed at the National Training Center in Fort Irwin, California. I spent a good four years of my life there in the Mojave Desert. Most of the places mentioned in the story—with the exception of the secret tunnel—are real, and have had a significant impact on my life. For instance, my eldest child and daughter was born at Weed Army Hospital.

In this story, I played with the ideas of first contact and pre-human civilizations on Earth. Of course, I had to add a twist—a parasitic species that had infected this ancient race—indigenous to Earth or otherwise—and the result was "Close Encounter in Coyote Canyon."

I sold this story to *Kasma SF Magazine* in May 2016, and it appeared online in June 2016.

I hope you found it both chilling and thought-provoking.

Murder and Mayhem

etective Joey D'Alessio gnawed on a toothpick in a seedy Tenderloin diner. He waited for the only jerkoff in San Francisco who knew something about the city's worst crime wave in over two centuries to quit bullshitting and start talking. So far, his informant had been about as useful as a football bat.

"All right, shitbird, tell me what you know," D'Alessio said with all the subtlety of a grizzly bear.

Sitting across from D'Alessio, Dorn Mather vibrated with the nervous intensity of a starving crow. His eyes had a jaundiced hue, and his hair was straw white–unnaturally so for someone with such smooth and delicate features. An oversized dark gray overcoat hung like a tarp over his scrawny frame.

In a voice reminiscent of Casey Kasem, Dorn cackled, quivering like a harlequin sprung out of a music box. "Murder, mayhem, and violence. Isn't it obvious? Welcome to our little intergalactic show where gods walk among men." He waved his arm in an exaggerated flourish.

Flashing police lights intermittently punctuated the diner's dim lighting.

D'Alessio reached across the table and grabbed Dorn by the throat. "Listen, dicklicker, people are dying. You promised answers. I'm either leaving here with wisdom or a piece of your ass. You're the guy gets to decide which. What'll it be, douchebag?"

D'Alessio relaxed his grip. He needed answers. Unlike prior crime waves, these murders had been spread fairly evenly throughout the city. Nowhere was safe. Anyone could become a victim.

Dorn exhaled loudly. His eyes lit up like Jack O' Lanterns on a moonless Halloween night. "Oooh, soooo many choices," he said in a voice oozing with sarcasm. "There's so much rage in you. I think I'll enjoy living in this savage city by the bay."

D'Alessio tossed his coffee mug at Dorn, spraying him with steaming coffee.

Dorn squealed, then covered his face with his hands. "What an intriguing sensation," he said with the dispassion of a scientist stripping legs off an insect. His sadistic smirk never left his face.

"Tell me what's going on or I'll break your fucking nose!" D'Alessio threatened. "What gang do you run with? Answer me!"

"Gang? Ha!" Dorn crowed. "We're just undesirables dumped on a third-rate rock. You better hope we don't get organized."

"What do you mean, 'we'? I need answers, dammit!" D'Alessio yelled, pounding his fist on the table.

"Officer down! I say again, officer down!" a frantic voice squawked over D'Alessio's handheld radio. "Need immediate assistance at 555 California Street on the corner of California and Kearney. Male suspect in vicinity."

D'Alessio grabbed the lapels on Dorn's overcoat and got in his face. "I'll be keeping my eye on you."

Dorn grinned. "And I, you, Detective D'Alessio, at your 988 Fulton Street apartment."

D'Alessio charged toward Dorn, but then stopped. An officer needed D'Alessio's help.

"I'll be back for you, pissbird." D'Alessio put on his coat and left the diner.

୫

D'Alessio parked his beaten up Ford Taurus behind an empty squad car and drew his service weapon. The car's strobe lights pulsated red and white. The driver's door was slightly ajar. Behind it, a pale, bald man squatted, chewing on something. Blood was everywhere. The air reeked of human filth.

A crowd had gathered on Kearney Street, recording video and snapping photos with their smartphones.

When D'Alessio saw what the man was eating, he struggled to contain his fury. "Put your hands where I can see 'em, you piece of shit."

Smacking his lips, the suspect huddled over an unresponsive police officer. It was Sergeant Wayne Murphy. Murphy and D'Alessio had graduated from the same academy class. The man had a wife and two children.

"I said, 'hands up', goddammit!"

The assailant ignored D'Alessio, continuing to devour Murphy's arm.

Wheeling into action, D'Alessio kicked the man in the face. The cannibal spun and landed on his back. A riot of bone, sinew, and shorn flesh hung from sharpened teeth. He hissed at D'Alessio.

Training his SIG Sauer on the suspect, D'Alessio yelled, "Hands up!"

The attacker leapt to his feet and lunged at the detective.

D'Alessio fired two shots, center of mass. The assailant fell back, hitting the pavement with a dull thud.

The crowd pressed in from all directions, their smartphone cameras flashing. D'Alessio holstered his weapon. He crouched next to the police officer and took the man's pulse.

Dead.

D'Alessio glanced at cannibal's body. Only then did he notice the man's sickly yellow eyes.

℘

It was eight thirty in the morning, and D'Alessio was late for work. As he was about to leave his apartment, the phone rang. It was Karl, an old buddy from D'Alessio's Brooklyn stomping grounds.

"You all right?" Karl said, his voice on the edge of panic.

"Sure," said D'Alessio, not sure what to make of Karl's out-of-the-blue call. "Why?"

"You don't know, do ya? Turn on your TV."

The carnage that unfolded on his television horrified D'Alessio. Shards of twisted metal rent their way through asphalt and mangled cars. Thick black smoke swirled over the scene as it mixed with choking gray dust. Scores of BART commuters stumbled through the haze, dead-eyed, despondent, and caked in dust like specters emerging from some nightmarish dreamscape.

The East Bay BART derailment was unprecedented. Casualties would be in the hundreds, not to mention the crippling economic cost to the region.

D'Alessio couldn't think clearly. His mind began to spin. But there was one hunch he couldn't shake: this derailment was no accident.

"Hello? You still there?" said Karl.

"I'm here. Let's catch up when I have more time. I need to get to the station." D'Alessio hung up. Seconds later, his phone rang again.

"What?" he said in frustration, as if the world were conspiring to keep him away from work.

"Sorry to bother you, Joe. I'm not sure if you remember me, but I'm Doctor Eli Rosen. I worked with you on the Red Oleander murders."

Despite his stress and frustration, D'Alessio couldn't help but smile. Rosen was one of the smartest and quirkiest people D'Alessio had ever met

"Sorry for my pissy mood, doc. 'Course I remember you. You still working for PEARL?"

PEARL stood for the Princeton Engineering Anomalies Research Lab, a research program that studied various parapsychological phenomena.

"Unfortunately, no. Princeton shut down the program in early 2007. Now, I just teach astrophysics. I also consult with various governmental agencies on the side. Speaking of which, I have a favor to ask."

"Name it."

"I'm working on a classified project for a certain government agency related to encryption and cybersecurity. I need the San Francisco Police Department's help."

"Sure, but why does the NSA need us?"

Rosen chuckled. "Whoever said anything about the NSA?"

D'Alessio raised his eyebrow. "C'mon. Seriously?"

"Fine, you got me," Rosen said. "To answer your question, I can't have the NSA tied to this case. It needs to be off book. It's related to today's BART derailment."

"When ya gonna be in town?"

"I'm already here. Can you meet me at the Starbucks inside the Bank of America building in about an hour?"

"Will do." D'Alessio hung up the phone.

∞

Inside Starbucks, D'Alessio checked his watch obsessively as he drank black coffee with the alacrity of a sloth. Ten minutes later, a balding man with ample girth, a prodigious beard, and a grease-smeared polyester polka dot suit shuffled through the entrance.

Rosen extended his hand. D'Alessio ignored it.

"Tell me about the case." said D'Alessio.

"I'm investigating a sophisticated zero day vulnerability in BART's operating software that enables a hacker to remotely control a train."

D'Alessio perked up. "What do you mean? BART officials are chalking the derailment up to operator error."

Rosen grinned. "That's exactly what the perpetrator wants us to think. The code was calibrated to mask the attacker's digital footprint."

"I bet this is related to the current crime wave," D'Alessio said. "Why exactly has a single hack gotten the NSA's attention? A bit too tactical for them, no?"

Rosen sighed. "Look, I don't want to say too much, but U.S. cybersecurity experts are alarmed. The attack exhibited an unprecedented degree of sophistication. So much so that NSA officials worry the hacker is capable of doing far worse. For instance, imagine if the hacker solved the traveling salesperson problem."

"The what?"

"The TSP is one of the more intractable problems in computing. Let's say there's a salesperson traveling to N cities. The TSP is finding the most efficient path for the salesperson to travel to each city in the least amount of time. As you add more cities, it takes exponentially longer to compute the optimal route. For just twenty cities, there are over two billion billion possible combinations."

"What's that got to do with national security?"

"Modern encryption systems rely on the TSP's inherent complexity to work. Let's say I have a password with twenty distinct, non-repeating characters, and it takes one second to enter this password. It would take over seventy-seven billion years to try every combination. This is why encryption is so effective.

"Now suppose I come up with an algorithm that identifies the right password combination in seconds. Imagine what I could do with this knowledge. I could hack into any bank account in the world. It would lead to the almost certain collapse of the global financial system. No encrypted data would be safe."

"Jesus," said D'Alessio.

"So, are you in?"

D'Alessio nodded. "You're goddamn right I am, and I know exactly where we need to start."

&

Rosen, D'Alessio, and Dorn gathered in the same decrepit diner where Dorn and the detective had met earlier that week.

With a demented grin, Dorn jutted his head toward Rosen. "Who's the plump turnip?"

Rosen seemed unfazed by the insult. "I'm Doctor Eli Rosen."

Dorn smirked.

"Look, dickbag," D'Alessio said, "we have a specific request. I strongly encourage you to cooperate."

Dorn waved his hand as if he were swatting a gnat. "Yes, yes. Sooo, what've you learned in the last few days, detective? Any closer to uncovering your make-believe criminal conspiracy?"

D'Alessio's face turned beet red. He was trying his best not to throttle Dorn. "We have something more pressing to discuss today."

"Oooh, what could be more important than the biggest crime spree in San Francisco's history?"

D'Alessio jerked his head toward Rosen. "Go ahead, chief."

Rosen unfolded a wad of paper from his wrinkled jacket. He spread the sheet on the table. Tiny blue equations peppered its surface.

Rosen said, "Are you familiar with the traveling salesperson problem?"

Dorn stared blankly at Rosen.

Rosen continued. "It's a classic optimization problem to find the shortest possible route for a salesperson traveling to N cities."

Dorn's eyes widened. "Ah, yes, yes. I'm familiar with this rudimentary riddle. The number of possible combinations is equal to N factorial or some such. We solved this problem hundreds of years ago. It wasn't so much an algorithmic solution as it was a quantum mechanical fix."

Rosen's jaw dropped. "Are you telling me you know of a technique to crack 256-bit encryption at the quantum level?"

"Of course. It's a routine function on any quantum computer. Just take the digital bits coming out of one of your primitive binary computers, translate them into qubits and run all the permutations through a quantum hypercomputer until the code is cracked. If the engineer is particularly talented, he could build a qubit-to-tachyon converter and run the calculations backward in time. Theoretically, he'd only have to run the computation once, rendering his attempt undetectable."

Rosen's face turned ashen.

"C'mon. You don't buy this, do you, doc?" said D'Alessio.

Rosen shook his head. "I honestly don't know what to believe, but theoretically the technique he laid out could work. We just haven't made enough breakthroughs in physics and engineering to get there yet. For instance, if one used Shor's algorithm on a quantum hypercomputer to factor large prime numbers, one could exponentially reduce the time it takes to decipher an encrypted code."

"Fine. Suppose what this chucklehead is saying has some merit. Who's got the technical chops to pull it off?"

"Oooh, wouldn't you like to know?" Dorn teased.

Leaping to his feet, D'Alessio rounded the table and elbowed his way into Dorn's side of the booth. Dorn giggled. The detective put Dorn in a headlock and said, "Start talking now. We don't have much time."

Dorn raised his hands in mock surrender. "Relax, detective. As far as you know I haven't committed any crimes."

"What the hell's that supposed to mean?" D'Alessio said.

"That's not your concern," Dorn countered. "I'd be delighted to help you find the suspect so long as you provide me with certain... assurances."

D'Alessio grabbed Dorn by the throat. "Why, you cocksucker."

"Calm down, Joe," Rosen said. "This man hasn't committed any crimes. And he seems to have knowledge that could help us."

D'Alessio released his grip. "Fine."

"Thanks for the assist, butterball," said Dorn. "As I was saying, I'm going to need a few things first."

D'Alessio braced himself.

Dorn grinned. "I want you to rent me a billboard on Highway 101 for one month. Should cost you around fifty-thousand dollars."

"What?" D'Alessio said, dumbfounded.

"A billboard. For advertising," Dorn clarified in the most condescending tone D'Alessio could imagine.

"What the hell could you possibly be selling?" The request was so far off the reservation, D'Alessio had to ask.

"Oh, some harmless spiritual claptrap that shouldn't concern you. But if you want my help, you'll make it happen. If you don't, I'll sit back and watch your civilization collapse."

The man had a point.

"Done," D'Alessio bluffed. He'd worry about making it happen later, and only if Dorn's intel panned out.

"Good. I'll hold you to it," Dorn said matter-of-factly. "Any who, you can find your man where they invented gene splicing."

D'Alessio balled his hands into fists. "That's it? That's all we get?"

"Now, now, detective, I'm operating on scout's honor. I have no real assurances you'll deliver on your promise. This is all a good faith effort on everyone's part, no?"

Holding up his hand, Rosen said, "Relax, Joe. Our suspect is at Stanford University."

"Stanford's a pretty big fucking place," said D'Alessio.

"I'm sure we can handle it," Rosen said. "Whoever our suspect is, he'll likely be within a square mile of Stanford's Computer Science Department." Rosen smiled at Dorn. "Thank you for your help, Mister Mather."

"The pleasure was all mine, doctor."

"All right," D'Alessio said, slamming two twenty dollar bills on the table. "Let's get cracking."

℥

D'Alessio and Rosen walked down Palm Drive toward Stanford's Main Quad. Orderly rows of palms flanked the road.

"Man, you gotta have some serious dough to pay for this joint," said D'Alessio. "Looks like a damn country club."

The beauty of the Quad was breathtaking. Even on a moderately cold autumn day, the sun shone on the complex of red-tile-roofed buildings nestled in the Northern Californian foothills.

"Have your colleagues made any progress figuring out who's behind the crime wave?" Rosen asked.

"Damn, doc!" D'Alessio grumbled, "You sure know how to piss on a man's corn flakes and call it syrup."

"I didn't mean to spoil your morning, but has the SFPD made any headway?"

"Nah. The department's got its collective head up its ass. Every swinging dick is pounding the pavement, responding to crimes in progress and arresting bad guys. The only connection officers have made, but aren't reporting, is that most arrests include suspects with no fingerprints and yellow eyes like Dorn's."

Rosen pressed. "You mean not one single officer's looked into that fact pattern?"

D'Alessio shrugged. "'Course they have. One lady in forensics did an autopsy on a yellow-eye killed in a police raid. She had a theory that the crime wave might've had something to do with a strange new disease that was similar to rabies. Turned out to be a blind alley. All I know is about two weeks ago, the crime rate spiked."

Rosen clammed up.

"What? Is it something I said?"

Rosen squirmed. "I'm sorry, but I can't talk about it."

D'Alessio spun toward Rosen and grabbed the man's collar. "What do you mean? People are dying, you got some intel that could help us, and all you can say is you can't talk about it?"

D'Alessio could see conflict and sorrow in Rosen's eyes. "I...I'm sorry, but it's classified. I tried to get you clearance. My request was denied."

D'Alessio pressed his nose against Rosen's. "Start talking, fatso, or I'm gonna break your balls."

"Fine," Rosen said. "I'll tell you, but you won't believe me."

"Try me."

"About two weeks ago, NORAD detected nearly imperceptible but distinct anomalies in the Earth's magnetic field, localized in the San Francisco Bay area. More precisely, there were two-hundred thirty-three distinct pulses."

"That seems kinda specific."

"Exactly. Turns out that number's a Fibonacci prime."

"A what?"

"A Fibonacci prime. A Fibonacci prime is both a prime and a Fibonacci number."

"That means dick to me. And even if it did, it's probably just a coincidence."

Rosen nodded. "That's what I thought too, but then I looked at the pulse distribution. The first pulse occurred one second before the second one. The second pulse, one second before the third; the third, two seconds before the fourth; and so on."

"What's your point?"

"The time between each subsequent pulse was equal to the next Fibonacci number in the sequence, which makes it highly unlikely the anomalies were random."

"What caused them?" asked D'Alessio.

"I don't know, but a few three-letter agencies in the U.S. government are freaking out about it."

D'Alessio was struck by a sudden insight. "What if two-thirty-three equals the number of yellow-eyed criminals on the streets?"

Rosen smiled. "Joe, have your colleagues done an inventory on how many suspects without fingerprints have been incarcerated over the last two weeks?"

D'Alessio smirked. "Hell, our forensics team has a running tally. Let me call my buddy, Larry."

Whipping out his phone, D'Alessio made a quick call. Thirty seconds later, he hung up and said, "Do you want the good news or the bad news?"

"The good news."

"One-hundred ninety-eight of the yellow-eyed nutjobs are dead or in lockup."

"What's the bad news?"

"Thirty-five of these shitstains are still loose, and they're the smart ones since they haven't been caught. I'll bet you dollars to donuts our computer geek is one of the thirty-five."

Rosen nodded. "I hate to say it, but you're probably right."

"Of course I am. Now let's go find this bastard. Then I can get back to my day job in San Francisco. Where exactly are we going?"

"I have a colleague who does some work on quantum computing. If anyone arrived on the quantum computing scene and started making radical discoveries, my friend, Tom, would know about it."

The duo wended their way towards Stanford's Gates Computer Science Building, an L-shaped sandstone behemoth. Rosen pulled out an ID card and waved him and D'Alessio in. The two headed to an elevator, making their way to the fifth floor. Once there, they walked down a hallway, passing glass-paned offices with dry-erase boards drowning in equations.

Halfway down the hall, Rosen knocked on a glass door. He waved at the office's two occupants. The first was a tall, thin, grandfatherly-looking fellow. He wore glasses that imposed order on the chaos of his wispy, white hair. The man smiled at Rosen, as if the two knew each other.

The office's second occupant sat huddled over a laptop. He too had wild white hair, but seemed much younger than his counterpart.

The older gentleman stood up and tapped his colleague on the back, motioning him to follow. But the younger man shook his head, his eyes fixed firmly on his screen.

The older man opened the door with a smile. "Eli, what an unexpected pleasure! What brings you to Stanford?"

Rosen beamed. "It's great to see you again, Tom. I'm working on a delicate matter. Given your expertise in quantum computing, I was hoping you could point me in the right direction."

"For you, Eli, anything," Tom said. His eyes shifted toward D'Alessio. "Who's this?"

Rosen put his hand on D'Alessio's shoulder. "Tom, this is my friend, Joe D'Alessio."

"Pleased to meet you," Tom said, shaking D'Alessio's hand. "I'd invite you both in, but as you can see, there isn't a ton of space in my office." He inclined his head toward his colleague and frowned. "This is Kip. He's the most gifted graduate student I've ever had, but also the most anti-social. I hope you'll forgive his rudeness. Kip, c'mon over here and introduce yourself."

"I don't think I will," Kip said, his eyes still locked on his screen.

D'Alessio tensed. "Hey, chief, your professor told you to stop what you're doing and talk. We're working on a criminal investigation and require your cooperation."

Tom's face tightened. "A criminal investigation? I didn't realize it was that bad, Eli. We'll assist you however we can."

Kip jerked his head toward Rosen and D'Alessio.

Yellow eyes.

D'Alessio reached for his service weapon.

Kip sneered. "Actually, we won't be helping." With the theatricality of a concert pianist, Kip tapped his keyboard with a single flourish. The glass-paned door slammed shut and locked, trapping Tom inside. Kip smiled, stood, strode over to Tom, and slit his professor's throat with a box cutter.

"You motherfucker!" D'Alessio yelled. He fired two shots into the door. The glass shattered. D'Alessio stomped toward Kip, training his weapon on the suspect. Tom writhed on the floor, covering his throat in a desperate but futile attempt to staunch the bleeding. Rosen rushed toward his friend.

"One more move and I'll shut down the Western Interconnection. The Western United States won't have power for a year," Kip threatened.

"Bullshit," D'Alessio said. Turning his head toward Rosen, he asked, "He can't really do that, can he?"

Rosen ignored D'Alessio. Tears streamed down Rosen's cheeks. "Why did you do this?" he screamed at Kip.

"Because I can," Kip answered, his tone calm and clinical.

"Rosen. Focus. Can he really shut down the grid?"

Rosen nodded. "That's the least he can do. We have to de-escalate this situation. If he shuts it off, thousands could die."

D'Alessio nodded. "You're right." He fired two shots into Kip's head. The man collapsed into a heap before he could tap his keyboard. "It was the least Kip could do," D'Alessio continued, "If we'd given him more time, he probably would've done worse."

₧

After closing the case, D'Alessio and Rosen went their separate ways. But D'Alessio still had to deliver on his promise to Dorn Mather. After all, the man's tip had panned out.

In the end, Doctor Rosen used his government connections to fund Dorn's billboard. The bureaucrats had been so ecstatic Rosen had averted digital Armageddon that they'd gladly cut a fifty-thousand-dollar check to a stranger.

Dorn had disappeared just before his billboard had appeared on Highway 101. That day, thousands of Bay Area residents went mad on the evening commute. Each swallowed his or her tongue. Those who'd survived the subsequent auto accidents reported a strange yellow-eyed man whose face had been posted on a Highway 101 billboard. They claimed he'd appeared to them in their cars and granted them wisdom. They called him Dorn and now worship him as a god.

Rosen went back to Princeton where he continued to consult for the government. D'Alessio returned to his beat, busting criminals in the Tenderloin. Neither ever figured out where the yellow-eyed crooks were from, but D'Alessio was pretty sure it wasn't here.

Soon, Dorn's followers began committing crimes in his name. D'Alessio swore if he ever found the bastard, he'd show 'em what's what.

END

Afterword

In "Murder and Mayhem," Joey D'Alessio and Dr. Eli Rosen once again combine forces to solve a mysterious crime spree. When Rosen shows up, Joey knows instantly that whatever is causing the spree, it definitely won't be something conventional.

In the D'Alessio and Rosen timeline, this narrative takes place some time after the events in the story, "Red Oleander," which was featured earlier in this collection. By this time, it's clear that D'Alessio's fondness and respect for Rosen has broken through the detective's normally gruff exterior.

From a technical perspective, I wanted to show the reader the impact that quantum computers could have on our society if our leaders aren't careful. In essence, they would allow criminals to rapidly break the most secure encryption protocols as easily as a hot knife can cut through butter. Obviously, the ability to solve things like the traveling salesman problem in real-time would have a radical effect on our civilization and would require massive structural changes in the way our economy runs.

In regards to how the yellow-eyed criminals arrived in San Francisco, I wanted to keep that part of the story a mystery so the reader could use his or her own imagination to fill in the blanks.

I finishing writing "Murder and Mayhem" and December 2015, and it first appeared in *MYTHIC: A Quarterly Science Fiction & Fantasy* in January 2019.

I hope you enjoyed it.

The Sultan's Cellar

I t all began in San Francisco—March '87, if I recall. After a night of debauchery soaking up King Diamond's wailing falsetto, concertgoers whispered of a mysterious gathering known only as the Sultan's Cellar.

Intrigued, I asked around, but most knew nothing. Those who did, knew little, but directed me toward the Tenderloin District.

Back then I was a young buck eager to make a name for myself. I had an ear for the next big thing; a sixth sense for what music the kiddos would be craving next. And I always found my way into the most exclusive parties. But in my entire career as a *Rolling Stone* journalist, no other event had proven as elusive as the Sultan's Cellar.

Desperate to learn more, I ventured alone into the Tenderloin's seedy streets. Then, as today, the Tenderloin was a hotbed of illicit activity, exacerbated by the crack epidemic infesting the district's twenty-three square blocks.

At Taylor and Eddy, I passed a ramshackle cluster of pornographic theaters, bars, and sex shops—a mélange of misery and pleasure. War-scarred Southeast Asian refugees shared overcrowded tenements with drug-pushers, prostitutes, and pimps. The sharp report of a gunshot occasionally interrupted a steady medley of Laotian, Vietnamese, and Cambodian chatter under flashing neon lights.

That night I saw the harlequin for the first time.

It skulked silently through the street's debris and gloom, seemingly seeking shadows. It slipped and shifted through the crowds with an uncanny, almost inhuman, grace.

Initially, I thought it just another oddity, a wayward costumed weirdo wandering in the night. But the more I watched it move, the more it seemed out of place.

The harlequin's face had a sickly pale hue. It wore a garish black and red costume caked with dirt and filth—a creeping checkerboard of diamonds marred by mildew. Three curved points sprouted from its black and red cap.

I tried to follow it. I had to. It was a curiosity so unusual there'd be a story in it no matter what.

So I pursued it through damp and dingy alleys, keeping a constant vigilance, lest some crack fiend murder me for my wallet. Yet, despite my diligence, the harlequin had somehow disappeared into the foggy night.

When I turned to go back to my hotel, I came face-to-face with the harlequin.

It grinned, exposing a row of needle-like fangs so rotten I nearly vomited from the stench of decay that washed over me. Its eyes were black pits. I wanted to run, but terror paralyzed me.

My vision faded to black.

The next morning, I awoke in a gutter several blocks away, robbed of my possessions with no memory of how I'd gotten there.

I returned to my hotel, showered and shaved, and packed my bags for my flight home. While getting dressed, I flipped on the television just in time to catch the end of a news conference about yet another horrific crime in the city.

଼

In subsequent years, the memory of the incident faded, and life's innumerable banalities took center stage. I got married, divorced, bought a home, sold a home. I suppose I managed the ups and downs about as well as anyone does.

Then in the spring of 2014, rumors of the Sultan's Cellar resurfaced at a Starkweather concert I was covering in Philly.

Its mere mention unearthed memories I'd suppressed over the past twenty-seven years. I still half believed my alley encounter had been a dream.

And so despite my skepticism, I did some digging and, in my research, I kept hearing one name over and over:

Greg Schauer.

⊗

When I entered Between Books, bells on the door jingled. Shelves were teeming with gaming books like *Dungeons and Dragons* and *Rifts*, and run-of-the-mill science fiction and fantasy novels. Racks of comics cluttering the store's aisles flirted with violating local fire codes.

A middle-aged man with glasses, long brown hair, and a beard flecked with gray greeted me from behind the front counter. "Anything I can help you find?" he said in a mild-mannered voice.

Taking it all in, I wondered if I'd come to the right place. "Um, I'm not sure."

He chuckled. "I get that a lot. Must be your first visit."

His manner was disarming, and I quickly warmed up to him. "Actually, I'm looking for someone named Greg Schauer."

Laughing again, he extended his hand. "I'm Greg. How can I help you?"

"This is gonna sound a bit odd, but someone told me you were a curator of certain occult books."

Greg nodded, then waved his arm forward. "Follow me."

We headed to the back of the store and through a door leading to a stock room. There, Greg wended his way through a maze of books until he stood beside a mangy olive rug. Lifting it, he exposed a hidden floor panel with a handle. Pulling on it, he revealed the entrance to a cellar just big enough for one person at a time to enter.

We climbed down a rickety ladder in near-darkness. After descending about thirty feet, Greg flipped on a light switch, and a generator whirled to life.

After my eyes adjusted, I found myself surrounded by shelves of dusty, old leather-bound tomes.

"What particular book are you looking for?" Greg asked.

I shrugged. "Not sure. It might be better if I told you what brought me here. I'm doing some research on the Sultan's Cellar."

Greg's eyes widened.

"What?" I said.

Greg lowered his head, digging his chin into his chest. He crossed his arms as if in consideration. He sighed. "I'm sorry, I just haven't heard those words in years. I might have something that could help you out."

He led me deeper into his subterranean library until we reached a vault with a massive, five-pronged banker wheel. He typed a code onto a small keypad, spun the wheel, and pulled open the six-inch-thick steel door.

When I tried to follow him in, he warded me off. "Stay outside. There's some nasty stuff in here."

Several minutes later, Greg emerged with a thick and battered tome. A symbol marked by a vertical line bisected by two parallel lines extending diagonally up and to the right was embossed on its rawhide cover.

"What's that symbol mean?"

He hesitated, took a deep breath, and exhaled. "This rune's traditionally been associated with abstract concepts like wealth as well as concrete things like cattle."

Leafing through the vellum pages, he continued. "Ah, here it is." He pointed to a black and white illustration of nine hooded bodies dangling from an oak tree. "The first recorded instances of the dread harvest were captured in Norse folklore when pagan kings sacrificed nine males every nine years during the Yule festivals."

Frustrated, I said, "I'm not sure I see the connection to the Sultan's Cellar."

"I'm getting to that." He resumed paging through the tome, then stopped at another illustration of a mass hanging. "The Norse weren't the only people who have partaken in these rituals. In 1825, Sultan Mahmud II lured nine janissary leaders into what came to be known as the Sultan's Cellar, where his palace guards hanged the janissaries from the rafters, but something else ripped their bodies to shreds."

"Something else?"

He shrugged. "Through the ages there've been eyewitness accounts of the caretakers—the beings behind the Sultan's Cellar. And in every instance, they appear in pockets of abject human misery within cities of great affluence. In other words, places that radiate negative energy—what most people would call evil. These sites often have foundations lying on ancient burial grounds."

That piqued my interest. "Tell me more about these caretakers."

"Accounts have described them as mad jesters with deathly white skin and harlequin caps that never sway or waver."

My jaw dropped. "Jesus."

"What's wrong?"

"I've seen one before. In '87. San Francisco."

"Let me guess," Greg said, adjusting his glasses, "it was the night before they found all those bodies strung up in the Civic Center station tunnels beneath the Tenderloin."

I shuddered.

His jaw tightened. "I'm right, aren't I?"

I slowly nodded. Until now, I had never connected the harlequin with the murders.

"And speaking of ancient burial grounds," he continued, "when workers were excavating the underground Civic Center BART Station in the Sixties, they exhumed a woman's five-thousand-year-old remains."

"Was that the Sultan's Cellar?"

Greg shrugged. "No idea. What I do know is that death trails the caretakers like stink on a corpse."

I tried a different approach. "Rumor has it the Sultan's Cellar's coming here. Any idea where?"

He folded his arms across his chest. "I might have a few ideas, but it's probably best I kept them to myself."

"Are you kidding me?" I said, immediately embarrassed at my outburst. I lowered my head and put my hand on his shoulder. "I'm sorry. I've been following this story for years. I'm just looking for answers."

Greg remained silent, then said, "Have you ever heard of the cult house?"

"No. Is that where I'll find it?"

"That's all you're gonna get from me. I won't be able to live with myself if I tell you more."

"I appreciate it."

We went back upstairs, exchanged a few pleasantries, and then said our goodbyes.

He grabbed my arm before I left. "If you're going where I think you're going, make sure you wear ear protection."

"What do you mean?"

He smiled. "Never mind. Have a great day."

ॐ

Local lore led me down a lonely country road at dusk through winding rows of warped and twisted trees. I was headed toward a place on the Delaware-Pennsylvania border known as Chandler's Hollow.

Atop a dark knoll, the cult house's rotten edifice scarred the countryside like blight on a spring bloom. I discreetly parked my Honda Accord on the roadside behind some dying lilacs.

The sun had set, and night's reign was now absolute. Two mangled colonnades of gnarled and sickly oak, ash, and maple lined the path. Their trunks twisted away from the ancient, dilapidated structure as if struggling to escape some unseen pestilence.

As I crept closer to the house, I noticed that not a single blade of grass grew within a hundred feet of it. Windows shaped like inverted crosses were chiseled into the dark temple's timber flanks.

Everything about it was wrong. A foul aura of corruption lingered on the wind. Using my iPhone to light the way, I felt a deep sense of trepidation as I approached. The house's decaying wood and splintered crossbeams made me confident its inhabitants had fled long ago.

I carefully opened double doors that creaked in the blackness. As I crossed the threshold, a gust of stale, musty air hit me square in the face. The ruin of what had once been pews littered the dark church's rotten floor.

The single-room structure had a spartan quality that made me uneasy. It was as if something had stripped it of its essence. Yet, armed with my obsession to uncover the Sultan's Cellar, I overcame my fear and pressed forward, anxious to find whatever clue I could, no matter how small or insignificant.

My efforts were rewarded when I stumbled across roughhewn slate stairs leading underground. As I traveled downward, a faint glow rising from far beneath the surface beckoned me forward.

After climbing down several stories, I reached a tunnel carved into the bedrock. Lanterns hanging along the walls illuminated the corridor.

The walls echoed with a distant piping. No matter how faint, the strange melody drew me deeper into the cavern. But before venturing further into its depths, and almost by chance, I remembered Greg's warning and put on my noise-canceling headphones.

In absolute silence, I followed the tunnel down a slight grade and through several twists and turns. My descent grew colder as I trekked deeper into the earth. Turning one last time, I stumbled into a cathedral-sized grotto. Three cyclopean blocks rose like mesas in the Sonoran desert.

Nine people swayed and writhed in a strangely hypnotic dance. From their soiled and frayed clothing, I assumed they were vagrants, shut-ins—people no one would miss. They seemed controlled by hidden strings.

Atop each block, their harlequin puppet masters stood. One played an ornately carved bone flute, another pounded on a skin drum, and the last strummed an ebony lute.

The vibrations from the music's harmonics made me feel a sense of weightlessness—my body resonating with a strange euphoria. I fought against an overpowering urge to remove my headphones. To distract myself, I raised my iPhone and began recording video.

The harlequins quickened the tempo. The walls shook, and dust drifted from the rocky ceiling. The dancers below responded with frenzied movements in sync with the redoubled beat.

Chains!

Like darting pythons, nine rusty chains zipped from the ceiling. Each chain terminated in a jagged meat hook.

Enraptured by the sinister symphony, the revelers seemed oblivious to the dangling iron links. The drumbeat slowed to the rhythm of a steady heart. In unison, the celebrants shed their clothing.

The dancers ripped the meat hooks into their shoulders. The chains went taut and pulled their quarry upward until the bodies dangled just above the platform blocks. Human feet swayed twenty-feet above the surface supported by nothing other than a hook lodged into flesh and sinew.

The music's vibrations faded. Turning toward their suspended prey, the harlequins removed their caps, each unveiling three bony horns. Like some bizarre arboreal species, the creatures leapt from their platforms and onto the chains where they rapidly converged on their victims.

Arterial sprays of blood heralded the culmination of the grim feast.

Stunned by the surreal and gruesome ritual, I was paralyzed by the spectacle for nearly a minute before the reality of the slaughter finally hit me. But by then, it was too late. The harlequins turned their heads toward me. And only then did I realize I was screaming.

They swung from the bloody chains and landed with catlike grace. I spun and raced through the tunnel, desperate to reach the surface. They loped after me on all fours like great cats on the Serengeti. They were closing the gap, getting so close I could smell their rank breath, soured with decay.

I bolted up the stairs. A talon swiped at my ankle, ripping off my sneaker. If not for an adrenaline surge, they would have taken me there, but I burst out of the stairway and into the hollow church. I sprinted toward the double doors. Once outside, I blundered through the darkness.

In minutes, I reached my car, fumbling for my keys. My hands shook as I frantically tried to insert them into the lock.

The mad harlequins charged out of the murk. Moments before impact, I slipped inside my Honda and locked the door. I thrust my key into the ignition and prayed it would start. A harlequin leapt onto the hood, baring gut-encrusted fangs. Its black eyes gleamed with a keen malevolence, an instant before it slammed its horns into my windshield.

Cracks snaked through the glass. I turned the key. The engine rumbled, but didn't start.

Another harlequin rammed into my driver's window, peppering me with shards of glass.

I turned the key again, and the engine roared to life.

My roof crumpled as the last harlequin landed on it.

I jammed my foot on the gas and made a hard right onto the road.

The force of my acceleration launched the first harlequin from my hood and onto the pavement. I heard a distinct crunch as my wheels grinded bone. The harlequin at my window hooked its talons on the door's upholstery as its legs scraped the pavement at over thirty miles an hour.

Barreling down the country road like a madman, I veered and swerved, nearly running my Honda off the road. But I couldn't shake off the last two predators. So I hit another curve and slammed on my brakes.

Gravity did the rest.

&

The next day I woke in my hotel room with no recollection of how I'd gotten there. I struggled to make sense of my experience. I'd witnessed the harlequins slaughter nine people, but I had no idea what I should do next. I somehow felt responsible for the deaths, but local authorities would never believe my story.

So I wrote down everything I could recall—pure stream of consciousness. I didn't want to miss a single detail while the nightmare was still raw.

Then I remembered the video footage. Actual, honest-to-God proof of what I'd seen. The police couldn't dismiss that, could they? But I had to be one hundred percent certain I'd captured enough evidence to be credible.

I watched the video just to be sure.

And when I did, I heard a song so beautiful, so sonorous, so sweet, it spoke to my soul. It lifted me above this mundane plane of existence toward the great beyond.

It changed my life.

In nine years I'll return to the Sultan's Cellar where I'll dance with the harlequins until they take me into their twilight realm forever.

END

Afterword

"The Sultan's Cellar" is another take on a local Delaware-Pennsylvania legend about a cult house near the Brandywine River. The first was a story called "Chandler's Hollow", which first appeared in the March 2015 issue of *Perihelion Online Science Fiction,* and you can now find it in my second collection *Necromancer: And Other Stories.*

Growing up, I had heard several variations of this story. In most of them, the cult house had windows in the shape of inverted crosses and trees bowed away from the structure, presumably because it emanated evil. Onlookers who dared visit the site frequently reported being chased by a strange black Bronco with stadium lights.

In this tale, I combine this local lore with medieval Christian accounts of a great pagan festival held every nine years at the Temple at Uppsala in Sweden, involving Norse Yule rituals that required nine human male sacrifices. Whether these ritualistic human sacrifices had actually occurred is a matter of historical debate, but in this story I assumed they were real and dedicated to particularly dark gods.

To add additional local flair to the story, I included a dear friend I've known since I was twelve years old and had first visited his bookstore Between Books at the Tri-State Mall in Delaware. That friend is Greg Schauer. As of this writing in September 2025, Greg continues to run a version of the store called Between Books 2.0 within an oddities shop today.

"The Sultan's Cellar" first appeared in the September 2017 issue of *Galaxy's Edge.* I trust it made you think.

About the Author

Sean is a technology and finance professional, and nationally bestselling award-winning author who writes science fiction and horror as well as nonfiction. Over fifty of his short stories in publications such as *The Year's Best Military and Adventure SF*, *Year's Best Hardcore Horror*, *Terraform*, *Galaxy's Edge*, and *Vastarien*, among others. He is the editor of the *Weird World War III*, *Weird World War IV*, and *Weird World War: China* anthologies. He is also the host of the YouTube channel, *Through A Glass Darkly*, where the paranormal meets military science fiction and fact.

Sean was a research associate at the Harvard-Stanford Preventive Defense Project where he worked on energy security issues. He won the 2006 Policy Analysis Exercise Award at the Harvard Kennedy School of Government for his work on policy solutions to Iran's nuclear weapons program. Sean also spent time at Booz Allen Hamilton as an intelligence analyst focusing on strategic war games and simulations for the Pentagon. Before graduate school, Sean was a cavalry officer in the United States Army where he trained American forces for combat operations in Iraq and Afghanistan at the National Training Center.

Sean holds a Master of Business Administration from Harvard Business School, a Master in Public Policy from the Harvard Kennedy School of Government, and bachelor's degrees in History and Electrical Engineering from Stanford.